MARK OF THE
RAVEN

MARK OF THE RAVEN

Pete Scales

SBR Press
Halifax, Nova Scotia, Canada

SBR Press
20 Keefe Road, Halifax, Nova Scotia, Canada B3P 2J1

MARK OF THE RAVEN
SBR Press Book
Published by Arrangement With The Author

Printed and Bound in Canada

Canadian Cataloguing in Publication Data

Scales, Pete, 1954-
Mark of the Raven

ISBN 0-9686449-0-2

I. Title.

PS8587.C3913M37 2000   C813'.54   C99-901642-3
PR9199.3.S254M37 2000

...to Tricia, Sam and Alex for believing.

For more titles from SBR Press
contact us at our web site or email us at...
Web Site: www.sbrpress.ns.ca
Email: pbscale@attglobal.net

Acknowledgements

You want to be an author? This is the question that none of the following folks ever asked. Rather, they wanted to know, "When are you going to get this puppy in print?"

First, many thanks to the people of Alert Bay, B.C. and the Nimpkish Reserve where the story was born. You provided me with an uncommon glimpse into a revival of your spiritualism.

To Ian MacSween, Dr. Don Eddy, Jim Clarke and Staff Sergeant Mike Clark, the Wednesday Nighters, a bunch of guys who sat around my kitchen table and made the story and the characters in it, live, thanks.

A lot of staffers at the Township of Langley offered up their time and efforts to pre-edit the book. Kudos to Kory Down, Arne Badke, Linda Floyd, Edie Mowat, David Wright for his great cover art of the raven totem, Judi Donald, Fred Peters, Sharla Mauger, now Councillor Mauger, Vicki Robinson and Cheryl Dickson.

To Margot MacDonald, who really can see what others can't, thanks for the insights.

We all need a mentor and somehow, Jack Whyte, best selling author of all the great books that started with the Skystone, chose to be mine. Thanks Jack.

Richard Sherbaniuk, my editor, a man who's red pen is mightier than one of Jack Whyte's swords gets the credit for flow, pacing and the art of describing really great snacks.

Karen Rempel of Vivid Page Productions Inc in Vancouver, as usual, has done a wonderful job with the cover and typesetting.

Most recently, my thanks go out to three folks in Halifax, Tom Donovan, Odette Murphy and Kirk ("don't call me Captain") MacDonald for helping me put the finishing touches to the manuscript.

And of course, my thanks would not ring true if I didn't mention my family. Heartfelt thanks to Tricia for reading manuscripts for the umpteenth time and still staying with me. And to Sam and Alex who are just now old enough for me to read *Raven* to them, and just hip enough to say, "Heh Dad, that's better than our normal bed time story."

If I have neglected to mention some names of all you others who have read the book and made your comments, trust me, its a matter of space, not memory. To all of you, thank you for your encouragement and great ideas.

PART 1

PROLOGUE
Alert Bay, B.C. Canada - Present

The blackness of the Big House was thick with the heat of too many bodies and their grief. Rain pounded on the wooden roof as if demanding to get in. Match touched gasoline with an explosive *Whomp* as the wood pile erupted. Ragged wavering fingers of light searched the corners of the cavernous room. Finding nothing of interest there they retreated to the glowing tower of luminescence that stood like a citadel over the crackling fire.

Dressed in dark robes, the Chief Councilor of the Nimpkish Band rose from a chair near the fire circle. With stiff dignity he walked to the microphone, incongruously modern in this ancient place. Squinting through the gloom at the five hundred souls gathered together, he soon recognized the grieving family. He nodded his head in respectful salute and began to speak.

His toneless words of condolence were steeped in sadness. Laden with grief, the cadence of his delivery slowed, finally stopping altogether as his eyes closed and his head drooped. Hundreds of eyes stared and there was not a sound in the great, dim hall.

Suddenly he began to speak once more. The words that came from his mouth were in the ancient tongue, Kwakwala, and the voice was not his own. Scratchy and weathered, it was the voice of an old woman.

Throughout the hall, elders leaned forward to better hear words that for so long had remained unspoken. Soon, the mysterious sounds began to sink in, their hypnotic rhythms penetrating deep into the thoughts of every soul present.

"Many dark winters have passed since the Spirit Talkers stood together to battle against the Season of Darkness and its Chief, the Man Eater. The lives of our people became disturbed by things we couldn't understand. We walked down strange trails and many lost their way. So many died that few were left to fight the battle, to act as the chosen voices of our Spirit Ancestors. Those few who did survive have waited a very long time, searching, always searching for someone to take over the fight.

It is prophesied that if the new Spirit Talkers are not found within this generation, the Guardians of Light will lose favor and in time, be cast from the earth by the powers of darkness."

The voice seemed to saturate the room as it spoke of the old things, of a time when the world was new. Dimly in the column of fire, the watchers could see a shimmering figure slowly appear, the vague image of an old woman.

"Many died violent deaths to protect the secrets of the Spirit Talkers. Yet their dying was not in vain . . ."

Suddenly the image faded to nothingness, replaced in an instant by ghostly things that rose out of the fire and drifted about the hall. Smoke trails the color of bronze marked their passage through the darkness. They swooped and dived, spiraling and pirouetting, then plunging back into the flames in a burst of embers. As sparks flew about the hall it seemed to become hotter and some in the audience began to panic.

The death place of one fiery phantom became the birth place of another. Soon, the fire things began to take on recognizable shapes. One, hovering over the crowd, was suddenly transformed into a man's face, then a body in shimmering traditional ceremonial clothes. Contagious terror spread though the crowd.

Soon, this ghost too was sucked back into the flames, only to be replaced by two more that hung at the outer limits of the fire's dwindling light, twisting aimlessly. Someone in the audience, recognizing the ghostly faces, screamed out the names of men long dead. As more ghosts escaped the fire, few in the audience were immune from recognition of at least one of the floating, dancing images. Names dusty and half-forgotten lived again as they were shouted in the gloom.

"Great are those who died willingly," spoke the old woman's voice from the mouth of the chief, "so that the battle be won and the darkness kept at bay . . ."

An image of a young man took shape, clearer and more defined than any that had appeared before. His face was strong and pleasant looking beneath his woven cedar helmet. Noble and confident, he spun slowly, as if blown by a gentle wind beyond the rim of time.

"And there were those who passed the test but were trapped in forces beyond the control of destiny. One of the chosen has left the world of the living. . . "

.

ONE
Vancouver, B.C., April 15, 1981

The ship was ugly. Cratered with rust over her entire length, even the S1244 designation number etched on her funnel was barely visible through the mess of corrosion. Only a crisp new red and white Polish ensign fluttering over her stern post provided any color.

Like many other vessels in the Pacific Polish fishing fleet, the S1244 used the Port of Vancouver every three to four months as a base to replenish supplies and give her crew much needed shore leave. It was a predictable routine for local authorities, to the point that surveillance of these Communist Block work horses of the sea had become lax.

The seventy-five Slavic sailors who came down the gang plank were a scruffy lot. Once through the Immigration Canada processing trailer they milled around waiting for friends to exit. In twos and threes they passed by the police cruiser, the two bored officers inside the car comprising the only security at the dock. They recognized faces from past landings, and this one seemed no different.

But within forty eight hours, twenty one crew members from the S1244 would jump ship, the biggest mass defection in Canadian history. The Special Operations Branch of the Royal Canadian Mounted Police initiated security checks on all the defectors, but there were too many foreign bodies and not enough RCMP.

Pavel Wasnoski's time in detention was unremarkable. Upon release he, like all the others, was taken in by a Polish Canadian family. Within a month of his arrival he was well on his way to successfully making the transition from refugee to immigrant. Getting a job as a plumber's assistant, soon he'd earned enough to rent his own basement suite in Richmond. Buying decent clothes and practicing to improve his English, it wasn't long before he looked like he had always lived in the West.

As always on Friday evenings, he left his suite and caught a bus for downtown Vancouver, some twenty minutes away. And as always, he was being tailed. The RCMP had been tipped off by an anonymous informant that Pavel was not all he appeared to be, and that he might well be a spy.

RCMP Sergeant Jerry Puchalski, a second generation Polish Canadian, knew that, as usual, Pavel was going to socialize with his fellow defectors at a downtown strip club. As usual, the Polish sailor got off the bus on the north end of the Granville Street Bridge, walked a block and entered the York Hotel. Puchalski drove his clapped-out Chevy van around the corner and parked in the alley. He entered the club just in time to hear the introduction of Vickie, a stripper with hair an improbable shade of red, who started her bored gyrations to a Robert Palmer song. He spotted Pavel in a rear corner, sitting with two friends, sipping a beer. As he waited for service, Puchalski pressed the clicker of the gold ball-point pen in his hand. Two metallic clicks sounded in his ear. The tiny transmitter switch was operating and he knew that somewhere just outside the hotel Corporal Douglas Baker was waiting and watching.

Two hours later, gazing at yet another stripper and nursing his third beer, he saw from the corner of his eye that Pavel had gotten up from the table, heading for the washroom. Puchalski sighed and returned his gaze to the sad flesh on stage. When he glanced back Pavel was still not back. Frowning, he took a closer look at the sailor's table. In the heat the sailors had taken off their jackets, all except Pavel. Puchalski remembered that Pavel had been wearing his leather bomber when he went to the restroom. Swearing under his breath, he clicked the transmitter.

"Doug. You spy anything Polish?"

"Roger," Baker answered laconically. "Just coming down the stairs from the back exit. Our man's on a mission."

"I'll be right there."

Puchalski was on the move, nearing the door when Baker's voice sounded again in his ear. "He's changed direction, heading for Granville and coming towards me. I'll stay in front of him, you take the rear."

Out on the street, Puchalski joined a throng of pedestrians waiting for the light to change. Once across, he took a route parallel with Pavel's on the opposite side of the street.

Pavel strolled casually, stopping to look in store windows. Puchalski spoke into the transmitter. "Ordinarily I'd say a blind man could tail this guy, but there has to be a reason he left the party like that."

"Yeah," agreed Baker. "Nothing like a little excitement in our lives, eh Jerry?"

Keeping their quarry neatly bracketed, Puchalski expertly wove his way through a stream of oncoming pedestrians eyeballing Pavel every two seconds or so. Once through the crowd he saw three punks pushing another. His dodge around them brought him up against the wall of the Lotus Garden Restaurant. Sliding past the dark entrance portico, believing he was in the clear he missed seeing a meaty fist smashing into his left temple.

Feeling abandoned his legs. He hit the sidewalk hard, dazed and nearly blinded with pain. Reflexively he reached for his Walther P.380 automatic, then remembered he was under cover. He staggered upright and searched the area with bleary eyes. Gone. The "fist" and Pavel.

He pushed the button of the transmitter still clutched in his hand. "Doug, I've lost him. Somebody just cold-cocked me. Maybe our mark knows he's being tailed."

"Got him," said Baker. "If he does, he doesn't know there's two of us. He just went into McDonalds. You okay?"

"Give me a couple secs. You take him. Something's going on. I don't believe this Polack bastard took a stroll just to grab a burger."

Doug Baker moved away from the counter with his tray, heading for a table where he could watch Pavel greedily devour his two Big Macs. A folded copy of the Vancouver Sun Baker had noted in the hip pocket of the Polish sailor's jacket was propped against his cup of Coke.

Finishing his food and licking his fingers, Pavel tucked the newspaper back into the jacket pocket. Seizing his tray and lurching up from his chair, the Pole bumped an older man, who dropped a fully loaded tray and his own folded newspaper with a crash.

Offering rapid apologies, Pavel bent down to help collect the fallen items. When that assistance was politely waved off he took out his wallet as if offering to pay for the man's food. When that too was refused, his hands spread in apology, Pavel moved toward the door, still talking. As he turned, Baker saw that the newspaper was still in the pocket. Something looked different. He looked at the other man, and at the newspaper on the tray with the remnants of the destroyed meal.

They'd made a switch.

With Pavel about to vanish into the night, twelve years of spy craft kicked in. Baker made what was destined to be one of the major decisions of his life – he gave up on Pavel and focused on the old man. The old guy was leaving the restaurant, newspaper tucked under his arm. Baker hung back a few seconds before leaving. On the pavement he searched the streets but his new mark had vanished. His earpiece crackled.

"Doug! What the hell's going on? Where's Pavel? It's like the earth swallowed him up."

"God damn it!", Baker swore. "Pavel just made a switch with another guy. Nice choreography, slick as Astaire and Rogers. Now the other guy's disappeared too. What the hell is going on?"

TWO

Vancouver B.C. February 18

One Year Ago

A lready dead tired, his shift only half over, new father and Vancouver Police Constable Reinholt's concentration wavered as he squinted through the darkness of the skid row back alley. Distracted by fat raindrops that blotted his windshield, he barely saw the dim figure running full tilt – into the hood of the cruiser, then flipping up on to the windshield with a fleshy thud. Reinholt stared at the face smashed against the glass. Time enough to note the expression of wild fear in the bulging eyes, before the body slid off, leaving a bloody smear.

Reinholt had the door open even before the cruiser stopped. His flashlight stabbed the darkness as he knelt, checking the carotid pulse of the fallen man. Catching a faint flutter, he called for an ambulance.

Five minutes later, as paramedics rolled the loaded gurney up to the flood lit back door of the ambulance, the constable got his first good look at the man who had run into him like a panicked deer. Native, in his late twenties, his skin was an odd bronze color and his hair, instead of being black, was also a bronze hue. Reinholt had never seen anything like it. He'd had enough experience on the force to know that all of the man's wounds couldn't have come from his run in with the cruiser. He'd recently suffered one hell of a thrashing. As Reinholt leaned forward for a closer look the victim's eye lids fluttered open revealing wide eyes of a peculiar radiant blue. His hand began twitching.

"Take it!" the man gasped.

"Take what?"

The hand, now steady and controlled, opened to reveal a gold amulet on a chain.

"Take it!"

When the ambulance pulled away, Reinholt fingered the finely crafted piece of jewelry. The front was intricately carved with mythological figures of birds and fish, traditional West Coast native art, and on the back was the inscription 'B. Johnson — Alert Bay'.

Four hours later the unidentified victim was resting quietly in an intensive care bed. Listed in critical condition from multiple wounds, most from a terrible beating he'd received in a lowrent bar, his prognosis was touch and go. Reports from the scene suggested that the man had gotten into an argument with another patron, and subsequently attacked by about ten of the assailant's friends. Half the bar had somehow been destroyed in the process. Then he'd run off into the night, straight into Constable Reinholt's cruiser.

During the night the man's condition deteriorated further. Already on a respirator, the EEG monitoring his brain waves started to register continuous high spikes. At five a.m., with the onset of severe convulsions, the resident on call summoned nursing staff for assistance. He also made one outside call.

They struggled to hold the patient down as the man began convulsing so violently that the bed began to shake. The glass in the wall of the observation booth vibrated wildly. The paper scrolling from the EEG monitor was black with scribbles and a mass of spiked lines filled the green screen.

The hospital staff put up a valiant fight to save the patient's life, their efforts closely monitored by a tall, aging stranger. Summoned by the resident's call, he gazed from the observation booth, his face a mask of misery, as the vibration of the bed reached a fever pitch. Then nothing. More white uniformed figures ran to the bedside. A defibrillator was fired, again and again to no effect.

Ten minutes later, sheets were pulled over the mutilated face. The lone observer held on to the window frame for support, his head bowed. And then, he felt it. He looked up. A bronze light glowed from under the white sheet covering the body. Then, against any rule of science the observer held dear, it seemed to shimmer up from the bed, forming a glowing column that hung in the air like smoke. Slowly the column resolved into an image — a young man with hair the color of bronze, hanging beneath a splendid helmet of woven cedar. A cloak of brown, gray and black patterned with the figure of a raven hung from his broad shoulders. His legs and feet were bare, his skin the color of bronze.

The ghostly image suddenly swirled as if caught in a gust of wind that tore it apart leaving wisps of bronze to spiral up and away.

Behind the glass, the man code named Reggie looked on in horror as the dream he had sought for so long died before his eyes.

THREE
Alert Bay, B.C. Canada

January 8. The Present

Michael Potter needed to puke.

Frothing spittle-like spray curled off the tops of leaden waves that heaved beneath roiling gray clouds heavy with rain. The view from the passenger lounge observation window of the ferry was typical north Pacific coast in the middle of a winter storm. As he stared at the white spray pelting against the window Potter swallowed hard. It wasn't often his lean, twenty nine year old, runner's body betrayed him. He pushed irritably at the damp blond hair that fell over his brow, to wipe away the beads of sweat. Why hadn't he thought to bring a dramamine patch?

Out of the murk a dark mass loomed. Thick forested slopes emerged from the whitecaps. His green eyes focused on the island with relief. It provided a stable visual anchor for his queasy insides and was evidence his ordeal was almost over.

Ten minutes later, when the ferry turned east into a protected bay, he paid more attention to the misty, rain-soaked landscape he would call home for at least the next six months. As he scanned the bay he wondered whether he had made a mistake coming to this remote place. Even in the gloom he could see both ends of the island.

He was soon off the ship and being thrown around in the back seat of a dilapidated Chev posing as a taxi, driven by a maniac. As they headed inland the driver barely cleared a couple of posts standing on either side of the winding gravel road. Despite the speed and bumpiness of the ride, Potter saw they were actually two age-ravaged totems of some mythological birds, their carved wings canting awkwardly in decay.

Without warning, the driver yanked on the wheel and stomped on his brakes, bringing the vehicle to a screeching, sliding stop in front of a flat roofed, two story building. Potter pushed himself upright and lurched unsteadily out of the car, his stomach still churning. He hauled out his three overfilled bags and dumped them on the wet gravel, then handed a couple of bills to the cabby. "Keep the change. Buy yourself a driving lesson."

As the car sped off, spraying him with mud and gravel, he picked up his bags and stared at the building. It had seen better days. Curls of white paint hung off the walls, half concealing a sign that said Nimpkish Band Office.

Potter climbed the stairs, opened one of the doors and tugged at his luggage. Needing to vent his rising frustration, the bags were convenient. Panting and cursing under his breath, he hauled them from the foyer up five stairs to the main hall. Suddenly he stopped swearing and stared.

In the shadows stood a man, arms crossed upon his chest, legs spread wide. He ambled forward. Around forty, he was of average height and skinny except for a small gut that hung over his belt. His dress was entirely western, a wide cowboy belt with a big, shiny bucking bronco buckle, new blue jeans, a red plaid shirt and cowboy boots. Black hair slicked straight back framed a ruggedly handsome face, one accustomed to an outdoor life. He looked at Potter appraisingly.

"Had better days, friend?"

"I was just terrorized by the local cabby. Where'd he learn to drive, Albania?"

The Indian laughed. "He's self taught. And he's a lousy student." As they decided they liked each other, Potter said, "Where can I find the band office?"

"Down the hall, first door on your right. Who're you looking for?"

"I'm not sure. I just got in from Vancouver and the only instructions I got were to report to the band office. I'm Mike Potter, the physician who'll be replacing Dr. Jeff Nelson."

"The new doc, huh? I hope you treat us Indians gentler than your luggage." He held out his hand. "Thomas Albert. I'm the chief here and I'll be signing your pay checks." He easily lifted two of the heavy bags and headed down the hall.

Inside the main administration office three women were sitting behind desks. "Ladies," boomed Albert, "This is Mike Potter, the new doctor. Based on what I've seen so far he's hot-blooded, so I wouldn't recommend you go anywhere near his examination table." The women laughed tolerantly, obviously used to their chief's sense of humor.

"I'm just heading down to my boat but I can give you a few minutes." He waved one leathery hand towards a chair beside an old oak desk. As he unzipped his red hiking jacket, Potter glanced around the office. He leaned toward a wall of photos and paintings. They were all of West coast fishing vessels, ranging from intricately carved dugouts to modern, large sized wood and aluminum seiners. Noticing Potter's interest, the chief pointed at one. "Mine. Northern Dancer. She's old and none too pretty but she catches fish real good."

Potter sat down, prompting Albert to say, "It's good to have you here. I know Doc Elliott'll be real happy to have someone else to help out. Things've been pretty hairy for the last little bit, what with Christmas and all. It's too bad about Jeff leaving. Must've got bush fever or something. It happens sometimes with you city guys.

Being trapped on this rock can get to you, especially if you don't drink, which he didn't. Three weeks ago, he just packed up his family and left."

"You married doc? No? Lucky." His chair creaked as he leaned back and studied Potter. "You're not one of those do-gooder white men, are you? Mind telling me why you're here?"

Potter shook his head. "Purely selfish. I wanted a change, and this is about as big a change from Vancouver as you can get. A professional acquaintance of mine, Dr. Harry Warner, told me that you were having trouble keeping physicians on the island and suggested I come."

Albert nodded. "Fair enough. Know where you're gonna stay?"

"No sir, chief. Preferably not under a tree. It's pretty wet out there."

Albert laughed. "That it is but about the 'sir', I haven't been called that since the last time I ate in some fancy restaurant in Vancouver. And don't call me chief, either - it's practically a four letter word around here. The old folks say the only good chief is a hereditary one, while the young ones favor elections but then don't like the person they elect. I'm more like a glorified mayor than anything else. So just call me Thomas."

Potter nodded. "I really don't know much about the job, or Alert Bay for that matter. I was told what you pay, that you have a place for me to live and that I won't need a car. Anything else you can tell me would be appreciated."

Thomas Albert had a disarming manner and considerable talent as a story teller. He explained that Alert Bay was an island community of approximately twelve hundred people, located some ten miles south-east of Port McNeill on the northern tip of Vancouver Island. The only access to the two mile long island was by water or air — it had a large, well protected harbor and was flat enough at the top to accommodate a landing strip. An invisible line divided the island exactly in half: to the north, the Nimpkish Indian

Reserve and to the south, the village of Alert Bay. At the turn of this century the area was a commercial center for logging and fishing operations, and at the same time attracted Church of England missionaries eager to save souls.

"So," concluded Thomas Albert, "Your wages are paid by the Department of Indian and Northern Affairs, and your housing too. All of your patients are Indian. That means they're at least one quarter native blood and a registered member of a band. We Indians can see either of you two doctors and since Doc Elliott has been here so long, Jeff still had some work to do to even up the numbers. You'll take over all of his patients and any you can steal away from Elliott. The old bugger's a crusty army guy who's been here for over thirty years. He's got no bedside manner and he drove Jeff near nuts. But the people on this island like him alot."

He glanced at his watch. "Damn. I talk too much. I've got to take my boat out."

He jumped out of his chair and bounded out the door. "Millie!" he bellowed. "Where's the new doctor staying?" A female voice said something Potter couldn't hear as Albert returned with a set of keys, pulling on a plaid jacket. He grabbed all three of Potter's bags and with a jerk of his head beckoned his guest to follow.

Outside, in the last of the late afternoon light, they got into Thomas Albert's late model Dodge pickup and roared off. As they passed some larger homes the chief suddenly hauled on the wheel, sending the vehicle into a skidding right-hand turn, past a half a dozen newly constructed townhouses. A second swerving turn into a driveway brought the truck to a wrenching halt inches from the door of unit 104. Albert flung himself out of the driver's door, threw Potter's bags onto the pavement, practically dragged the physician from the truck. Slamming the gears into reverse he yelled out the window, "Home sweet home, doc!" The set of keys flew out and hit the wall as the truck disappeared in a hail of wet gravel.

"Well, at least I know who taught the cabby how to drive," mused Potter out loud as he walked toward his new home.

****

After his first week Michael Potter began to settle into a comfortable routine.

An average working day was a 6:15 a.m. wake up, a quick shower, breakfast, then a fast paced walk a mile and a half south to St. George's Hospital to start rounds at 7:30. Normally he was finished at 9:30 and on his way back to the reserve to start office hours at the clinic an hour later. The rest of the time was spent alternating two day stretches of on-call with Dr. Elliott.

The old physician left him pretty much to his own devices so he quickly came to rely on the unflappable Linda Jarvis, assistant head nurse.

Linda was gorgeous. As a registered Kwakiutl she did not fit the norm, taller than most, perhaps more slender, with a speech pattern that was all big city.

In addition to everything else, Linda was instrumental in providing Potter with a social life, mostly in the form of the Wednesday Nite Beautiful Losers Club.

The Losers, a loose association of people from the community's administrative and professional sector, met each Wednesday evening in the Bayside Inn pub for a social drink and chit chat. The group included teachers, Linda and other nurses, business people, the local Royal Canadian Mounted Police detachment commanding officer, Sergeant Jim Glinnon, and various band councilors. Chief Thomas Albert was a member, as was his friend Dan Lucas, an ex chief who had lost his seat to Thomas in the last election. Bitter political rivals from battling family groups, they still remained close friends.

There were others in the small community who came within

Potter's sphere and for the most part, they were his patients. In the beginning, the few who came to see him were there to evaluate him more than for any specific medical problem.

He soon learned that the most respected resident on the island, as well as the oldest, was Mary Hill, or Auntie Mary as everyone called her. From the first time he visited her they got along famously. Thomas Albert told him that she knew more about the old ways than anyone and he was fascinated by her tales of Indian life and lore.

When she invited him for Sunday lunch, he jumped at the opportunity.

FOUR

Auntie Mary's home was a tiny weathered cabin shingled in cedar, standing wreathed in mist at the edge of the forest. Potter climbed the rickety stairs to the porch and knocked on the door.

"Come on in, Doctor Mike. Door's open," came the faint, scratchy welcome.

Entering the small, spartan living room he immediately felt the overpowering warmth of the place and struggled to get his coat off. He saw her rounding a partition between the living room and the kitchen. Auntie Mary was slight and frail, her back heavily bowed with age. Thin, yellow-white hair, parted in the center and collected in two long braids, hung over each of her bony shoulders. Her heavily wrinkled face featured a hawkish nose and a generous mouth, which was usually twisted into the start of a laugh. But the most startling feature was her piercing black eyes. From the deeply sunken eye sockets they seemed as old as time and as young as tomorrow.

She hobbled with the characteristic bent kneed, wide-footed stance of the very old. Her fingers, gnarled, twisted and sheathed in olive-purple skin, clutched at a full tea tray. Her determined approach was slow and wavering but she was not spilling a drop. She reached the old fashioned coffee table and placed the tray down in front of him, then sat stiffly in the armchair.

She poured the tea, then settled back in her chair, squirming to get as comfortable as her bony old body would allow, and began to talk.

Throughout the afternoon she spoke of her long and eventful life. She told him of her early days in the original Nimpkish village. She spoke of her father, a powerful chief and how he had arranged her marriage to the chief of the Gilford Island band. She talked of her life as a young bride and her membership in the last of the secret Hamasta societies, the Cannibal dancers. There were times when she actually made Potter feel he was back in time.

Finally ending a period of silence, the silence of the very old, she said, "Doctor Mike, I want to tell you the story of my people. It all started with a black whale. He lifted his huge head up from the world under the ocean and saw land that made him happy. He swam up to the shore and touched the beach with his head. He gave a big push with his tail and wouldn't you know it, he landed way up on the beach. You see, because he had great nawalakui, or magic power as you would call it, he could do such amazing things."

She talked on and on. Finally she said, "My people believe in the sort of magic power that whale had. We believe that great magic, wherever it comes from, is needed to help humans fight the spirits of darkness. The chief dark spirit is their leader, 'Man Eater at the Mouth of the River.' Those of my people who've seen him say he's a horrible man-like creature with many mouths, all over his huge, ugly body. To feed all them mouths, he has lots of helpers that're real terrible creatures."

"Like what?" asked Potter.

"From the skies, Man Eater depends on the powers of the Thunderbird, the chief of all the birds of heaven, a huge creature with wings of great length. From the sea, Man Eater sends Winalagilis, the War Spirit. He is a creature seen by my people as a beautiful dugout canoe coming from the north, the land of the House of Death. Winalagilis travels the world searching for any chance to bring humans to war. On the earth, in the dark forests up north, lives many of Man Eater's helpers. Their chief is Sisiutl, a fierce, double headed creature who's part snake, part man. The human part of this horrible thing lets it live in the worlds of the dead and the living. It's said that he hides beside trails in the woods, tricking humans by appearing before them as a beautiful, shiny spring salmon. Then, when they walk too close to look at his beauty, he turns them stiff like stone."

She fell into another meditative silence. Potter let it go almost surprised when she started to speak again after only a short pause.

"And the raven," she whispered. "The trickster. Able to change shape and soar high."

She wagged a bony finger. "In my younger days, the Man Eater and all his helpers had to be stopped, somehow. It was a real tough job, one left up to our great chiefs. Often times they'd have to ask for help from people like the shaman and secret dancing societies like the Hamasta. These were usually kids of chiefs or other close relatives. They all had to pass some really terrible tests to know if they would be useful against the forces of the Man Eater. Like the shaman, they too could see into the spirit world. They were Spirit Talkers."

She shifted her weight, attempting to find a more comfortable position. Not finding one, she slumped back and regarded him with a pained expression. "That was when the power of our chiefs, our magic and our people was real strong. We could hold back the power of darkness, then. But times got real bad and our chiefs lost their magic. Soon, there were no Spirit Talkers left to hear, to tell the rest of us what was said in the spirit world. Yeah. We once had strong magic." She closed her eyes as her head drooped in sleep.

He looked down at his watch and was shocked to discover that the old woman had kept him spell-bound for more than three hours. He pulled at a colorful blanket lying over the back of the chair, wrapped it around her and let himself out.

FIVE

All hell seemed to break loose on the anniversary of Potter's first month in Alert Bay.

An intimation of what was to come was the morning, which was different from the endless rain and fog of the previous few weeks. The rain had finally stopped and so the walk south to the hospital was a pleasure. The sun shone and there was no wind. The water in the boat basin was a perfect mirror for the reflections of moored fishing boats. And there, across the Sound, were the mountains, craggy and lush with forest and he could smell the fresh iodine tang of the water and feel the cool morning air on his face.

That evening, while he prepared dinner, his beeper went off. A quick telephone call to the hospital told him of an unscheduled labor by one of his patients and that a cab was on the way for him. Two hours later a small but healthy baby girl was born one month early. A couple of the nurses remarked that it was the full moon but Potter paid no attention.

His second call back to the hospital was at almost midnight. A car crammed with six drunks from the Bayside Inn bar had collided with a motor bike and a general melee had ensued. After the mud and blood settled, Potter and the emergency team set two arms, stitched one man's face and cleaned up the effects of a severe case of asphalt rash on another.

Stepping outside for a breather at around two a.m., he was startled by the sight of the moon, a shimmering bronze globe tangled eerily in the limbs of two huge, scraggly spruce. By 3:00 a.m. and his fourth emergency in five hours — more than they would normally get in a whole month — he was fast becoming a believer in full moons. He had also figured out why Doc Elliott chose that particular weekend to go off-island.

By ten the next evening, after two more deliveries, patching up the results of a bar fight and handling a nearly continuous stream of assorted minor injuries, he crashed on the couch in his front room and fell instantly into a deep sleep.

A loud banging jolted him. He forced himself upright and stumbled to the door, fumbling with the lock. When he pulled the door open a white light blinded him.

"Turn that damn thing off!"

"Mike, it's Jim Glinnen, RCMP. There's been a stabbing. We need you."

Moving back into the room to collect his things, Potter called out, "Reserve or town?"

"It's right around the corner. Let's go!"

A hundred yards from Potter's apartment a crowd had gathered on the front porch of the featureless, government issue prefab house. The big cop pushed through the crowd and Potter followed.

Inside was carnage. The whole living room and the hallway to the kitchen was drenched in blood. By the front door, next to a grimy couch, a motionless man lay stretched out. Kneeling beside him, two volunteer ambulance attendants were working vigorously with bandages and an oxygen unit. In the far corner of the room two uniformed police officers stood over a bloodied second man lying face down on another couch, his hands cuffed tightly behind him.

Potter squeezed his eyes shut and took two deep breaths. When he opened them again one of the ambulance attendants was talking. "The party was in full swing when Georgie Jack went berserk and attacked the old guy who's his room mate. Nobody knows why.

Then he stopped, like he'd just come to his senses, and the others started beating the shit out of him . . ."

It was hours later, at first light, when Potter and Linda Jarvis stood on the front lawn of the hospital, their faces turned away from the buffeting roar of the ascending Search and Rescue Labrador helicopter that was taking Georgie Jack's room mate to the mainland. The old man was luckier than Georgie. An hour after he was arrested the RCMP had called Potter to the cells when Georgie's body was discovered lying on the concrete floor in a pool of blood. Shortly thereafter Potter had pronounced him dead from self inflicted wounds suffered from repeatedly banging his head against the lip of the stainless steel toilet bowl in his cell.

"This is strangest couple of days I've ever had," he said to Linda as they trudged wearily back into the hospital. "This island is so beautiful, and it's been so quiet for the month I've been here, and in one night it's like everyone turned into werewolves or something."

One hour later, back at his apartment, Potter lay staring at the ceiling, his body craving the sleep that his over stimulated brain wouldn't allow. Finally, he decided to slosh his way down to the Umista Cultural Center, the Nimpkish history museum. He had discovered the place his first week in Alert Bay. The photos and written history he found on the back shelves helped him to better understand Mary's stories and all the characters she talked about. After two hours of studying the books on Kwakuitl myths he was close to exhaustion but even further away from sleep. When focusing on individual words became a task, he finally decided to brave the elements and went for a walk in the rain.

He slogged up the hill toward the townhouses and then across the road to the Big House, the reserve's official meeting hall. It was a long structure built in the traditional Kwakuitl style of rough hewn vertical cedar posts supporting a low peaked roof. On the front wall was painted a huge thunderbird, its outstretched wings guarding the narrow doorway. Thinking of the strange history of the island and its people, Potter didn't notice where he was going.

With a start he realized he was standing across the road from the scene of the previous night's bloodbath. He flinched from the memory and walked away toward one of the few streets on the whole island he hadn't yet explored. It soon petered out on a rocky shoreline, exposed and windblown. He stopped to get his bearings. To the south, the view was a scarred mess of stumps and woody debris, the result of recent logging. To the north, a cold, biting wind caused his eyes to blur. The only landmark was a grove of gray, leafless trees extending down to the beach. On the water side, to the east, gray-green waves marched sullenly past the shoreline.

He stood in exhausted indecision, trying to decide which way to go. He shook his head to clear his fogged brain. Having decided to walk south, away from the north wind, he found that he had in fact turned and was walking into the howling stream of cold Arctic air. A strange blackness pressed his temples as his eyes teared with the cold. He told himself that he would turn around, but somehow he couldn't. It was a peculiar sensation, so odd he smiled in spite of himself. Christ, he thought, exhaustion's made you like a robot. Soon it was easier just to keep walking than to try and figure out why he was doing it.

Every few steps on his strange, impulsive march he had to lower his eyes to weave through the football sized rocks under his feet. Ahead he could see an overgrown road bed cratered with overflowing potholes and littered with the twisted limbs of dead alders. Farther in, the trees on either side of the trail grew so thickly they blocked any view of the water, so dense the upper branches arched across the trail like the nave of some organic cathedral.

Soon the track narrowed to a mere footpath bordered on either side by tangled undergrowth that pawed at his shoulders like persistent, mossy panhandlers. Finally he stopped, breathing hard. The overhead canopy was now so thick only wan threads of light reached down to the gloom of the forest floor. It was completely still, and Potter suddenly found it airless and claustrophobic. He looked quickly around and realized he couldn't see more than a few feet in any direction.

What the hell was he doing here?

Suddenly from behind came an explosive Crrraaack! He started convulsively as if a gun had just gone off in his ear. He searched the trees the way he'd come, and heard nothing but the reverberating silence that remained after the thunderclap of sound.

Then he heard it. Laughter. Not human, but the screeching of some enormous predatory bird. The sound was so loud it was agonizing. He put his hands over his ears and started a clumsy, stumbling run away from the noise. He surged forward, lashing out at the dull green undergrowth that seemed to be grabbing at him from the sides of the trail.

Panting, he leaned for a moment, enmeshed in thick vegetation like a man snagged in barbed wire. The sound drew closer and he lowered his head, lunging again, now so tangled he was barely moving at all. Frantic, he saw just ahead of him a tiny silver-green patch of light and thrashed toward it.

Something suddenly grabbed his feet, binding his legs together. Forward momentum kept his upper body moving, and slowly he pitched forward, falling with the heavy inevitability of a tree overwhelmed by some primeval force of nature. He pawed at the air, falling, falling into blackness.

SIX

The rough rasping noise was everywhere, the sound of some heaving creature.

It took Michael Potter a few moments to realize it was his own breathing, exaggerated by the absolute silence of the ancient drenched forest in which he lay. He opened his eyes and saw dripping ferns. Gingerly, he lifted his head and strained to look back at what had caught him. A hump of rotten root insinuated out of the mossy soil like a petrified snake, crowned incongruously with one of his yellow rubber boots.

He laid his head back again and mentally checked his body. All systems go. Suddenly there was a croaking, woody laugh followed by a peculiar wheezing, as if the forest was so old it had emphysema. His eyes quickly searched the canopy as he painfully propped himself up on one elbow. High above, he saw branches rubbing together. The movement of branch against branch, plus wind gusts funneling down into the trees, created the eerie sounds.

Slowly he got to his feet and put on his boot, feeling like an idiot. He realized the silver green patch of light he had fought toward was a small clearing. He tried to brush off the mud and moss that caked his yellow slicker and found himself looking around. Thank God he'd had no audience, although it seemed the forest was still breathing smoky laughter at his panicked stupidity. "Glad you enjoyed the performance," he said as he bowed to the trees and trudged into the clearing like an actor taking the stage for an encore.

Plunging once again into the underbrush, he pondered the reasons for his flight from nothing. But the sound he'd first heard had been deafeningly loud — his ears still stung from it. And the screeching laughter hadn't been just branches and breeze. It bothered him that he could make no sense of what he'd heard or his own unreasoning panic, and soon concluded he was far more tired and stressed from the past two days than he realized. Home and to bed. And he'd have a few words with Doc Elliott about who was going to be on island and on call during the next full moon.

Finally he caught sight of the shoreline of Broughton Sound — the west side of the island — and knew exactly where he was. He could just see the clearing that housed the two most northerly buildings on the island, the old float plane hangar and next to it the Nimpkish band's fishing net loft, an old Quonset hut.

Walking into the clearing, a flash of white alternating to black caught his eye. A soccer ball. He watched as it bounced in the wide open space, then suddenly stopped.

Stopped by nothing, as if some invisible player had pressed down on it with his foot, or it was a video someone had suddenly put on pause. "Oh, no," he moaned. "I've had enough hallucinations for today."

"Can't you pass the damn thing without sending it into outer space?"

A tall, gangly Indian kid was jogging toward the inexplicably halted ball as another voice reached Potter's ears. "Jesus, Belly. Don't get so excited," shouted a small muscular boy. Also headed for the ball, he had broad Indian features but odd bronzed skin, and his hair was the color of bronze, his eyes icy blue. He was followed by a third very large male as all three converged on the black and white object. The gangly one reached it first.

"Hey, Beebo! You're not in the damned circus. Stop stunting so we can play a decent game."

"Yeah," said the big kid in a near perfect imitation of the other's whine, "No more showboat stuff. What do you think you are, a white man?"

As if on cue the two bigger boys grabbed the smaller one by the arms and heaved him skyward — where he stayed, hung in mid air, thrashing his arms in protest, as if defiance of gravity was an every-day event.

"Let me down, you assholes!" he yelled.

Potter blinked, then rubbed his eyes. Had he hit his head when he fell? He was now genuinely concerned about the state of his own health, with the same clinical detachment he would have given a patient who claimed to have conversations with little green men.

Starting again he realized he'd been mistaken — the little guy was in the air but the other two were holding on to him. Of course. He was seeing things. They let go and the boy tumbled to the wet ground, cursing to gales of mocking adolescent laughter.

Potter turned away towards home, suddenly overwhelmed with fatigue. He'd be no good to either himself or his patients if he did-n't get some rest. He smiled wearily, remembering that he had some single malt scotch. Just what the doctor ordered.

SEVEN

The alarm ripped Potter from a dreamless sleep. His third fumbling effort succeeded in stopping the noise and he peered groggily at the LED of the offending radio alarm. He'd slept for fifteen hours straight.

The world seemed back to normal as he made breakfast and left his apartment. Work at the clinic was uneventful and he had almost forgotten the events of the previous day when the receptionist told him about a last minute appointment. As she left Potter opened the patient's file. Johnson, Samuel James. Fifteen years old, born at St. George's Hospital, Alert Bay. Height five foot three, weight 125 pounds.

He learned that the boy had been a regular visitor to the clinic since childhood. The list of injuries was long and suggestive — multiple fractures, nose broken (three times), facial contusions, mysterious bruises, cuts, requiring stitches. Potter didn't even have to see Johnson to recognize the telltale signs of physical abuse.

He noted that for the past three years the injuries listed seemed mainly due to fighting. Not unusual, since the abused tend towards aggressiveness and abuse of others. The most recent entries indicated severe headaches with related blurred vision and severe dizziness. Two notations by Jeff Nelson, the Band's previous physician, indicated that the cause of these symptoms was unknown and did not seem related to head trauma. The patient had not responded to drug therapy.

Potter walked down the hall to the examination room. Entering the cubicle, he froze. Standing and smirking at him was the small, well-muscled boy he'd last seen hanging in mid-air. The contrast between the aboriginal features, bronze hair and skin, and blue eyes was even more striking up close.

He nodded curtly to hide his surprise, then over-compensated with a big false smile. "Please sit down."

"No thanks. Standing's fine."

"Very well. What's the problem?"

"Headaches. Getting worse. Sometimes I can't see."

"I've read your file," said Potter, waving the manila folder. "Can you tell me what you think might be causing them?"

The kid snorted. "You're the doctor."

Five minutes of subsequent consultation wasn't much more productive. The kid's arrogance began to wear on Potter's nerves. *Damn it you little creep*, he thought, *I'm the one who's supposed to be in charge here and I'm trying to help you.* People with genuine pain are always more cooperative than obstructive, and it occurred to him that maybe the purpose of the boy's visit wasn't medical at all. The boy kept staring so intensely with his bizarre blue eyes that Potter felt he had to continually look away.

Finally he'd had enough. "If the headaches continue then obviously there's something wrong." For the first time he dropped his helpful bedside manner and stared directly into those glacier blue eyes. "You don't look like a neurotic to me and I don't believe in phantom pain. Or phantom anything."

The boy's grin was crafty and at the same time genuinely amused. "Sure you do." He extended his hand, and the small grip was strong as a vise. "Name's Beebo. You a soccer fan, doc?"

Speechless, Potter watched the small figure march down the hall.

EIGHT

Potter caught the afternoon ferry to Port McNeill. Grateful for the break from his medical duties, he wandered around the tiny town center, browsing stores, visiting the library, and stopping for a beer with Thomas Albert at the too-cute-for-words Haida-Way Motel. Unable to forget his meeting with Samuel James Johnson, AKA Beebo, he was going to mention it to the laconic chief and decided it wasn't wise. He'd try to find out more about the kids first.

Dinner time. He'd ended up at the Bavarian Deli. As he gazed idly out of the fogged-up window onto the dark parking lot, a movement outside the window broke his reverie. A group of high school kids had huddled in front of the restaurant and were peering in. A pair of black eyes in an angular face above a narrow, beaky nose stared straight at him. It was the gangly kid from the bizarre soccer game, the one called Belly, and his burning, unblinking gaze was one of flat hostility.

Staring back, determined not to blink either, Potter's fingers loosened their hold on his coffee cup and it slipped from his grasp, sending a sheet of scalding liquid all over the table and the woman sitting at the next table. As he helped her, he heard mocking laughter as the teens moved off.

Disturbed and angry at the encounter, Potter headed back to the Haida-Way bar. Thomas Albert and his group were still there, playing pool with a group of loggers. As he joined them, it was obvious the tree-cutters took the strange white man as a city boy, and Albert said nothing to disabuse them of the notion. Once at the pool table, Potter's still lingering anger made him drink a lot of beer and play aggressively, and he lasted twelve games undefeated. This was taken as cause for general celebration, which lasted the whole ferry trip back to the island, and Thomas and Potter ended up closing down the Bayside Inn.

He had considerable cause to regret his overindulgence the next day. When he showed up at the clinic after scraping the fur off his tongue and gulping a gallon of orange juice, the receptionist greeted him with, "You look sicker than most of your patients. What were you drinking, fuel oil?"

After enduring a day of sympathy from his patients, who winked as they recommended a variety of home remedies for 'the flu', he'd had enough and decided to go on a gut-breaker of a run to sweat the rest of the poison out of his system and punish himself for his stupidity.

He'd been running for about fifteen minutes, feeling awful, when he entered the back road that connected the village and the reserve over the hump of the island. Every step he took sent stabbing pains through the sides of his head and he felt nauseated. The road had been shaded by trees but as he rounded the corner next to the gravel pit he was blinded by the late afternoon sun reflecting off the glistening, rain-soaked greenery, which only added to the pain he already felt behind his eyes. Still partially blinded, he missed seeing a darkened blur in the middle of the road. At the very last instant he dodged away, barely avoiding a collision with whatever it was that was standing in the way, fell heavily onto the gravel and began to vomit.

At first all he could make out was that the blur was not an elk or a deer. It was several seconds before he realized it was three human males and several more before he regained enough breath to wipe the sweat from his eyes well enough to recognize the three boys from the soccer game.

"Oh man, is this repulsive or what?" exclaimed a voice he recognized as that of Beebo.

"Yeah, I heard he really tied one on last night. And they say Indians can't hold their liquor."

The ringing laughter clanged painfully in Potter's head. He managed to lift himself onto one knee but couldn't be sure of rising any further without fainting. He wiped his mouth with the back of his hand. "Well, if it isn't the Hardy boys," he riposted feebly.

"C'mon doc," said Belly, as he leaned down to lend a helping hand. "You look kind of pitiful like that."

He'd had enough of their remarks and condescension. "Get away from me!" he snarled, pushing away the hand and finally rising to his feet. He assumed a crouching attack position. "All of you, get away from me now!" They backed away.

"Jesus, he thinks he's Jean-Claude Van Damme," said the big fellow.

Beebo was looking at Potter narrowly. "Shut up Dickie. Hey, doc, cool down. We're just kids, you know."

Potter's breath was coming easier and he was starting to feel a little foolish. He lowered his fists. "Then why are you trying to terrorize me?"

"Terrorism is what Arabs do," said Belly. "No comparison. You just happened to see something that struck you as kind of strange. We just wanted to make sure that you were a little off balance, you know. Scare you a bit. That's why we sent Beebo to see you. We like to be alone."

"Saw what?"

"You saw us playing soccer," said Dickie accusingly. "You *saw.*"

"I saw what couldn't possibly be. I figured I was hallucinating. Are you telling me I wasn't?"

The three boys looked at each other with a peculiar intensity, as if having a conversation no one else could hear. Finally Belly sighed. "When we realized you'd seen the thing with the ball, we decided to throw Beebo into the air. Just for effect, you know? Then we sent Beebo to see you and let you know we knew you were watching. After that I made you do the thing with the coffee cup in Port McNeill. We wanted to scare you a little. We figured it'd do one of two things — shut you up so you wouldn't tell anybody else, or rattle you so bad that even if you did tell someone they'd think you were off the deep end."

Now fully recovered, Potter looked at the boys. They weren't joking. "Well, I have to admit it rattled me a little. Why are you afraid of me?"

"We've seen the movies," said Belly. "About what happens to people who can do stuff like we do. Those CIA guys come after you, or even the Russians. And we're not too sure about the whole thing anyway. We're scared."

"I'm not!" shouted Beebo.

"Shut up," said Belly. "Doc, there's something wrong with us. We need help and someone to trust."

"We're different," said Dickie eagerly. "We can do weird things, but weird things also happen to us, especially Beebo. He gets dreams and headaches, real bad ones, and they're getting worse. You're the only one who's ever really seen us, and you're a doctor. Maybe you can help us. Maybe we could trust you. You know, the Hypocritic Oath."

Potter almost smiled, but a thought occurred to him. "And what if you decide you can't trust me? Do you hang me in the air and leave me? Or worse?"

No one answered. Potter had regained his confidence in one area and was losing it in another, as he realized that he had actually seen the impossible at the soccer game near the hangar. *These weird kids could do damn near anything to me and I probably couldn't stop it,* he thought.

"We just want to find out what's happening to us," said Belly. "If people find out about us, they might do something to us. Maybe split us up. Or worse."

There was silence as Potter contemplated this. What did he have to lose? And if there was one thing they taught you at medical school, it was how to reassure the nervous, if only by misdirection.

"All right, I promise I won't tell anyone what I saw. And I will do my best to help you." As they started to grin he played his authority card. "But I can't do that unless you are absolutely truthful with me. For example, how did you know I was going to be at Port McNeill?"

In unison the boys turned toward the side of the road and started waving their arms. Two small black heads popped up from behind a gravel pile and suddenly two young girls were running toward them.

They were grinning shyly as they reached them, and began to giggle. The first was a thirteen year old. She was pretty, five feet tall and her thick wavy hair was short and matched her athletic build. Potter immediately recognized her as his next door neighbor, Brenda Johnson. The other was a small girl of eight, her angelic look made slightly awry by a shiny silver front tooth. "You were funny when you went on your walk in the woods and started running and fell down."

Potter was about to ask how she knew about it, then decided his recently recovered dignity was too fragile to risk another battering.

"Right," he said with authority, as they all grinned. "Why don't I walk you home?"

More than once on the walk back to the reserve Potter questioned his judgment. A pushing match between Dickie and Brenda resulted in her apparently falling over into the ditch. He lunged to break her fall, then saw her downward momentum halted magically. At a forty-five degree angle she walked confidently, impossibly, as Potter stared in disbelief. The closer they got to the reserve the more serious and guarded the youngsters became. No one spoke, each absorbed in thought.

They left each other with nods and smiles, and Potter turned to walk back to his home on this odd rainy place with its strangely gifted children. His meditations made it seem as if the walk took no time at all, and suddenly he was bending down at his front door to unlace his shoes. Opening the door, he spotted a pair of white nursing shoes and a trail of women's clothing leading up the stairs. He stepped back outside and checked the address. It was his house, all right. Wondering if his new-found friends had a more adult sense of humor than he was inclined to give them credit for, he followed the scatter of white pantyhose, pastel pink uniform, green lacy bra, and filmy, emerald green panties, on tiptoe, like a man stalking a large and potentially dangerous animal. The trail ended at his bedroom door. Sitting in his bed under his comforter was Linda Jarvis. She smiled at him, then frowned.

"Oh dear. Here I thought I was planning a lovely surprise for a man I know is crazy about me but too shy to say it, and he shows up looking like he was just mauled by a cougar."

The following three hours made him almost forget the events of the previous day.

NINE

Two days later, returning from a run, Potter noticed Brenda Johnson loitering with intent outside his townhouse. His invitation to come in was accepted eagerly and she squeezed past him into the living room, moving over to the couch. She sat down and looked expectant.

No sooner had he closed the door when a faint knock sounded on the other side. He opened it to see Belly and Princess standing there. Without a word, they too pushed past him, sitting on either side of Brenda.

He meditated for a moment, then flung open the door and peered outside. Nothing. But just as he was about to close it he heard shuffling sounds and an instant later Beebo and Dickie were stalking up to the door.

After they too had sat down, Potter closed the door for the final time. "Do we wait for the Pope, or is this it?"

The kids grinned. "Just us," said Belly. "We've been talking. About you, mainly. You said we had to tell you everything. So we will."

Potter nodded and sat down. "As they used to say on TV, why don't you start at the beginning?"

It was obvious that Belly was the designated spokesman. He shrugged. "We knew you were coming."

"How"?

"Saw it in a dream."

"Uh huh. Do you stop soccer balls in your dreams too?"

Belly glared. "It's true. You know about Beebo's headaches. Well, he dreamed about you. Months ago. We knew you'd come."

He looked so hurt that Potter said, "This is all a bit much for me. I was trained to be a skeptic. I'm a doctor, a scientist. All this dreaming, foreseeing the future, being able to influence events in the real world, all this She-Manitou, Great Spirit stuff takes a little getting used to. I know it's been an effort for you to try to trust me. Remember that trust is a two way street."

He looked at them suspiciously. "Can you read minds? If you can, then you know you can trust me, and this is all pointless."

"No. But we can read people pretty well, I don't know how."

Something else occurred to Mike Potter. "That terrible thing that happened at Georgie Jack's place. You didn't have any reason to terrorize him, did you? Or have a grudge against the old guy who was his room mate?"

Belly looked horrified as the others shook their heads. "We aren't killers." He hesitated. "Although there's something you should know."

Potter nodded patiently.

"Like most dreams, Beebo's aren't very specific. He dreamed a healer would come to us, one who would understand. We assumed it was the other guy. He had hair and eyes kind of like yours. Tall too."

Potter frowned. "What other guy?"

"The doctor before you. Dr. Nelson."

Suddenly Potter recalled what Chief Thomas Albert had said about Jeff Nelson's sudden departure from the island.

"We sort of tested him," said Belly hesitantly. "You know, like we did you. And he sort of freaked out. I guess he was pretty religious, didn't drink, stuff like that. We didn't mean any harm. But we had to know. Then, just like that, he left."

Potter shrugged. "Well, now I'm here. What do we do? This kind of thing isn't exactly covered in medical school."

"We think we're going crazy. We can't tell anyone, but we need help. It's all getting worse. The really strange stuff started happening to Beebo three or four years back."

"Okay. So tell me about it. I have to understand before I can help. This actually is kind of like medicine, where you learn how to listen to a patient and take a case history. But you have to tell me in your own words. Maybe Beebo should go first, since he's the one having the most problems."

Beebo and Dickie looked at each other, having one of those wordless conversations Potter found so eerie. Finally Beebo spoke.

"Name's Beebo Johnson. Me and Dickie Cook are cousins. We look out for each other. We both come from small villages over towards the mainland. Figured we'd be loggers or fishermen, like our dads. My dad was a drunk, beat me up all the time when I was little. But I always fought back."

Potter nodded encouragement, remembering the medical file, as Dickie said, "Beebo has a temper, always gets into fights."

"So I took up body building."

"I don't have to body build 'cause I'm big enough already."

Potter appraised Dickie, who even at his young age tipped the scales at more than two hundred pounds. With a shambling, slope shouldered walk like a bear, he didn't look particularly agile, but once he got a firm grip there wouldn't be much you could do.

"We both like practical jokes," continued Beebo, grinning at Dickie. "The elders get kind of slivers-up-the-bum about it."

An answering smile appeared on Dickie's round face. Despite his name his look was total Kwaquitl, one now normally seen only in sepia-tinted museum photos from the last century. "And we also felt like we knew each other, like we shared a secret. But we didn't find out why for a long time."

Beebo continued. "It was a Friday night, summer. Dickie and me were hanging around trying to score beer from guys coming out of the Nimpkish Hotel bar. But we couldn't score so we headed for home. We were on our bikes. We got to the new housing development at the south edge of the reserve when we heard a car behind us."

"It passed us real fast, and we could hear guys hollering as it went around the bend," said Dickie. "Then we heard it reverse and come back toward us. Right at us. We had to throw ourselves into the ditch."

"We couldn't believe it," added Beebo. "Until I saw who was in the car. It was Jimmy Albert. I'd sort of made a pass at his girlfriend the previous week and I'd heard he was pissed off. As he got out of the car I saw that he was also pissed up."

"Not just him, but five others," said Dickie. "They blocked our way, said they were going to beat the shit out of us. Which they proceeded to do."

"I lost sight of Dickie," continued Beebo. "And I was being held down and beaten up by several guys. Beaten up pretty bad, but I could still hear Dickie calling my name as he was being pounded."

The muscular teen took a deep breath. "Because I couldn't thrash around physically, I found somehow I was doing it in my thoughts, out of panic like. And suddenly I could *see* inside the car. Like I was seeing it from above. It was an old piece of junk and I saw that the brake handle was on. So I kinda lifted it."

Dickie said, "I saw he was doing it so I popped the gearshift into neutral."

Potter interrupted. "Let me get this straight. You both influenced mechanical objects from a distance, with your minds?"

"Yeah," interjected Beebo. "The car was on a slope so it was edging forward. The guys beating on me didn't see it, not until the last moment, and Jimmy Albert last of all. He was too drunk to get out of the way and it hit him in the hip and shoved him over a retaining wall on the side of the road. He was flat on his back, with one of the tires pressing down on his chest just hard enough to pin him there but not hard enough to crush him. It was strange that it just stopped like that. I know I didn't stop it."

"Me neither," said Dickie. Suddenly the two boys looked at Belly, who gazed calmly back.

"Anyway," continued Beebo, "some of the guys hitting on us ran off, and we were standing there looking at Jimmy, who was screaming like crazy. Dickie had just reached in and turned off the ignition when one of our own Native constables came by. Constable Murphy. They patrol the island all night Friday and Saturday because of the drinking and fights and stuff. Murphy called an ambulance."

Dickie shrugged. "Jimmy was unconscious by then. We all worked to get the car off him, but couldn't. Then we realized Belly had appeared out of nowhere. He suggested jacking the car up, so we did."

"Then the ambulance came and took him away."

"End of story?" asked Potter.

"No." Now it was Belly's turn.

"I was home that same evening when I heard car tires screeching and the whooping and hollering. I live in the housing development they told you about, close to the road. Went out on the back porch and saw six guys beating up on two. Suddenly I could see in my mind's eye the inside of the car and the brake handle being lifted with nothing lifting it. I was somehow above the car, but seeing inside it too. But I was also still on my porch. Anyway, the car started to move and I could tell it was going to hit Jimmy and he was going to be hurt real bad. So I *made* it stop. Then I went over to help. I mean, then I *physically* moved my body to the road to help jack up the car."

The kids stared at Potter as he struggled to find something sensible to say, but couldn't.

Finally Belly said, "Me, Dickie and Beebo just looked at each other. I knew from past experience that I could do this kind of stuff." He nodded at Princess, sitting silent and solemn beside him. "But apart from my baby sister I had no idea anyone else could. And since they were freaked out, I could pretty much tell what they were feeling and I knew they could do the same. But it didn't make me feel uncomfortable or anything. It was just a fact."

"We didn't even say anything out loud," concluded Beebo. "We just nodded at each other and went home. That was about a year ago."

"Well," said Potter carefully, "I've heard of Yury Geller, the spoon-bending guy, but this is ridiculous."

****

For the next two hours Potter listened to the stories, stories of how these children had discovered the strange powers that existed within them, and how they had discovered each other.

It turned out that Belly's real name was William Lucas, and at seventeen he was the eldest son of senior Nimpkish Band Councilor Dan Lucas, as well as the oldest member of the group.

He'd always been a loner. Liked computers as well as anything mechanical. Knowing he was somehow different, he began to construct barriers around himself. But never did the barriers exclude his little sister Molly, or Princess as everyone called her.

Potter learned that Beebo's dreams, visions and nightmares had started when he was quite young, usually at night. Now they could come at any time.

The three boys had become fast friends and the early testing of the limits of their powers accidentally led them to test Princess.

They gathered in the basement of the Lucas home one Saturday evening to play miniature pool. They worked on a trick shot so that once the rack was hit, a ball would sink in each of the six pockets. By choosing two balls and two pockets each, they could direct the balls into selected holes. As they were about to begin, Princess came downstairs.

Beebo hit the cue ball. It struck the pack on the right-hand side, three balls down. As if in slow motion, six balls traveled towards the intended pockets and one by one, plopped in. When the last ball hit its target Beebo grinned.

Princess was excited. She pointed at the nine balls still on the table. "But what about these?" Slowly at first and then faster, they all rolled to four corners of the table and fell neatly into pockets. The boys gaped.

The group of three became four. Yet still they felt incomplete.

Until late one wintry Saturday night, when a wild storm was thumping down Broughton Sound.

Brenda didn't like the thought of making her way home through the gale, but she was more frightened of the storm she'd face from her mother, who would be home from a dance at around midnight. She was on a strict curfew, even though her mother socialized a lot these days, now that her father was gone.

After waiting half an hour for a taxi at her friend's house, she decided to leave and brave the storm.

She was instantly drenched and cold. She caught the hood strings of her heavy jacket and pulled them down, lowering her head. After walking briskly for almost fifteen minutes , she heard music coming from the Bayside Inn Pub.

She reached the Pub entrance just as the door snapped open, exposing the smoky interior of the crowded establishment. Two beefy patrons staggered out. A quick sideways glance at them convinced her that she recognized them.

A week before, when she and her mother were grocery shopping in the Island Center department store, two men came up to her mother and started to give her a hard time. Dorothy Johnson got rid of them in no uncertain terms, but Brenda had been frightened. Asking who they were, she had learned they were Yugoslavs who used Alert Bay as a fishing base. Her mother had added that they were probably just having a little fun and were nothing to worry about. Brenda didn't find that explanation comforting — they looked pretty scary to her and she had absolutely no idea where Yugoslavs came from.

Without looking back, Brenda continued walking, increasing her pace. She heard hoarse laughter and a couple of shouted comments.

She started to run. She heard pursuing footsteps, then a hand grabbed at her hair, jerking her violently backwards. As she tried to scream a huge hand that smelled like fish, beer and cigarette smoke clamped over her face.

She heard another shout. Suddenly the hand was gone, revealing her two attackers and a large, muscular blond man who was running toward them, obviously angry. Arguing with them in a foreign tongue, as if he knew them and that he was somehow their leader. It appeared he was getting them under control when one of the men threw a sucker punch and hit the big blond full in the face. He crashed against the wall and slid to the ground. Dimly she could see blood flowing from a cut on his forehead.

They were dragging her toward the alley. She fought but they were too strong. Suddenly she was on the ground and a pock marked face was in front of hers. She thrashed as he tore at her clothing. "NOOOOO" she screamed.

It was a scream heard by no one! For Brenda, time shifted into a slow, nauseating jumble.

Suddenly, that ugly face touching her's wasn't there any more, flashing away into the darkness. The body attached to it pirouetted away from her in a sluggish arc and seemed like long, agonizing moments passed before the head made contact with the wall, that horrible, fleshy face contorting into a confused grin as a flush of crimson welled up in the nostrils. The back, waist and legs hit in succession. His head slumped forward and his torso slithered down the rough wall boards.

The other one stared at her terrified, dumb enough to try for her again, only to be thrust out of the way. Dimly she saw men struggling, fists thrown, a body with its head slammed with tremendous force against a wall. It was the blond, his face a mask of blood and rage come to her rescue. The other man tried to run and the burly blond tackled him and threw him on his back. Sitting astride him, he threw his fists into the Yugoslav's face. Finally he sat back on the now inert body, exhausted, then got to his feet.

Painfully, he limped over to Brenda, who was trying to gather her torn clothes around her and regain her feet on shaky legs at the same time. He stopped a few feet away and wiped the blood and rain from his face. Handsome through blood, he looked to be in his mid-forties and very fit. In some heavy foreign accent he said, "Animals."

He looked at her closely. "You okay?" She shook her head no. "You are trembling. "Here, take my hand. We'll get you a car."

She pulled back from him in panic. "OK. OK Take my coat and stay here. I'll be back shortly." Waiting for her nod, he turned and ran back towards the bar. The instant he was out of sight, she jumped to her feet and ran in the opposite direction. She ran and ran until she couldn't feel her body any longer.

Responding to the voiceless call and the running imagery, stronger than anything they had ever experienced, Dickie, Beebo and Belly ran into the stormy night. They found her an hour later, carrying her home and getting her calmed and clean before her mother returned.

And the group of four had become five.

TEN

A forest, a raging stream. Nowhere and yet everywhere. Silent, shaggy sentinels stand, guarded by barbed undergrowth and lurking shadows.

The narrow track begins to rise more steeply, its far end vanishing into gloomy mist and murk. It is cold yet hot, dry yet sweaty with humidity.

As the dusk deepens sounds grow louder, sounds that are not forest sounds, nor animal, nor human. As the thickets thicken the sentinel trees lean closer, old angry bearded men peering down with envy at something young and free. He peers through the tendrils of mist that reach out to him with their cold caresses.

Slowly, slowly, long spindly arms rise, fall, rise again and with a woody groan reach toward him. But there is no wind, and fog thick as the death exhaled from an open grave blots out the ground. There is a shriek like an angry tropical bird, in a place where there can be no tropical bird. Another shriek, much louder. Suddenly all the branches reach for him all at once, as if to grasp him in some terrible marriage embrace. He knows somehow that their touch is fatal. He begins to run.

It is hard to breath, the mist is now thick and foul, heavy with the stench of rotting vegetation and putrefying corpses. He feels he is being chased, but dares not look around. Feeding on his fear, the forest pants around him as he suddenly gags at the graveyard stench.

Suddenly a fibrous knotty arm with a hand-like clump of clawed twigs lashes at his face. Then another, and another. He dodges and weaves but they fly at him faster and faster. Panicked, he sees a pair of plant hands reach for his throat. Where they touch him the pain burns like fire, like acid, like acid fire. His eyes tear uncontrollably and he stumbles.

He knows he is weakening. Stumbles again, falls. The hostile forest seems to move in like a mob scenting a kill, as fear makes him weak.

Suddenly there is no fear. Something touches him and he touches it back. A star-burst of energy fills him, emanates from him, so strong it bleaches the color from the now cowering trees and the mist hisses as it is burned away by the power.

He stands, ready now to fight, to survive. As he tears at flailing branches, ripping them from their shaggy sockets, the acid fire burns even worse than before. But because he fights, it is only the pain of a battle well-fought, not the agony of fear and death.

Suddenly the forest vanishes in a whirl of flaming embers. The way ahead is clear and shining. In a clearing, in the shadows between two cedar trunks is a towering, glistening creature. . .

"What kind of dream was it this time?" asked Michael Potter gently. He always waited for several minutes after Beebo awakened from his dreams, always convulsively, always drenched in sweat, always with a pounding headache.

Beebo gave a wan smile. "For the first time I had them scared. I was in control, not just running forever and being devoured." He closed his eyes and heaved a sigh so deep it was as if he thrust his soul from him. "The pain was the same, though. Jesus, the pain ..." He struggled to describe it before falling into an exhausted sleep.

Potter rose from the chair by the bed, stretched and walked toward the journal in which he had been recording these episodes for almost two months. It was an important day, the first where Beebo had been able to take charge in a dream, at least up to a point. As he wrote down what the boy had said, he glanced back at the bed, more worried than he cared to admit. The dreams seemed to take so much out of the boy, strong though he was.

At the very beginning he had told them what he thought they should do. He had walked with them out into the forest and collected six thick twigs. He had handed one to Beebo. "Break it." The teen had snapped it effortlessly. Potter had then handed him a bundle of five twigs. "Now break these." Beebo had strained mightily before giving up. Potter explained, "When Genghis Khan was a boy he, his mother, and just a handful of friends were being hunted by their clan's enemies. They were quarreling about what to do. His mother Holun called them all together and had Genghis do the same thing Beebo just tried to do. Then she said the words the world's greatest conqueror never forgot: 'A single twig is easily broken. But many twigs together can never be broken.' I think all five of you will have to stick together, learn together, fight together, or the world may break you."

So they all worked together to help Beebo with his debilitating dreams. There were three types — regular dreams, nightmares of terrifying vividness, always accompanied by excruciating headaches, and what Potter described in his journal as visions or premonitions. The nightmares were the worst.

Potter wasn't sure what could be accomplished through these sessions, which he referred to in his journal as 'psycho-non-analysis', but hoped that soon some sort of breakthrough might be achieved. And his worries about the state of Beebo's health weren't the only things bothering him.

The previous week he had been at the clinic staring out of the staff room window at a group of kids playing with a heap of oyster shells. He heard the door open and looked around. It was Thomas Albert.

"What're you staring at?"

"Kids. Oyster shells. Nothing in particular."

"Actually Mike, that's kind of what I came to talk to you about. Got a minute?"

"Sure. What's up?"

The normally loquacious chief looked uncomfortable. "Mike, you and I are friends and, well, if somebody was saying things about me I'd like to think you'd come and tell me, you know?"

"Of course I would."

"Okay. Well, it's basically a word to the wise, if you know what I mean. This is a mighty small place and everybody sooner or later knows everybody else's business."

He paused as Potter waited, mystified. "So?"

"So it seems there are some people who think you hanging around with that group of kids all the time is kind of unhealthy."

"Oh, come on, Thomas . . ."

Albert held up his hands as if pushing the protest away. "Personally I don't see it. Any guy interested in Linda Jarvis isn't likely to have the inclination — or the energy, if you don't mind me saying it — to be interested in kids."

"I am interested in this group of children, but not for that reason."

Albert was watching him closely. "Mind me asking what the reason is?"

Potter thought of the promise he had made to his young friends. "Yes," he said flatly.

The chief waited a moment, then said, "Fine. Just a word to the wise. Forest has eyes and all that. See you around."

ELEVEN

Over weeks spent with the kids, Potter had devised a number of tests to determine the precise extent of their powers. He wanted to be scientific about the process, so they had started small. But even from the beginning it seemed obvious the possibilities were practically infinite. Albert Einstein had once described his journeys through space and time as 'thought experiments', and so were these — literally. They were often complicated by the fact that the kids were easily bored, tended to regard them as games, and had an adolescent fondness for practical jokes.

Like the day of the ferry incident.

It was a Sunday in April, rainy and squally. They headed for the exposed bluff on the northwest end of the island. As they trudged along the muddy trail, Brenda and Princess led the way. Dickie, Belly and Potter followed, while Beebo struggled in the rear, still suffering the effects of a particularly bad headache. Potter looked back occasionally in concern, while the others tried to pretend not to notice he was doing so.

At their destination on the bluff they overlooked a rough and sullen sea, as black clouds overlooked them.

Potter's plan was to throw pieces of driftwood off the bluff and then have individual members of the group try to keep the wood stationary in the current. He would call others to assist until, as a team, they were able to gain full mental control over the movement of the wood. His goal was to sharpen their concentration and coordination.

At first all went well. Brenda was unable to control a large chunk of driftwood, but Dickie's assistance slowed the wood down and Princess's mental contribution stopped it dead. The results were much the same when Beebo started and Belly and Brenda were brought in to help.

Twenty minutes later, Potter could tell the test was starting to lose its appeal as the magnificent sight of the ferry plowing its way north up the Sound shattered their already wandering concentration. He looked at the five of them, staring raptly at the huge ship as it thrashed through the stormy sea. Slowly the ship began to come around, deviating from what he knew was its usual course, unsteady in the heaving waves. After only a couple of minutes it was heading straight for them, at full speed, toward the cliffs.

"Jesus Christ!" he shouted. "Do you see that? There's something desperately wrong!"

Shrieks of laughter exploded behind him. He turned to see the five kids wildly jumping around, high-fiving like members of some lunatic basketball team in the poltergeist Olympics.

"Have you gone completely off your collective rocker?" he yelled. "You're going to kill someone! And you're jumping around like a pack of idiots for the whole world to see. Let that ship go!"

Both Belly and Princess pointed to the ferry and shouted, "Whale on the beach!"

"Aw, doc, it's fun to play God," said Dickie.

"I wish I could see the crew's faces," giggled Brenda.

"Beats playing with driftwood like the rest of the dorks," jeered Beebo.

Potter turned and saw that the ferry was now slowing down and making a wide arc to turn back on course.

He grabbed at the two yellow rain slickers closest to him and pulled hard. Dickie and Belly toppled on him in a heap. The others kept hooting and jumping, then decided they liked the sight of the human pile better than the circling vessel. They dived on top and their weight caused the writhing mass to slide over the grassy fringe of the bluff into dense undergrowth.

Potter's muffled, angry yells could barely be heard over shrill schoolgirl screams, hoarse male howls and the shrieking wind.

****

Back at Potter's apartment, they explained.

"Explaining's hard," said Dickie. "Just for fun I threw out a thought rope — a sort of spiraling, filmy thread. Mine's like copper and green."

"And I helped," said Princess, "with a silver-blue one. That's how we wrapped around the bridge."

"Mine is blue and gold," said Belly, "Beebo's was crimson-mother of pearl and Brenda's was bronze-green. Mine found the wheel on the bridge and hauled on it."

"I made the helmsman *relax* so the others could make the wheel spin out of control," said Brenda.

Potter listened to them and tried not to believe, his expression like that of a skeptic at a seance who suddenly realizes the ectoplasm is real and happens to be talking directly to him. After a stern lecture on the merits of secrecy and controlled scientific experimentation, they departed and left him alone with his thoughts and his journal, scribbling furiously.

TWELVE

Potter was all trussed up the following Saturday, tied to a spine board.

He had found that all work and no play made his five charges dull boys and girls. He had also discovered they had almost as much interest in medicine as he had in their strange powers, so he would occasionally give impromptu medical lectures and demonstrations. As this rainy Saturday was a perfect day for first aid practice, he was in his apartment, bound to the spine board, pretending to have a fractured pelvis.

There was a knock at the door. "Would one of you get that, please?"

"This is your place, doc. You should do the greeting It's rude otherwise."

"In case you hadn't noticed, I'm bound hand and foot."

"Wouldn't have bothered Houdini," laughed Dickie.

"Houdini never had to deal with you lot," said Potter. "Door, *s'il vous plait.*"

Dickie opened the door to reveal a tall man in his sixties, with a perfectly rounded shiny head like a billiard ball, fringed with gray hair. His calm eyes were blue beneath bushy eyebrows, and if he'd been smoking a pipe he would have looked every inch the professor. He thrust his hands into the pockets of baggy brown corduroys beneath his too-short orange floater jacket and contemplated Potter lying bound in the middle of the living room floor.

"Hello," he said dryly. "I've just arrived with the ransom and I assure you the police haven't followed me."

Potter frowned upon hearing the familiar voice with its plummy English accent, barely tempered by years in North America. He craned his neck to see. "Harry? Is that you?"

The tall man looked up at the sky, squinting into the light drizzle that dropped gently into his eyes and beaded on his shiny domed head. "You know, children, when you have as little hair as I do, you can actually hear the rain drumming on your skull. Shall I stand here and listen to it until it drives me insane, or may I come in?"

"Harry, this is completely unexpected. Come on in. Kids, get me out of this thing."

Finally free, he stood stiffly and walked toward the older man, extending his hand. "Come in, take off that wet stuff. What are you doing here?"

"I needed a break and thought I might come to the island. I've known Dr. Elliott for a number of years and I also wanted to see how you were doing. If you say you hate it here I'll be consumed with guilt."

"I love it here. Wish I could say the same about Elliott, but we can talk shop later. Anyway, let me introduce you. Guys, this is Dr. Harry Warner, a professional colleague of mine and the man who suggested I should come to Alert Bay."

As Potter expected, the kids were polite enough, but only the boys would return Warner's friendly, alert gaze as the girls shyly averted their eyes. Given their wariness around strangers, it would be interesting to see how long it would take Warner, famous for his soothing bedside manner, to make them open up.

"What was your name again, young man? My memory isn't what it used to be."

"Beebo."

"Ah yes. Beebo and Belly. Sounds like a vaudeville act from my youth. How'd you ever get handles like that?"

Beebo shrugged irritably. "Dunno. Just happened."

"I know what you mean. When I was a boy in England, my family hung strange names on my sisters and me. We could never figure the exact significance of the names but it's interesting how such things stick with you. Mine at least made sense, they called me 'Stretch.' Anyway, it's very nice to meet you all."

"Have you seen Elliott yet?"

"Just came from there. I really must apologize for not letting you know I was coming. Didn't want you to put on the dog and whatnot. But surprise has its downside, as I discovered to my chagrin. Elliott and his wife are not getting along at present and frankly the lady and I have never much cared for each other. She greeted me as if I were the bubonic plague incarnate."

Potter could tell from the way the kids intently followed this barely understandable exchange that they could at least deduce there was some sort of problem with Mrs. Elliott. Since she had taught them all at school, and all had gotten into trouble with her, it was apparent that Warner was already building a tiny beach head of sympathy with the kids.

"Harry, you have to tell me what you've been up to. How long are you here?"

"Two days. I'm on my way up to Prince Rupert tomorrow afternoon."

"Take a load off. What can I get you to drink?"

It was almost supper time when Harry said he had to leave. Potter got the kids to help clean up the debris of beer cans, pop bottles, and several different kinds of junk food that had accumulated over the previous several hours and, as the kids waved goodbye, offered to walk with Harry back into the village.

As they trudged along the road, Warner said, "Really, Michael, how do you like being here? Did I make a mistake in suggesting that you come?"

"It's not exactly bright lights, big city, but now that I've gotten used to the rhythm and the laid-backness of it all. I must admit I enjoy it."

"Any surprises? Culture shock? I'm a little taken aback to see that those children like you so much. You never struck me as the scout leader type."

"They're okay. More than that, actually. As for culture shock, there's been a little more than I expected." Briefly Potter considered confiding in Warner, who he suddenly remembered was a psychiatrist and an expert in brain dysfunction. It dawned on him that Harry might very well be able to diagnose Beebo's dreams and headaches. Then he recalled his promise to the kids, which he now regretted. But a promise was a promise.

"But I've adapted pretty well, I think."

Harry Warner's friendly but alert gaze appraised him for a few moments. "Very glad to hear it. I must say you're looking well. Now what's this about you and John Elliott?"

Potter filled him in on the difficulties he had with the crusty old physician — he was stubborn, rude, no longer read the literature and couldn't abide advice, no matter how well-intentioned.

Warner nodded. "He was always a bit like that. A person's traits tend to get exaggerated as they get older and they end up a hopeless caricature of themselves. Personally, I intend to turn into one of those old men who's always pinching nurse's bums, sneaking drinks from a hip flask hidden under the spare linens, and generally being a terror."

"Amen," answered Potter.

They shook hands as they parted at the edge of the village. "Sorry I can't see you again tomorrow, Harry. My day of on call at the clinic."

"I understand completely." Warner's eyes searched his face. "And remember, if you run into any difficulties here, anything you can't handle, need someone to talk to and all that, I'm not far away.

"Of course," smiled Potter. "If I catch a terminal case of bush fever and go completely nuts I'll let you know."

THIRTEEN

The next day for Potter was near murder — literally. He burst through the Emergency Room doors to face a cluster of worried faces and started scrubbing as Linda filled him in.

"Fishing boat accident. Maimed, some loss of blood. Patient is in shock. It's the chief's son, Jimmy Albert."

"What happened?"

"Fell into a seine net. Hand got snagged, dragging him all the way up into the pulley block at the top of the mast. Severe chest trauma, right arm and hand practically crushed. We're waiting for x-rays, Doc Elliott can help and the patient is on IV."

Potter worked most of the afternoon to stabilize Jimmy Albert. The boy was unconscious the whole time as Elliott helped to clean up the chest cavity and set the hand and arm. Mike grudgingly had to admit that the old guy still knew his stuff. Later an air ambulance helicopter came and took Jimmy off-island.

At 6:30 p.m. Potter was lying on the staff room couch when Linda poked her head around the corner.

"Mike? Thomas Albert and Dan Lucas are here to see you. From what I can tell it isn't going to be pleasant."

Rolling off the couch he saw that her pretty features were strained with something other than exhaustion. He knew it was neither professional nor advisable, but he put his arms around her, drew her close and kissed her. Holding her at arm's length, he asked, "What do you mean?"

"This is a small island. Thomas Albert and Dan Lucas are political rivals, but they've been friends since childhood. It's hard to explain. They slap each other on the back and do all that other guy stuff, but their kids don't like each other. What an understatement. You know, Jimmy and Belly. And both of them were on the boat this afternoon. You can cut the tension out there with a knife and I'm getting real bad vibes. Be careful. And it doesn't help that they've been waiting for hours."

Potter kissed her on the forehead. "If I'd had someone like you to look after me my whole life, I'd have won the Nobel Prize by now. Let's go."

Thomas was rigid as a statue as Potter entered the room. He leapt to his feet and was across the floor in two bounding steps. "I heard he's off-island. Mike, we're friends. Give it to me straight."

Potter was about to speak when Dan Lucas entered the room, followed by a pale Belly. Lucas was big and handsome and always impressed people as a highly skillful politician. Potter had eaten many times in the Lucas household, with Dan and his wife Yvonne, and of course Belly and Princess. He knew good people when he saw them, and these were good people.

Knowing both Thomas Albert and Dan Lucas so well, he was unprepared for what followed.

"You son of a bitch," roared Albert. "You stood there and did fuck all as my boy was being dragged to his death!"

With the agility that makes big men so scary, he was across the room in an instant, a fist the size of a softball heading for Lucas's face. Dan dodged the blow and threw one of his own. Then both men stood and stared at their respective hands, held immobile by Michael Potter.

"This is a hospital. A place where injuries are cured, not caused. Knock it off."

Both men heaved simultaneously at Potter's grip. Thomas

attempted to swing with his other arm but its trajectory was interrupted by Potter's right forearm blocking the punch.

The two combatants looked at him in amazement, panting.

"Any more of this and I'll have to give you both a good spanking."

He turned suddenly and glared at Belly, who had the sort of listening-to-a-voice-no-other-can-hear look that he'd seen too often before. "Stay out of this. This is adult stuff and not a game."

Confused by the remark, the two men relaxed and Potter thrust them away as hard as he could, to remind them of his hidden skills, then motioned them all to sit down.

They all moved tentatively to chairs, sat down stiffly and stared at each other. Potter gave it a few seconds.

"Look, everyone's upset. I understand. But Jimmy's going to be fine. Now can someone tell me what happened?"

Dan Lucas spoke first. "I couldn't stop the damn winch! Jimmy just kept going up, his arm getting closer to the block. The damn thing wouldn't respond. And that's the truth." He looked at Thomas Albert defiantly. "I wish I'd never gotten that contract in the first place."

Potter knew the Nimpkish Band had been chosen by the federal Department of Fisheries and Oceans to complete a contract to study local spring salmon migration patterns. Finally it had been decided that Dan Lucas and his boat Northern Warrior would do the job, and the craft was fitted with a new net and sensing equipment. To spread the wealth, the crew from the runner-up vessel was hired to assist — Thomas Albert and his son Jimmy.

"We were cruising off Broughton Island when we hit a big one. Net filled with a thrashing silver mass, loveliest sight on earth. I was manning the winch. Belly was on the wheel and Jimmy and his dad were bringing in the net. All of a sudden I heard a sound like a gun going off! Damned if we hadn't caught a mother of a sinker hemlock branch, hiding water-logged under the surface. It flew in over the rollers, completely unexpected, and whacked Jimmy right across the chest. It threw him into the net and his hand got caught between the lead line and the web and he started going up the rope, right for the block. I jammed the winch lever into reverse but it wouldn't go. Frozen solid. He was screaming, knew what was coming."

Lucas suddenly turned and pointed at Thomas Albert. "You saw I was banging on that fucking lever like it was the devil's cock and it wouldn't budge. Then you came and helped me and it still wouldn't move. I yelled at Belly to throw the engine into reverse, take some pressure off the net. Didn't help a bit. Jimmy's hand was being eaten by that block and he was screaming and screaming. I could hear his bones snapping."

He put his head in his hands. "Then somehow he was just hanging up there, limp as a flag in August heat. Then the winch kicked loose and Jimmy and the net started falling back onto the deck. I stomped on the brake but it didn't work neither, and then just inches before he would've hit the deck at thirty miles an hour it just stopped."

He turned to Thomas Albert. "It was all just so strange. That winch lever's never been a problem before. The brake neither. You really think I'd try to kill your boy?"

Slowly the chief turned to face his friend. "There *was* something weird going on out there. And when the winch let loose and we got Jimmy down, he was bleeding like a fountain. And then it just stopped. Didn't it, Belly?"

Silently, gaze averted, Belly nodded yes. As he looked at the boy Potter could feel the tightness of rage in his chest.

After a few more minutes of discussion, Albert and Lucas shook hands and went to leave. As they did, Lucas turned to Potter. "Hey doc. Where'd you learn that kung fu stuff? You could catch a cobra's venom in mid-spit."

"Watching television," said Mike curtly, wanting them to go. Lucas shrugged and followed Albert out the door.

He grabbed Belly's arm as the boy tried to follow his father. "We're going to play Twenty Questions. Tonight, at my place." The boy pulled away as his eyes filled with tears.

****

Later that night he got the story.

Gathered together in his apartment, he heard from the five kids how human passions, assisted by strange powers, could almost result in murder.

Apparently the idea of Thomas Albert and Dan Lucas working together on the same boat just wasn't a good idea. Fishing was a cooperative business, and to have political rivalries and male egos competing was a recipe for disaster. But what had made it even worse was the presence of Belly and Jimmy together in the same confined space.

It was obvious that Jimmy Albert was a nasty piece of work. After the incident where he had been pinned beneath his car after assaulting Beebo and Dickie, he'd made it his business to hound the two of them and any of their friends. He wouldn't let up. And although the boys could handle themselves, his cruelty to the girls enraged them.

From the moment Belly had reluctantly come on board the boat that morning, prepared to mind his own business and pretty sure that Jimmy wouldn't dare be too aggressive with the two men present, he knew it was a mistake. Muttered insults, the occasional shove, and spitballs rapidly made the day intolerable. By noon Belly was on edge and there was no way to escape the torment. And he certainly wasn't going to whine to his father.

So when the sunken hemlock branch catapulted Jimmy into

the net and he caught his hand, Belly mentally let it keep happening, *interfering* with the machinery.

"But I didn't realize how fast it was moving," he whispered softly, his head in his hands. "It's hard to monitor movement, control the machinery and make up a plan all at the same time. I didn't mean to hurt him, just scare him a little. Honest."

Potter believed him but was still angry. "This can't go on. You're going to kill someone, whether you intend to or not. And I don't want to be involved in anything like that. You can't seize control of ferry boats or people's lives like that. I save lives, I don't take them. I'm through with all of you."

Five pairs of frightened eyes gazed at him so beseechingly he finally had to look away.

"Doc, you can't," said Beebo, close to tears. "You can't leave us. If you do I'll die, I know it. You said we had to stick together, be unbreakable like Genghis Khan's twigs, but we can't figure this out on our own. And we don't want to lose control either."

The others murmured agreement. "We have to find out why we are the way we are. Were we born this way? Were we made this way? You're a doctor. You made a promise in doctor school to help sick people. We're sick so you have to help us."

The logic was childishly simple. It was also true.

FOURTEEN

As the spring advanced Potter's experiments continued as Beebo grew steadily weaker and his dreams steadily stronger. Desperate to help the boy fight his demons, he recruited the other four twigs of the unbreakable bundle to help the muscular teen fight something his muscles couldn't.

The five of them lay against the sun-bleached drift logs littering the beach. They listened as Beebo recounted, for the fifth time, a recent dream. Like precocious theologians, they tried to gloss its meaning.

"The guy's image just rose and turned. It shimmered from the bed, a glowing column that hung in the air like smoke. It was a young guy, like us, with hair the color of bronze. He was wearing a cedar hat and a cloak that was brown and gray and black. He had the same coloring as me, you know, bronze skin, pale hair. But there was another guy, behind glass. It drives me crazy that I can't see him clearly, but it was somebody I know I've seen before. Then it was like wind tore it apart and it disappeared."

They mediated on what Beebo said as the physical world manifested itself in squawking gulls, silver slivers of light from the sea, and the sleepy warmth of a sunny day in May. A far cry from the dream world that increasingly was, for all of them, almost as substantial as reality.

Belly looked at his watch. "Time for another session. You up to it, Beebo?"

Pale and smaller than he had ever looked before, Beebo was still defiant, still a fighter. "I'm up for anything. How about you?"

The four gazed out to sea or plucked at the grass. Recently, under Potter's direction, they had crowded around Beebo's bed as he dreamed, began to dimly share his nightmares, if not his pain. The dreams were bad enough, and each wondered in that secret cowardly place everyone knows but few acknowledge, whether they would have had the courage to do what Beebo did.

"Sure," said Dickie, eventually. "Let's go."

Having entered Potter's apartment with the key he'd given them, they waited almost half an hour. "So he's not here," shrugged Belly. "Today's his day at the clinic, maybe there's an emergency. We've done this before. So let's do it."

It was agreed. Beebo lay down on the bed, his friends gathering in a circle around him. As his eyelids grew heavy they closed their own eyes and concentrated.

. . . . A horrible arm thing slices out of nowhere. He's seen this before, knows how to deal with it. Bats it away as it leaves a slimy scream of pain lying on his skin. He's felt this before. Ignore. He hears an old voice. Heard before. Listen.

He pushes on through the foul mist. Everything is familiar, seen before.

A bush undulates as if pushed by undersea currents, beckoning him. The old voice protests. Confident in his power, he ignores it and steps closer. Before his eyes, the shimmering salal leaves are suddenly a huge rainbowed salmon that swims sensuously towards him. Closer.

Suddenly the fish becomes a two headed green-red snake demon coiled at the base of a huge cedar tree. Its gaping mouths reveal filthy dripping fangs.

Another swirl of mist reveals another creature. He sees the opening and closing of mouths, thousands upon thousands of starving death holes. And the sounds from them are clotted screams, rank with the stink of putrefication.

He did not listen and now he is trapped.

The old voice comes to him. He forces himself to listen.

A snake head thrusts at his chest. He dodges it too late, pushed back violently against the mouth creature, grotesque, fleshy lips clamp onto his neck. The pain is excruciating as his life force is sucked out of the wound in his neck.

His thoughts begin to fade.

Just as his vision flickers to nothingness, he hears the old voice calling to him. He struggles. The voice tells him that he must warn his friends, or all will be devoured by the ravenous powers of darkness. Summoning all his will, he twists away and breaks the suction of the pulsing lips.

He stumbles through the mist, hearing the slither of a thousand scaly bodies pursue. There is light ahead and he knows the light is life. He runs as hard as he can, screaming, screaming . . .

Beebo bolted upright into a full sitting position on the couch, that last terrible scream still scorching his throat. His hands were pressed tightly against his face to shield his eyes from the brilliant blue flame that burned in his brain. His heart pounded wildly and his body was soaked with sweat.

He stared wildly at the four sets of eyes, all big with fear, that stared back. "I couldn't stop it," he whispered. "The old voice was speaking to me but I couldn't stop it."

Brenda suddenly sat on the bed and took Beebo in her arms as he sobbed. As he leaned into her the others saw it.

"Oh man," whispered Dickie. "What the fuck is that?"

Stretching from Beebo's jaw line all the way down his neck to his breastbone was a purplish welt oozing a rank mucoid slime.

The smell was so bad that Princess bolted for the bathroom and started to retch into the toilet. Belly's mouth was a thin line as he strode to the kitchen and grabbed a roll of paper towels. He tore off several sheets, soaked them in warm water and returned to the couch. He dabbed at Beebo's neck as the boy flinched and sobbed convulsively, as Brenda stroked his soaked bronze hair.

"Call the clinic," he said curtly to Dickie. "Dr. Potter has to come here now." Examining the wound as gently as he could he heard Dickie's urgent tone. "This is Dickie Cook. There's an emergency at Dr. Potter's house. Tell him he has to come right away. Tell him Beebo's hurt real bad."

Gradually Beebo stopped crying and Brenda gently laid him back on the cushion. Princess stood in the doorway, his hands to her mouth. "Did you see it? I saw it."

"Part of it," said Dickie grimly. "It was vague. At least we didn't feel it. Jesus Christ Almighty, look at his neck."

It was less than ten minutes later when they heard pounding footsteps and Mike Potter burst through the door.

"What happened?"

Potter examined the boy's neck as they explained how they had conducted a session on their own, and their recollections of the dream they had dimly shared with Beebo. It was like nothing he'd ever seen before. The circular wound pattern was characteristic of a parasite, like a tapeworm, that uses the spikes in its round muscular mouth to seize tissue and puncture it so it can feed. But no tapeworm could possibly be this big. And the ugly abscesses in Beebo's skin still oozed smelly green-brown pus.

"Belly, get that black bag of mine from upstairs."

The gangly teen was up the stairs almost in a single bound and back again almost as fast. Potter opened his bag and took out swabs, bandages, a bottle of antiseptic, two ampoules of clear liquid and two syringes. Rapidly he tended to the wound, making sure it was clean. He filled one syringe and injected it into the boy's arm. As he filled the second one Brenda said, "What are you giving him?"

"Morphine for the pain and tetracycline in case he's got blood poisoning." He administered the antibiotic, gathered up his things and put them in his bag.

"Is he going to be all right?" whispered Princess.

Potter sighed. "Yes." He pointed at the now bandaged wound. "Let me get this straight. He got this wound from his dream?"

As they nodded, Potter looked grim. "That's it. As far as I'm concerned, this is out of control. Beebo's dreams are getting worse and he's getting weaker. Now he's having physical manifestations of dream events, which my medical experience tells me is impossible. My notes don't make any sense and basically I don't know what the hell I'm doing anymore."

He turned to face them. "I'm leveling with you. I'm a doctor but I'm not trained to deal with this kind of shit. My friend Harry Warner is. I'm going to take all of you to the mainland, to Vancouver, so he can look at Beebo. It might mean telling your secret to someone other than me. I won't do it without your permission, but it may be necessary. What do you say?"

The four kids stared at Beebo. Finally Belly spoke as the others nodded agreement. "If it has to be done it has to be done. What reason are you going to give our folks for taking us to the mainland?"

Potter shrugged. "I'll say it's just something I want to do to introduce you guys to the big wide world. A cultural excursion, an educational thing. I'll tell them I'm paying for it and that you'll call home every day. I don't think it'll be a problem."

Turning to take his bag upstairs he said, "In fact, I'll do it right now. You stay here with Beebo. On the off chance he starts to dream again, you do anything you can to wake him up. For all we know, next time he dreams he'll die."

As they waited for Potter to return, they did not know that Beebo has started dreaming again. A good dream. It was a dream he had had many times, but never told Potter or his friends because it wasn't a nightmare, and it intrigued him. This particular dream felt very close to him, almost part of his body, and he would no more expose it than break up the group.

Just as she had for as long as he could remember, she came to him . . .

The vast Arctic landscape was snow-shrouded and bitterly cold.

The string of gray concrete fence posts supported rusting security mesh and barbed wire crowns. The waning light of afternoon shone on the gold-backed red stars on the soldiers' fur caps, their heads pulled tortoise-like into the high, upturned collars of their winter issue greatcoats as their gloved hands gripped the AK47 assault rifles slung diagonally across their chests. They stamped their feet in a vain attempt to defeat the chill that had penetrated their thermal snow boots.

They were too cold to feel curiosity about the child they were guarding as they stood shoulder to shoulder, united in misery against the piercing cold wind.

The child seemed unaware of them. Bundled in thick, formless clothing, she could have been any age from five to ten. She stared unblinkingly into the wind, seemingly oblivious to the cold. She wore no hat, her head protected only by a plain brown scarf that bound her hair and covered part of her elfin face. Beneath the scarf's edge, flattened against her forehead, were the ends of a straight fringe of bronze colored hair. And her eyes were a blue of an unimagined intensity.

The soldiers watched as the doctor emerged from the concrete block enclosure and trudged into the wind toward the child. She called "Nakita! We have more work to do in the laboratory. Come, child."

Slowly she turned and obeyed. She paused and turned once more to look into the vastness of the Siberian wasteland. A single tear spilled from her right eye as she continued walking back to the doctor, away from the emptiness without and toward the emptiness within.

FIFTEEN

The five days before their departure were busy ones. All of the parents thought the journey to the mainland was an excellent idea, and Chief Thomas Albert's warning to Michael Potter several months before about how his interest in the children was perceived seemed to have vanished. Beebo's wound, explained as the result of falling into a stand of poison ivy and accepted because Potter kept it bandaged at all times mysteriously, healed faster than expected.

Harry Warner had not only been welcoming but positively excited when he called to see if the specialist could manage to see Beebo. Potter had simply told him that the boy had nightmares associated with severe headaches that were getting worse, and that he was bringing the other children with him as well. "Headaches and nightmares at that young age, eh? Very interesting indeed. Glad you called. I'll very much look forward to seeing the boy and doing whatever I can."

Much of his time during the five days was spent seeing all of his patients to make sure they were okay before he left, including Auntie Mary. This proved difficult to do, as there was a major celebration planned, in which the whole of the native population of Albert Bay was to participate. As the custodian of the Nimpkish band's old ways, Auntie Mary was reveling in her role as advisor and choreographer.

She was in rare form, buoyed by the prospect of that evening's celebration, and her health for someone her age was better than could be expected. "So tell me, O wise one," Potter said. "What exactly is this shindig about, anyway?"

She explained that it was to be a 'handing over' ceremony to celebrate the end of years of negotiations — all Nimpkish lands formally transferred to the United Church by the federal government decades earlier were to be handed back to First Nations control. VIPs from around the province were coming and Potter promised that he would be there as well.

"So tell me, doctor," the old woman said in conclusion, her depthless black eyes searching his face. "How long will you be gone?"

Potter shrugged. "A couple of weeks."

"And you're taking the children to the mainland as a cultural excursion?"

"Yes," lied Potter, uneasy at having to dissemble the real purpose of the trip to the old woman.

"An untruth is like a badly measured door frame," she smiled. "You keep banging your head on it."

He stared at her, amazed.

"But if it will help Beebo with his dreams then it will be a good thing. It is not often a good thing comes of an untruth."

Finally he found his voice. "You know Beebo dreams?"

She nodded. "Of course. What is that stupid phrase they have Indians say in the movies? Many moons ago? Well, many moons ago our people had many shamans. They dreamt, they saw the future. We let them lead us because they had powers. Many powers. They had to be trained to use them."

He couldn't read her inscrutable gaze as she sighed. "And then the white men came and the missionaries said none of it was true. As if there are not many truths. This from people whose god could perform miracles and who rose from the dead. And slowly the knowledge of how to use the powers was lost. Even the knowledge that they ever existed. But it is still alive in some of us, from a time beyond the rim of time, before we even came to the these forests from across the Bering Strait, at a time when it was earth and not water."

"If in fact the poor boy's dreams are spirit dreams, I pity him. To fully understand them, he will have to pass many terrible trails. Only then will he be free of his pain."

Although Potter pressed her, she would say nothing more.

****

He was still brooding on the old woman's remarks when he walked into the Big House later that evening. It was all spruced up. The central performance area, a dirt floor, was raked and in its center, directly under a single vent hole in the roof, was a huge stack of wood. At the far end of the floor, two lines of tables were piled high with food. On either side of the hall, tiers of rough, wood benches angled up the walls. On the left, about midway and three rows up, Potter spotted the chief waving at him, beckoning him up into the stands.

Potter made his way through a happy crowd to Thomas. On the way, his hand was shaken by several people who told him to hurry back from the mainland. For the first time it occurred to him that he had been accepted by these people, that they regarded him as a friend. The thought brought a lump to his throat. Just as he slipped into the seat next to Thomas Albert the chief stood. "I'll be back soon. Got to get this show on the road."

A few minutes later his voice came crackling over public address system asking for everyone's attention. He began by introducing the seven band elders. As their names were called they moved from the far back of the room to a position across from the wood pile. Each was dressed in a cloak of rich, red serge studded with abalone shells in the pattern of the animal spirit protector of their family. The last to be called was Auntie Mary. Her cloak was by far the most beautiful, decorated with intricate patterns forming the shape of a raven on her back. Next the visiting dignitaries were introduced, and Auntie Mary took the mike to explain the religious significance of the celebration. Silence fell as she spoke of the decline of the once great Kwakiutl culture and how as a young girl she had witnessed the last great potlatch ceremony in the early twenties.

She began to chant an ancient prayer in the Kwakwala language just as Thomas returned to his seat. "Christ, I hate being an emcee."

"What does the chant mean?"

"Damned if I know. Might as well be Greek, all that old stuff."

There was dead silence as the last haunting notes faded. Finally there was a cough and Dan Lucas was on the mike, introducing a provincial politician who was to say a few words. The few turned out to be many, every one of them a resounding cliché. Other dignitaries spoke and Potter found himself fighting to stay awake.

"Christ, I hate speeches," muttered Thomas Albert. "Shut the fuck up and let's get started."

Finally the hollow speeches were over and suddenly the Big House was plunged into darkness and moments later the center of the floor erupted into a pillar of blue-orange flame. Slowly the wavering light receded and hunched figures moved into the ring of light. It was the elders, each beating a skin drum. Then five dancers entered, bare legged and bare footed, each wearing woven blankets of gray and black, on their heads wooden masks. Potter could make out the long beak of the thunderbird on one, a bear on another, a raven and a two headed thing with a human face where two snake bodies intertwined. He thought of Beebo's dreams, and the snake-like things that had attacked and maimed him.

The dances were spectacular, the dancers skillful, particularly the big man in the thunderbird mask.

He turned once more to Thomas Albert. "What's it all about?"

"Don't know," he shrugged. "Most of the people in this room don't know. I bet a lot of them would rather be home watching TV. Hamasta, the Cannibal dancers, I think."

When the number finished a few minutes later, the dancers all bowed to cheers, taking off their masks and turning to the crowd. With a shock Potter realized that the best of the bunch, in the thunderbird mask, was Dickie Cook.

Staring at the slight smile on the broad Kwaquitl face, the one that had first reminded him of the photos from long past, it occurred to him how little he knew of these people and their traditions. It cast him into a gloomy mood for the rest of the evening, and when the party broke up he made excuses about needing to pack and left early.

The sun was a hot golden ball sinking into the molten bronze of Broughton Sound. It cast an eerie glow over the landscape as he passed the island's main cemetery. There, weathered burial totems, standing amongst ordered rows of concrete and granite headstones, threw long, jagged shadows to meld with the darkened spires of the tall conifers at the graveyard's edge.

In the soft, fading light, the faces of the mythical creatures on the poles seemed to come alive. The painted eyes of thunderbirds, frogs, cormorants and killer whales no longer stared sightlessly, but searched the horizon as if looking in vain for something long lost. He felt a little lost himself as he brooded once more on what Auntie Mary had said. It struck him how peculiar this island was, with its silent dripping forests and the slowly decaying evidence of a once vigorous culture. He had a sudden vision of the island as a patch of ancient green sanity in the midst of the white man's world, all neon and asphalt and electronic pulses. Perhaps it was some sort of dream, and the five children's strange powers would evaporate like insubstantial mist once they found themselves in the throbbing concrete reality of a modern city like Vancouver.

This mood was still upon him as he prepared a special dinner for himself and Linda, who had been unable to attend the ceremony because she was working late at the hospital. He stared at his watch as supper cooled. She was never late. He was about to call the clinic when the phone rang. It was Linda.

"Mike, it's Auntie Mary. She was just admitted a few minutes ago."

At St. Georges Hospital, the old woman was lying on her side in bed. Her eyes were closed but he could hear her ragged breathing, could see the pulsing green screen that said she was still alive.

"Looks like a minor stroke," whispered Linda. "Dr. Elliott says the excitement and the hard work of planning for the ceremony must have been too much for her. She seems fine but there's aphasia. She can't speak."

Potter bent over the bed. The old woman's eyes suddenly opened. He took her hand and she gave him a feeble tug and painfilled smile. Her mouth began to move, but no sound came.

"Don't try to talk. You're going to be fine. We'll take care of you. No way you're ready to join your ancestors just yet."

There was still formidable intelligence in those piercing black eyes, and they seemed to be trying to tell him some message he couldn't understand. Finally, with that inadequacy even physicians feel, he patted her hand and said, "You'll be okay. I promise. I'll phone from the mainland every day to see how you're doing. And by the way, the ceremony was fantastic and so were you." Tears welled in the old woman's eyes as he turned away.

After giving some instructions to the night nurse — "I don't give a damn what Dr. Elliott said. The last time he treated cerebral hemorrhage it was the War of 1812" — he and Linda went back to his apartment and ate the now cold but still delicious dinner before going to bed and making slow, languorous love. The sight of her beautiful Kwaquitl features seemed infinitely mysterious in the moonlight, and he never wanted to leave her.

When her breathing deepened in sleep he silently arose and went to his desk. He wrote down his thoughts in his journal. He paused, staring out of the window at the surging sea, unable to shake the sensation that Auntie Mary's stroke was some sort of terrible omen.

PART 2

SIXTEEN

"Well, if it isn't the people of the forest primeval," boomed Dr. Harry Warner as Michael Potter shooed the five wide-eyed children into the specialist's office.

It was a huge room with an old green leather couch and an even older teak desk. Above the desk were a large number of framed citations, medical certificates and photographs of Warner with an impressive number of dignitaries, including four Canadian prime ministers. In the center of the untidy expanse was a table heaped with papers.

"Harry, how do you find anything in this mess? Hire a team of detectives?"

Warner grinned. "Some might say it's messy. But I like a little creative disorder."

He leaned over to greet each of the children individually, taking their hands in his and gazing directly into their eyes. Not for the first time Potter marveled at the specialist's technique. It was obvious Harry could tell that the kids were overwhelmed by their first experience with a big city and he was doing his subtle best to make them feel welcome and secure. He paid special attention to Beebo.

"Can I get anything for you?" he asked the muscular teen. "There's a pop machine down the hall. Candy machine too."

He turned to Belly. "Perhaps you could take the others and buy them something as Dr. Potter and I have a chat with Beebo. I need to take a medical history. You brought the file?"

Potter nodded. "Actually, I think it might be best if they all stayed to keep Beebo company. They're very close friends."

Warner looked at him keenly and got the message. "Of course. A little unusual, but then a foolish consistency is the hobgoblin of little minds, as Emerson used to say."

While he busied himself to clear papers off the room's chairs Brenda leaned over to Potter and whispered, "Goblins?"

"Figure of speech," he whispered back. "Nothing to worry about."

During the five days before they left Alert Bay, he had coached them on what to do and say. "Based on what I've seen, particularly the thing with the ferry and what Belly did to Jimmy Albert, it's obvious to me that you have extraordinary powers. Individually, certainly, but together you are capable of coordinated action. It would be inadvisable to let others know about it. Your kind of power could attract the interest of some very unsavory people, and be worth a lot of money. The main purpose of our visit is to find out why Beebo has nightmares, visions and especially headaches. We can't mislead Dr. Warner about that because otherwise he can't help Beebo, but I don't think its necessary to tell him about the powers you have. If it does become necessary, I'll tell him in such a way as to minimize it. That means you have to trust me. Okay?"

They had all agreed.

After reviewing the medical file and asking Beebo a few questions, to which he received inadequate answers, Harry Warner leaned back in this chair and made a steeple with his long elegant fingers.

"It's important for you to know what I do here and not to be afraid of anything. Like Dr. Potter, I too am a physician but I'm more of a medical researcher. I study what we call brain disorders — epilepsy, Alzheimer's, that sort of thing. We research using something with a rather scary name, although it's not nearly as bad as it sounds. Beebo, for the next week we're going to put you through lots of tests, taking pictures of your brain with a Nuclear Magnetic Resonance scanner. We'll monitor your sleep patterns and so on and generally look you over. Apart from the tests, which are completely painless, you can enjoy the city. Any questions?"

There were none.

****

The next day, leaving the other children at the motel where they were staying, Potter accompanied Beebo on his first test at the Nuclear Magnetic Resonance unit. He knew what the boy's reaction was likely to be and thought it unwise to leave him alone.

"It looks like something from *Star Trek*," muttered Beebo when he first caught sight of the muted lights, shiny steel, and computer terminals of the great hollow tube into which he was going to be inserted. The attendants in their white lab coats had obviously dealt with reluctant patients before and Potter was impressed with their professionalism — they were as soothing as a double dose of Prozac.

Beebo lay down on the bed which would slide him on silent rollers into the tube of the scanner. Nurses applied the restraints that would ensure he wouldn't move his head and blur the three-dimensional picture of his brain the scanner was trying to take. Potter was holding his hand as they administered a sedative when Harry Warner bustled in, emanating warmth like a Caribbean sun. After some final instructions both the machine and Beebo were ready, and as the boy was rolled into the heart of the scanner he closed his eyes and tried to ignore the low-pitched purr the tube suddenly voiced, like a big metallic cat about to eat a mouse.

Beebo's routine was the same for the next five days - tests and more tests. Potter didn't have to accompany the boy after the first day, as the teen realized that the most spectacular thing that was going to happen to him was a chance to nap. Every day after the tests, Potter would collect Beebo and show him and the other four kids around Vancouver, from the aquarium to the beaches and the Pacific National Exhibition grounds. Although they relaxed a little as the days went by, it was obvious they were still intimidated by the roar and movement of big city life, and Potter couldn't blame them.

In the evenings they'd go out for pizza, and often Harry Warner would join them. The tall Englishman's efforts were paying off — the children started to let down their guard and it was obvious they were coming to like and trust him. He asked them many questions about life on the island and about Alert Bay. He told them his wife Alice had died several years before and that as a result he found he did little but work. The kids told him he had to visit them at the Bay when Beebo's tests were concluded and he enthusiastically agreed.

At the end of the first week, when Potter went as he always did to pick Beebo up at the hospital, Warner met him at the door of the NMR unit holding a sheaf of photographs and EEG printouts. Potter hadn't asked the specialist any questions about how things were progressing, knowing Harry would tell him when he felt ready. From the frown on his face, he was ready now.

"Michael, as Beebo gets dressed I'd like you to have a look at these. Come down the hall to my office."

Two minutes later Warner threw himself into a chair and gestured for Potter to do the same. "To put it simply, there's a great deal of unusual activity going on in Beebo's head. He's dreamed every day, although there were only a couple that appeared to be violent nightmares."

He leaned forward and fanned the sheaf of photos. "Look here. Wave pattern is normal until he starts to dream." He pointed to a bright blue area next to a bright red one. "Anterior of the medulla. And here, the hypothalamus. Tremendous synaptic activity." He pointed to the EEG printouts. "Look at those spikes — tall and sharp as a punker's hairdo. Absolutely bizarre."

"Have you ever seen anything like it?"

Warner shrugged. "This kind of EEG reading, yes. But very rarely and only in certain patients, usually suffering from crippling epilepsy. I've tested hundreds of people with a wide variety of brain disorders on the NMR and have never seen anything remotely like these photos. But the technology is still too new for me, or anyone else, to have built up a proper database."

He rubbed his face. "The bad news is what you've already told me — the headaches are getting worse and the boy increasingly suffers general debilitation. Eventually he'll be completely incapacitated. And this kind of brain storm, this spontaneous burst of electrical activity, is only controllable through surgery. We take off the top of the skull, sever the corpus callosum that holds the two halves of the brain together, then excise half of the medulla."

"Jesus," breathed Potter.

"Exactly. It would be a last resort, I assure you."

Harry Warner appraised Potter, his hooded eyes shrewd. "According to the data I've gathered, the boy's brain crackles with excess energy, yet it doesn't manifest itself as seizures. That's impossible. All that energy has to go somewhere, show up somehow. Which means only one thing."

He leaned forward and stared deeply into Potter's eyes. "There's something you're not telling me, Michael. Given the gravity of the boy's condition, I have to know everything."

Potter hesitated, recalling his promise to the five children. But then, they had agreed he could tell Warner if he thought it necessary. It seemed pretty obvious that it was.

"You're right, Harry. I didn't mean to be deceptive, to hide anything from you. It's just that I'd promised the kids I'd keep their secret unless divulging it was absolutely necessary."

Warner frowned. "Kids? As in plural? Secret?"

"Yes. They can all do it, but they're much more powerful in concert. Also when they're motivated. It's a synergistic thing. And they're scared of what might happen if people find out about it."

"Forgive me, Michael, but you're not making a great deal of sense. They can all do what? And what does fear have to do with anything?"

Potter took a deep breath. "The kids are scared of what's happening to them. As individuals they have the ability to influence objects at a distance. Collectively they can do the same thing, only more powerfully."

Warner nodded slowly. "Objects at a distance. Telekinesis. Lots of anecdotal testimony in the literature. Many professionals don't accept it because it's not easily reproducible experimentally, which as far as they're concerned means it simply isn't evidence."

"Do you believe in it?"

"Yes. I've seen some of the laboratory demonstrations Russian researchers performed and released here in the West, in the late seventies and early eighties. All on film. Hard to dispute. Mind you, film can be faked. What would the movie industry be without special effects, eh?"

Harry Warner stood and paced the room. "So. Telekinesis. Like that spoon-bending chap Yury Geller, I suppose?"

"Actually, no," said Potter carefully. "A bit larger scale than that."

Warner peered at him. "Larger scale?"

"Harry, can we just leave it at that. Let's just say they can do things that would make you shit your pants!" The Englishman stared, absolutely still, then blinked like a stunned owl.

"So," concluded Potter. "I know it sounds impossible, but I

swear I've seen it. I've been keeping a record of everything, including the control experiments.

Warner nodded abstractedly, lost in thought. "Of course." Slowly his head lifted. His heavy-lidded gaze was the coldest Potter had ever seen it. "Hiding more evidence that might help me save Beebo's life?"

"God no," protested Mike. "I'm a physician, Harry. Somethings I just can't divulge, even to you."

Warner's smile at this lame joke was an effort. "Of course. As you think best." He paced again around the room, banging into a chair and swearing softly.

Finally he turned to face Potter again. "Remarkable story. So glad you told me. Only thing to do is continue testing. Your information gives me a couple of very interesting avenues to explore. Very interesting indeed." He glanced at his watch. "I'm sure Beebo is anxious to go. I'd love to join you tonight but I have to make some phone calls and generally tidy things up. You understand?"

"Of course," said Potter, rising to leave. As he headed for the door Warner suddenly clasped both his hands, his bedside manner in overdrive. "Michael, I want you to know that I fully understand the importance of what you've told me today. These children could very well find themselves in grave danger. It will go no further. Understood?"

Even though Potter knew Warner was bound by his Hippocratic Oath, he felt a sense of relief as the tidal wave of the older man's earnestness washed over him. "Thanks, Harry. See you tomorrow."

SEVENTEEN

The next day was hot and cloudless, apparently no different from the previous seven. The plan was that Potter would pick up Beebo after testing, as usual, take him to visit places around the city, then they'd all go to Sami's on Cornwall Street for dinner at 5:30. What Beebo didn't know was that the others would already be at the restaurant waiting for him, because it was his birthday. Potter figured that after all the kid had been through the previous week he deserved a treat— even though his real birthday was a full week off.

Harry Warner wasn't present during Beebo's tests, which had become so routine the boy barely noticed the Englishman's absence. When the tests were done, at 2:30, Beebo waited for Potter. He didn't arrive. After an hour Beebo was edgy. He knew where Warner's office was and went to look. Harry wasn't there.

The nursing staff were now so used to seeing him that they didn't see him. He sat and waited, wondering what to do. He took out the twenty dollar bill Potter had given him as emergency cash, then thrust it back in his pocket. Dejected and more than a little scared, he waited another half hour, then stood and walked out.

Standing uncertainly on the pavement, he thrust his arm in the air like he'd seen Potter do. A cab pulled over and he told the driver to take him to Sami's. The cabby's eyebrows lifted a little at the thought of an Indian brat going to such a place, but the sight of the twenty dollar bill clutched in Beebo's fist was reassurance enough.

At Sami's Beebo paid the driver, got out of the cab and walked uncertainly into the restaurant, staring at the clock behind the reservations desk — 5:25. What if Potter wasn't there?

"May I help you?" said the kindly hostess.

"Please," said Beebo. "Dr. Potter's table."

She checked the reservation list and smiled. "Of course. This way, sir."

The restaurant was an L-shaped affair with a large open-air seating area that faced onto Cornwall Street, the grassy park and tennis courts of Kitsilano Beach, and the waters of English Bay. Beebo was astonished to see his friends sitting and waiting.

"What are you doing here?"

"It's supposed to be a surprise for your birthday, idiot," said Belly. "Dr. Mike arranged for a pre-paid cab to pick us up at the motel and bring us here. He was supposed to bring you. Is he in the can?"

Beebo shook his head. "He never showed up. I came here from the clinic on my own."

As the others gawked at his bravery, Brenda frowned. "Then where is he? We can't sit here and eat because we can't pay for anything. What are we going to do?"

"Wait," said Dickie, with more confidence than he felt. "There was probably some kind of emergency. He'll be here soon enough."

They sat with downcast eyes for ten minutes, feeling increasingly out-of-place as well healed dinner patrons streamed in. A couple of them sniffed and muttered remarks about Indians, which made Belly grind his teeth, Brenda look thoughtful, Princess's eyes tear and Dickie look aggressive. Beebo just looked pale, withdrawn and worried.

"Thank God you're here!" It was Dr. Harry Warner bounding to their table. The childrens' sense of relief was palpable. The Englishman was sweaty as he threw himself into the only vacant chair at the table.

"Have you been waiting long?"

"Yes," whispered Brenda urgently. "We don't belong here, not without a white person. It's horrible the way people look at us, like we're trash."

Warner seized her hand. "Don't worry. I'm here and I will protect you. You all look famished. Let's get some service. Ignore my friends, indeed!"

He raised a long arm and snapped impatient fingers. A waiter bustled over and Harry barked orders in his best, no-nonsense imperial English voice. Having eaten with the children many times before, he knew unerringly what dishes and refreshments to order for each of them.

When he had finished, and as they waited for their food, Belly leaned forward. "Dr. Harry, what are you doing here? And where's Dr. Mike?"

"I knew you would be here tonight. Michael told me. The problem is, others may know you're here as well."

"Others?" said Belly.

"Michael told me about your strange powers. He also said that it would be possible to make a great deal of money, and asked me if I'd be willing to help exploit your abilities. Of course, I turned him down flat."

Warner looked around conspiratorially. "And now he's vanished. Up to no good, possibly. We may be watched even as I speak."

Five pairs of eyes rounded with shock and fear stared back at him.

"But don't worry," Warner assured them. "As long as I'm here you'll be fine."

Suddenly, the monotonous background noise of the traffic on Cornwall Street was shattered by the sound of screeching tires. Everyone turned to look as two police cruisers screeched to a halt in front of the restaurant. At the same instant an unmarked cruiser skidded to a loud stop at the far sidewalk, effectively cutting off all traffic. Uniformed officers armed with assault rifles burst out of the cars, scrambling for cover behind the hedge.

Across the street in the tennis court parking lot a dark blue panel van screamed to a stop and the back doors burst open. Twelve figures in black and gray camouflage fatigues, black wool hats and flak jackets bristling with communication gear and ammunition piled out and scurried for cover. Each carried an automatic rifle and had side arms slung in black webbing hip holsters.

Everyone stared in disbelief.

Anxious restaurant patrons, wanting to get the hell out of there, standing, making runs for the exits were stopped dead in their tracks by a blaring bullhorn.

"In the cafe, stay in your seats! I repeat, stay in your seats! This is the Vancouver Police Emergency Response Team! No harm will come to you if you stay seated and remain calm! The area is now totally surrounded!"

Everyone complied in a daze as a small black van pulled up behind the crouching police. Two men got out as Harry Warner pointed and said, "My God. Look!"

The five children strained to see. Belly saw first. "It's Dr. Mike!"

Exclamations from the others as they too caught sight of the tall figure. He was wearing dark wraparound sunglasses and a Vancouver police baseball cap, but there was no mistaking the red hiking jacket, khaki slacks and Kodiak hiking boots with the reflective tape flashing on the ankles. He was wearing a high tech headset and speaking into the microphone that curved in front of this mouth as he held one gloved hand to his earplug. Although he was well behind the ERT squad's position he was waving with his free arm as if directing more men, out of their line of vision.

The bullhorn blared again. "This is the Vancouver Police

Department. We know you're in there. Surrender immediately — there is no possibility of escape."

"Bastard!" hissed Warner. "He's told the authorities about you and they've come to take you away!" He leaned over to the children staring at him. "If you have the abilities Potter claims, you'll have to use them to get out of here. Now!"

In an instant the group was up and running for the kitchen. As they burst through the swinging doors they saw four black and gray clad figures bobbing between the stoves and sinks, handguns drawn. "Stop!" shouted the leader. Suddenly he was flying backwards through the air as if struck by a train. He landed on his back on a stove, then crashed to the floor. The three others spun and fell like pins hit by a supersonic bowling ball.

Directly behind Dickie, Beebo followed. Brenda, dragging Princess along with her, came next. Belly tugged at the arm of a stunned Harry Warner as he paused to look at the fallen, unconscious officers. "Jesus . . ."

They burst through the back exit into the alley. "Doc! Where's your car?" cried Belly.

"This way!" shouted Harry Warner, breaking into a spindly but surprisingly fast run. Fanned out behind him, the kids struggled to keep up. They reached Warner's Mercedes and he fumbled for his keys, panting.

"C'mon doc!" shouted Beebo, gazing wildly around. From down the street they could hear the pounding pursuit of heavy boots.

Finally the car doors were open and they all piled in as the engine roared to life. In the rear view mirror they could see uniformed figures surging up the street.

Warner gunned the engine and pulled heavily on the wheel. In an instant the big car was weaving wildly on the asphalt, away from the police. There was a loud pop and a circular crater appeared on the back window, trailing spidery cracks. A second shot shattered the glass sending a hail of stinging white glass particles at them.

Struggling to control the car, Warner juddered around the corner of Yew Street, barely missing an oncoming police cruiser. It spun around like a toy, lights pulsing, then tires screamed as it gave pursuit, following them toward the ocean.

"We'll never outrun them," panted Warner. "This isn't a race car and I'm not Stirling Moss."

He looked into the rear mirror. All he could see was the backs of five heads, not the intense concentration in the five sets of glassy eyes that stared at the rapidly gaining police car. As he barely rounded the corner Point Grey Road running along English Bay, horn blaring, the pursuing cruiser inexplicably failed to take the corner. As if fired from a howitzer it shot straight across the street, smashed through the railings and sailed into the ocean, landing with a soggy *whud*.

Astonished at the sight, Warner almost collided with an oncoming Toyota, just nicking the left front clip and sending the vehicle spinning.

"Keep your eyes on the road, doc!" shouted Beebo.

Harry continued driving like a madman for another ten blocks and then hauled on the steering wheel, sending the car into a sliding skid down a back lane off Broadway. He nudged the Mercedes between two dumpsters and parked. Eyes closed, he lowered his head until it rested on the steering wheel.

"Dr. Harry?" asked Princess anxiously.

"That was the most amazing thing I've ever seen in my entire life," said Harry, eyes still closed. "When Michael told me I wasn't sure, but now I'm a believer."

"What do we do now?" asked Belly. "The whole police force will be looking for us."

Warner raised his head and nodded decisively. "Potter has

betrayed you. And me. And not just the police are involved. Who knows how high up his treachery reaches."

"Just like in the movies," breathed Dickie.

"You all are in grave danger," said Warner grimly. "You obviously can't go back to the motel, and I can't go back to the clinic. As far as the authorities are concerned, I'm an accessory to your escape. If Potter hasn't already told them about me then they've seen my license plates. And going back to Alert Bay is out of the question too. Believe me, these people will stop at nothing."

Tears were streaming down Princess's face. "What can we do? Where can we go?"

Harry Warner nodded thoughtfully. "I have an idea. When my wife Alice was still alive, we used to go to the Olympic Peninsula in Washington State. It's peaceful, quiet and people mind their own business. We can go there and formulate a plan."

"But they know this car."

Warner shrugged. "It's just a car. They make cars in factories. You can't make friends in factories. I'm your friend and I will look after you. We'll ditch it and rent another one."

"I can't tell you what this means to us," said Brenda, as the others nodded agreement.

"We'll have to get the car and scoot over the border fast before the authorities put out an APB."

"A what?" asked Beebo.

"All points bulletin," said Dickie. "I heard about it in the movies."

****

That evening they left Vancouver and crossed into the outlying community of Burnaby, driving the late model Ford van Warner had rented at the Brentwood Shopping Mall, close to where they had abandoned the Mercedes.

"We'll cross at Blaine," explained Warner. "It's the busiest border station and with any luck we'll be over in no time. American TV stations rarely carry Vancouver news, so once we're in the States we'll be anonymous. Unless of course the intelligence community is on to us."

This remark ensured silence for most of the drive to the border. Warner frowned in concentration most of the way until Beebo suddenly said, "How could he do it? I thought he was our friend."

Warner shrugged. "Frankly, I never knew him all that well. Our relationship was strictly professional. It's astonishing what people will do for money and power." He shook his head. "And to think it was me who suggested that he go to Alert Bay in the first place. I'll never forgive myself."

"It's okay, Dr. Harry," soothed Brenda. "There's no way you could have known."

"He just thought we were a bunch of ignorant Indians and he could do anything he wanted with us," said Belly bitterly. "It's like those white people at the restaurant making remarks under their breath."

"The western world is a very strange place," agreed Warner. "The idea that people aren't really people at all, they're just consumers. I thought a lot about this kind of thing when I was still in England, in school. I decided then that I'd do my best to help people threatened by our crazy capitalist society. People like you."

Warner explained how his late wife Alice had gotten him interested in the history and traditions of aboriginal west coast culture. "In fact, I first heard about the kind of powers you possess from the old tales of shamans that my wife researched. Your ancestors were a great people, living in harmony with the land. They could be a great people again, but the white man's world won't let them. It's a terrible injustice."

Five black heads were bowed in thoughtful contemplation as they entered the line of vehicles waiting to cross the border.

"Remember," Warner said as they inched forward. "They may be waiting for us. Or they may just ask questions. It's their job to try and trip us up. I'll do the talking. If they ask you a question, defer to me or play dumb. Okay?"

The green light came on and Harry edged the van forward. A customs officer was in the booth, eyes watchful as he peered into the back of the vehicle. "Evening, sir. These kids always stay up so late?"

Harry smiled, his bedside manner once again in overdrive. "They'll be put straight to bed once we get to Bellingham officer."

"This a business trip or personal?"

"Professional," smiled Harry. "I'm with B.C. Social Services. These children are my wards. I'm taking them to visit an aunt who lives on the Lummi reserve."

"And how long will you be in Washington State?"

"Just a day."

"Very well. Have a pleasant stay."

"Thank you, officer."

They were in.

EIGHTEEN

Late the next morning, after spending the night at a motel, they took the twenty five minute car ferry ride from Keystone Jetty to Port Townsend, Washington. They spent the day sightseeing.

Harry Warner found an amusement park and paid for the kids to take the rides for several hours. He left them alone to wander the grounds, saying he had to make a couple of phone calls to check up on the situation back in Vancouver. He was all smiles when he rejoined them.

That evening, they drove in the van for dinner at the Salal Cafe, one of Harry's favorite haunts in Port Townsend. As they ate he held them enthralled with stories about the town, and about aspects of their own culture even they had never been told about by the people at Alert Bay.

"So you see," he concluded, "appearances can be very misleading. Just as they were with Michael Potter. Take this town, for instance. We're in a pleasant, peaceful pocket of Puget Sound, and yet the area bristles with military installations. Remember that naval air station we passed?"

The kids nodded. On route to Port Townsend they had passed the gates of the Whidbey Island Naval Air Station. Belly had snickered at the wording on a large sign out front which read, *Please excuse the noise but it is the sound of freedom,* until an A6 bomber had screamed overhead, seemingly out of nowhere, like a thunderbird.

"Well, that naval air base is just one of eight major installations in the area . . ."

"Listen to that asshole windbag," came a jeering voice.

The children looked around and Warner frowned. Close by there were three sailors sitting at a table. They were obviously drunk and looking for a fight.

"Yeah, like some bald fuck like him knows fuck all about the navy."

"Fucking windbag."

"Fucking civilian windbag."

One of the sailors leaned over and wagged a half-empty beer bottle at Brenda. "I hear squaws take it up the ass for a bottle of beer. Maybe for half she'll suck my cock."

"Fucking Injuns," said the second.

"Haw!" laughed the older sailor. "Hey Tonto," he called to Beebo. "Where's the Lone Ranger?"

The first sailor stood, hitched the belt of his navy whites and rubbed his crotch suggestively. "Hey squaw. Wanna visit my teepee? Or maybe we could do it in the bushes. You'd feel right at home there."

The second stood as well. "Little squaw's kind of pretty too. It'd be her first time, I bet."

"Nah. On the reservation their uncles make 'em sniff glue until they pass out, then cornhole 'em before they're out of diapers. Old Indian custom."

The third sailor stood and grabbed an empty beer bottle by the neck. "Hey grandpa," he called to Warner. "You fuck them both at once? Or do you like those boys instead?"

The three swaggered slowly over to their table.

"Now look here. I've had enough with you young toughs causing trouble." It was the restaurant's manager, grabbing the first sailor's arm. Without even turning around the drunken seaman placed his hand over the face of the elderly man and shoved. The manager flew across the room and hit the wall with a dull thud, sliding unconscious to the floor.

Now Warner was standing. The children were completely terrorized, all except Belly. The seventeen year old had a look of pure hatred on his face but his eyes were turning glassy. "You think Jimmy Albert got hurt bad . . ." he panted. Warner turned to him and spoke sharply. "Belly! Not here."

He rolled his head like a boxer warming up. "I'll handle this."

"Handle what, you old fart?" jeered the first sailor. "I bet you have trouble handling that squaw's tit."

"Handle this!" roared Harry Warner, throwing a right cross. His bony fist smashed into the seaman's face with a sickening crunch. With a half step to the left the physician dodged the second sailor and threw a left hook to his kidney so hard the swabbie screamed before doubling over. Seizing his collar with both hands, Harry heaved the sailor across the table, then ducked as the third seaman threw a looping haymaker. From his crouch he pumped a right hand into the sailor's solar plexus, then straightened him with an uppercut so powerful Warner's knuckles actually scraped the floor before impacting on the point of the seaman's chin so hard he jumped two feet off the ground before landing spread-eagled on his back.

There was a moment's thunderous silence. "Screaming Jesus," whispered Belly.

The light of hero worship was beginning to dawn in Dickie's and Beebo's eyes. "Where'd you learn to fight like that?" asked Belly.

Warner rolled his head again. "Cambridge. Boxing team. It's like riding a bicycle. You never forget."

He walked over and helped the manager to his feet, asking if he was okay. When the man said yes, Harry pointed to the still unconscious sailors. "Some garbage for disposal."

Back at the table he took Brenda and Princess in his arms. As they clung to him, Brenda whispered, "What were those horrible things they were saying?"

"Doesn't matter now," said Warner. "I'm here. I'll protect you." He held her at arm's length, searching her eyes. "And I will, so long as God gives me strength."

He called to the manager. "Bill please."

The manager walked to them, rubbing the back of his head. "On the house." He pointed at the still unconscious seamen. "I'm phoning the shore patrol. These guys'll be in the brig until they're gray."

They shook hands and Warner and the group left.

NINETEEN

Over the next several days, as they traveled around Port Townsend and the surrounding area, the kids listened as Warner talked. He told them more about their heritage than they had ever heard, and more about white cruelty than they had ever imagined.

He told them about his wife Alice, and how they had always been inseparable. "It was Alice who always made sure that my feet were firmly planted on the ground, even if sometimes my head was in the clouds as I did my research. As I said, she was the one who got me interested in the stories of your people, their past greatness, and the terrible wrongs that have been done to them. Never could abide cruelty. Always an idealist, my Alice, trying to make the world a better place."

They were standing high atop the fortified walls of a decommissioned army base called Fort Wardon where, Harry informed them, the movie *Officer and a Gentleman* had been filmed. As he spoke, his blue eyes searched Puget Sound from their vantage point high above the sand dunes and their sparse tough grasses. A stiff breeze laden with salt and the tang of the sea stung their faces.

"She would have been infuriated by those three disgusting men at the restaurant. And unfortunately their kind are throughout the military. Brutal, racist, sneering white supremacists — just the sort of people who ruined your great ancestors and their culture. It hasn't changed much in all these years. Not many gentlemen amongst them, not even the officers."

Brenda took the tall physician's arm. "But you're white and you're a gentleman. You saved us all from those terrible men."

Warner nodded sadly. "I'm different because of what I believe in. There was once a very great man, so long ago young people like you have never heard of him. He wrote a book that perfectly describes what I've tried to do with my life, and what my dear Alice tried to do with hers. It's called *My Silent War,* and tells of this great man's struggles to fight the oppression of Western culture."

"I'd like to read it someday," said Belly.

"Me too," said Beebo, as Dickie nodded agreement.

"But it is very hard to fight injustice, because there are so many who are unjust. If it were in my power, I'd save everyone, everywhere. But I don't have that power."

He turned suddenly to face them, as if the thought had just occurred to him. "But you do. You have such power."

Brenda looked confused. "Us?"

"Of course. Think of what you did at the restaurant. And what Belly could have done to those three sailors, if I hadn't intervened. Imagine what could happen if you tried to use that power for good instead of just for games or personal vengeance."

"I'm not following you, doc," said Beebo.

"Imagine fighting back against the white man's world, against his machines. Against the betrayers like Michael Potter."

Belly spat into the void that yawned over the wall of the abandoned military base.

"What kind of machines?" asked Princess.

Warner turned to face the interior of the old fort and swept his arm to encompass its emptiness. "Like the ones that used to be here. Machines of war. Imagine if all of the forts in the white man's world were as empty as this one. Empty of machines of destruction, empty of the smirking drones who run them and make the lives of innocents like yourselves and your ancestors so miserable. There would be peace and harmony, as there was in your ancestors' time."

Dickie frowned. "Fight the US army, navy and air force? Gee, doc, I don't know. All those weapons? I've seen the movies."

Warner didn't have to lean over far to gaze into Dickie's eyes. "What's a battleship but a big ferryboat with a few guns on it?"

There was silence as the children contemplated this idea and Warner resumed gazing out to sea, a small smile playing on his lips.

TWENTY

By the next day the uneasy possibilities inspired by Warner's remarks had turned into a generalized disquiet that manifested itself in a predictable way.

"I'm homesick," whimpered Princess. The three boys looked thoughtful as Brenda bent down to comfort the youngest member of their group. "So am I," she said. "We've been here for days and the last time we phoned home was from Vancouver the day of the police raid on Sami's."

"I know," sighed Dickie. "But Dr. Harry's right. We can't call and tell them where we are because we're being watched. Maybe Dr. Mike arranged for the police to visit Alert Bay and they've tapped the phones and could trace a call. Maybe they're even holding our folks so that . . ."

Beebo punched him in the arm, hard, as Princess started to wail. "Anyway," said Dickie, rubbing his arm, "it's possible."

"If even part of what Dickie says is true, then they'll be able to find us. Even here. In fact, I'm surprised they haven't found us already. We have to talk to Dr. Harry," said Belly decisively.

Harry Warner listened attentively. "Belly is absolutely right, and I sympathize completely with Princess and Brenda. To avoid detection we should leave this place as soon as possible and find another haven. In fact, I've already made plans for us to leave by this afternoon's ferry. Fortunately I have access to money here so we don't have to worry about paying for things. I'm also monitoring the situation in Vancouver, but I'm afraid it isn't good and we might not be able to go home for some time. Not unless we have something to bargain with."

"Bargain with?" asked Beebo.

"Yes. We bargain to get all of you back home with your families, safely and without fear of ever being bothered again. To bargain you must have something to bring to the table. Some sort of power. Or powers."

The children averted their eyes, knowing what he meant.

"Anyway," said Warner hastily, "we're leaving this afternoon so we better get packed."

****

The outside upper deck of the ferry was crowded with vacationers. Harry chose to sit inside where seats were still available. The kids pushed their way through the crowd to find a sunny spot by the rail.

A few minutes into the voyage, Beebo and Princess opened the door into the salon and crossed the compartment, eager to see the other side of the ship. Standing at the rail, black and bronze hair streaming in the breeze, they laughed and pointed at anything that caught their fancy as the sun warmed their skins.

Suddenly Princess pointed. "Look! What's that?"

Receiving no answer, she turned and saw Beebo's bulging blue eyes staring with a look of total disbelief. She looked again at the strange sight as Beebo reached out and grabbed the handrail for support.

As if in some sinister marine crucifixion, a tall black cross was slicing through the opaque water of the channel, coming towards the ferry at a thirty degree angle. Closer inspection revealed that behind the cross trailed a hump and then a flat deck that barely cleared the waterline. At the very end trailed a black fluke.

Beebo was panting. "I've seen this before. In my dreams. Get the others."

Within moments the other children and Harry Warner were beside him. Craning his neck, the tall physician could see better than the rest. "It's a submarine. Nuclear. Probably a Trident. Must be over five hundred feet long."

"I've seen it before. I know what's going to happen next," whispered Beebo.

Warner pointed with a long arm. "That thing carries sixteen missiles. Enough to destroy numerous cities and millions of people."

"And what's a submarine?" said Belly softly. "Just an underwater ferryboat with a few weapons on it."

Beebo looked around distractedly. "There's supposed to be a big ship, like a freighter. And animals."

"Animals? What kind of animals?" asked Harry Warner.

With more than a hundred feet of her forward deck submerged, the submarine's bow wave was pushed back to a point just forward of the cross-shaped conning tower. The passage of the black monster was so imposing that the gawking crowd on the deck of the ferry failed to notice the white and red superstructure of the massive freighter approaching from the north west — but the group was aware of it immediately.

Gasps of wonder issued from the crowd. Heads turned in the direction of wildly gesturing arms, to a point quarter of a mile to the north east. A killer whale cow and her calf arched gracefully through the sea's smooth swells.

Harry saw the animals and said urgently to the children, "the contrast between the beauty and grace of nature and the unnatural menace of the white man's machine of destruction!"

Beebo made a mental image of the submarine on its northerly

course, then imagined it veering to the west, towards the freighter. Then, over that image, he superimposed one of the Alert Bay ferry on a stormy day. He was showing them the method, just like before. Aware that they were tuned into his thoughts, he added to the image Dickie's mental rope as well as Princess's blue and silver flamed signature filament.

After tacking south, the ferry moved back to its original easterly heading and in the process, crossed the submarine's turbulent wake.

Though Brenda's mental energies were preoccupied with what Beebo was doing, she distractedly put a comforting hand on the old man's shoulder. The plan was in motion — the sight of the whales and Warner's remark committed them to it.

Beebo's thought flash exactly matched what the rest of the group now saw before them. Dickie threw out a thought rope to the submarine. Princess helped him get it there. Belly and Brenda let their thoughts follow along the shimmering mental filament.

Belly mentally searched the conning tower of the Trident and the four men on it. Not finding what he wanted there, his mind moved downwards through the microscopic spaces inside communication lines until he was inside a wide, low chamber packed with a dazzling array of instrumentation. He searched the chamber, investigating each station he found there. He took in all the dials, the readouts on all the equipment and the location of the crew members. He soon found what he wanted.

The helmsman.

He *pointed* the man out to Brenda so she could squeeze his mind. Moving to where Belly directed, she found the helmsman and surrounded his head with her thoughts. Belly's mind entered the panel behind the helm controls, letting his thoughts move through the circuitry he found there.

Within seconds he found what he wanted. He created a circuit to turn the vessel to the left and held it there, preventing further current from reaching the wiring in the console.

Brenda twisted at the inside of the helmsman's head, causing him to give up his hold on the wheel and grab for his temples instead. Two other sailors jumped to help him as he collapsed to the floor.

The crowd on board the ferry gawked in wonder as the submarine's graceful passage was violently altered. The wake flared up in white torrents. The conning tower dipped sickeningly, forcefully enough to fling one of the four tiny figures up in the tower out of his protective perch, to be left dangling against the black superstructure. The vessel began an awkward veering maneuver to the northwest.

For a full fifteen seconds the submarine continued on its swerving course until slowly, nauseatingly slow, the tower started to came back to vertical. The wake flattened as the submarine plowed ahead, on a new course — directly into the path of the oncoming freighter, two kilometers in the distance.

For ten very long minutes the two monsters continued on their collision course. As they drew ever nearer, the bristling superstructure of the merchantman dwarfed the stark, black sleekness of the submarine. The Trident continued its blind rush with no deviation in direction or speed. Too late the freighter tried to take evasive action but it was clear to all who watched that a catastrophe was in the making. The freighter would not be able to turn away because the shore north of Port Townsend prevented any maneuvering in that direction.

Belly was exhausted. Trying to maintain mental control of the steering position, while at the same time preventing activation of the auxiliary station and stopping the captain's efforts to initiate a dive — a maneuver that was not part of the dream and could not be allowed — had taken him to the limit of endurance.

He felt his strength slip away from him. He couldn't continue to control a monster machine of this complexity, even though it was a symbol of all they had recently come to hate. He flashed a signal to the others and they all let go simultaneously. The mob of sailors and officers that swarmed over the wheel, trying to wrest control of it from whatever mysterious force prevented it from turning, suddenly plunged to the floor in a confusion of legs and shouts.

The stern of the freighter loomed over the silhouette of the black undersea monster. Suddenly, the conning tower pitched sickeningly to the east and again the submarine's wake became a billowing plume as the vessel entered another wild turn, this time away from the freighter. At the last possible second, the submarine's submerged bow finally veered away from the dark mass of plate steel looming less than one hundred feet away. Mighty bow waves from the monster freighter smashed against the submarine's tower, sending visible shudders through the smaller vessel.

There were shouts of relief from the wide-eyed crowd on the ferry deck.

Mentally withdrawing from the Trident, the group scanned the conning tower and for the first time saw the blood of the one injury sustained in their assault, the crewman tossed out of the tower. The sight of the man's injuries almost overcame their sense of exultation and power. It alarmed them because Beebo's dream of the event never showed anyone being hurt, but in the instant it took them to return the mental distance from the Trident to the ferry, they all reasoned that while the dream wasn't entirely correct, the sailor was not badly injured. A small price to pay for the panic they had just caused, the task they had just accomplished.

Twenty minutes later, the submarine completed a slow turn to the northeast, a maneuver that took it out of the shipping lanes. Scores of blue clad figures and a small number dressed in green fatigues swarmed out of the stranded monster, rapidly ringing the deck, automatic rifles in front.

TWENTY ONE

The ferry docked at Keystone Jetty. Harry Warner had been silent for almost an hour. His blue eyes occasionally rested appraisingly on the children, but sometimes he just gazed out to sea, looking thoughtful. He was still silent as he drove the station wagon off the vessel, past the lines of parked vehicles waiting to make the crossing.

The children didn't mind not having to talk. They were exhausted, mentally as well as physically, but mixed in with the fog of fatigue was a pleasant, comfortable warmth, the feeling of having power and being able to exercise it whenever they wanted.

The mind picture they shared communicated one overriding feeling — they wanted to do it again. Soon.

After about fifteen minutes of driving, Harry turned off the road into an observation area. He stopped the van and turned off the ignition. With both hands firmly on the wheel, he gazed straight ahead.

"Enough beating around the bush. You did that, didn't you?"

They stared at him silently, unsure of his anger, sure only that his blue eyes were very cold.

"I know what I saw in the restaurant and after, when we escaped from the police," continued Warner. "But making a getaway from a food establishment is small scale compared to controlling a Trident submarine, one of the most powerful killing machines ever invented. And I know you were responsible because all five of you looked like you were in a trance."

"It was your idea, doc," said Belly defensively. "You're the one who talked about stopping the white man's machines of destruction. Of getting back at them for what they did to our people."

Harry Warner nodded slowly. "I did say that. And I meant every word of it. It's just that I didn't think I'd see a demonstration of such awesome power. You realize what this means?"

Belly shook his head as the others stared intently, subdued by the doctor's intensity as he stared out of the windshield.

"It means the white man's world, the world of industrial capitalism and oppression, or death and destruction, is not invincible. You have the power to change the world. We should live in a world at one with nature, with the whale and her calf, not with some killing machine that stole nature's design for the purposes of destruction."

He turned to face them again. "What I saw today makes me feel that the causes Alice fought for all those years were not as futile as I often believed. Things can be accomplished. And they can only be accomplished with the five of you. Won't you help me make a difference in this world? And for your people as well?"

The children were too young and inexperienced to realize how skillfully Harry Warner was manipulating their emotions. Suddenly, from fierce, cold-eyed professional and idealist, he was suddenly all compassion and warmth.

"Oh my strange young friends, I know a great deal about you. I've known for some time that you are very special people. Michael told me."

As Warner had intended, his words further reinforced the sense of betrayal they felt towards Michael Potter.

"What did he tell you?" demanded Belly angrily. He could tell that there was something not quite right about Warner's emotional zigzags, but he couldn't figure out precisely what. Still, he was determined to find out whether or not the old man represented a threat.

"Nothing concrete," answered Harry. "Before he left for your village any communication I did have with him was of a social nature and there wasn't a lot to that. Yet, on the odd occasion, he did ask specific questions of me, usually as they related to my work with seizure patients. He wanted to know if I, or anyone else, had come across reports of concentrated seizure activity in coastal native populations. When I asked him why he wanted to know he was vague and evasive — something about researching traditional medicine men. I must admit that his questions piqued my interest — and my suspicions. He must've stumbled on to something."

Warner was all warmth, sympathy and flattery. "When he telephoned me to make the arrangements for Beebo to come down, things started to come together a little better in my mind. Then when I got to know you all I could see that you possessed a number of qualities which are uncommon among others your age. For instance, your undying compassion for Beebo and your ability to act as you do in unison, to mention just a couple."

He gazed again out of the window. "I'm convinced the episode at the restaurant in Vancouver was due to someone knowing who and what you are. And that someone could only have been Michael. I don't know why he wants to possess you and your powers, but you can be assured that what happened at the restaurant will happen again."

The wily doctor's comments stirred up the darkest fears in each of them and their expressions showed it. "You possess magnificent powers, the limits of which I can't even begin to imagine! But they must be used for the betterment of mankind, which means they must be protected. I want to help, if you'll let me."

Belly looked at the old man, then turned to the others, imploring them with his eyes to help him, to give him strength in the gamble he was about attempt. "What's in it for you?"

"A chance to help you, to help humanity. I'm old, my beloved wife is dead and I have nothing to lose but my life. And you don't have a plan at all, do you? Well I do."

"Talk to us, doc," said Dickie quietly.

"Thank you," said Warner. "As I mentioned at Fort Wardon, you can use your powers for three purposes. The first is for the good of humanity. But you can't help other people if you're dead."

They were listening intently.

"And that means finding out who is behind all this. Potter is obviously involved, but he must be working for someone. We must find out who. And finally, we must have something to bargain with, to ensure your safety and the safety of your families. A show of power, to scare them and make them leave you alone forever."

Warner rubbed his bald head thoughtfully. "I would suggest a strategy that will force your enemies into the open. Do the totally unexpected, create diversions, make them guess and be afraid. If you know your enemy, you'll know how to defeat him."

"What do you mean by strategies and diversions?" Beebo asked.

"Just like what you did this afternoon, with the Trident submarine." Warner was watching them closely. "It was fun, wasn't it?"

The eye contact between the children and a giggle from Princess told him he was right. "And believe me," he continued, "there's nothing the capitalist machine fears more than attacks on its very heart, its industry, especially the military. With your powers, you could have the entire power structure of the United States tied up in knots. Panicked meetings in the White House, all of that. Make a mess, have some fun and get what you want all at the same time. But it's very important that no one gets hurt."

He started the van. "That's food for thought. And by the way, I'm hungry and you must be too. Let's all think about what I've said."

Twenty minutes later they were in Oak Harbor. The others kept looking at Belly. He obviously didn't like Warner's ideas and they couldn't figure out why.

They stopped at the *Skipper's Seafood* restaurant located in the small shopping center north of town. When their food arrived, Harry Warner scooped up his fish and french fries and said, "I'm going to stretch my legs. I believe you should be alone so you can freely discuss my proposal. When you're ready to leave come and get me."

Belly waited a few moments before crossing the room to the window. He saw Harry ambling down the walk, browsing idly in shop windows as he ate. He returned to the table and sat down heavily, forcing out a loud sigh. He surveyed his friends with concern.

"What's up?" inquired Dickie from across the table. "You look pretty bugged."

Belly didn't answer instantly, obviously collecting his thoughts. Finally, he spoke up. "There's something wrong here. This guy's too good to be true. He just steps in and wants to take over our lives. I just can't stop thinking that he wants something more than he says he does."

Beebo reached out and patted his friend on the shoulder. "Belly, nobody's going to take over anything. We can crush that guy any time we want. We know it and he knows it. And you gotta admit that what happened today was totally excellent."

The others knew exactly what he was feeling and giggled. Belly still looked thoughtful and concerned.

"Nothing personal," continued Beebo, "but what the hell do we know about staying alive outside of Alert Bay? We're kids and Dr. Harry's this famous bigshot and wants to look after us. And everything he's said so far makes sense to me."

"I know you trust the guy," said Belly, "but what does he know about running from anything? And all this strategy and diversion bull. What the hell does a medical doctor know about that? I just think something's wrong. Dickie, what do you think?"

"I like the guy," shrugged Dickie. "He's like my grandpa or something. And I know that since we been with him, I don't feel like I have to be looking over my shoulder all the time. Going to Port Townsend was a good idea because nobody found us there, right?"

Belly turned to Princess. "What about you, baby girl?"

"Doctor Harry's nice to me and I think he can help us. But Belly, I really miss mommy and daddy." There were tears in her dark eyes.

Belly reached across the table and touched her hand as Brenda gave her a warm hug.

Brenda spoke next. "He seems like a real nice man most of the time, and then he goes all cold. I can't read him very well. It bothers me that he's with us, knowing what he knows, especially with everything happening so fast."

She paused as she sucked the salt from another french fry. "And we trusted Dr. Mike too, and look what happened."

The others all looked thoughtful as she continued. "At the same time, I like what he got us thinking about, the things we can do for our people you know."

"Yeah," said Beebo. "And he doesn't call the police, he protects us from them."

"Okay," said Belly decisively. "He knows too much about us for us to let him out of our sight. He's thinking he'll keep an eye on us, we'll keep an eye on him. And I like what Beebo said - the guy gets out of line, wham! I just wish Dr. Mike was here so I could do it to him. Besides, he's got a plan and we don't. What he says makes sense. Fair enough?"

The others nodded.

Once they finished what was left of their meals they went in search of Harry Warner. They found him at the far end of the mall, sitting on a bench, finishing his fish and french fries and lost in thought.

No one spoke during the drive east along Route 20 and as they got closer to the intersection for the I 5 north to the border the group got progressively more tense. Belly still hadn't told Harry of their decision and the doctor hadn't asked. Just as Belly was about to speak they heard a siren approaching from behind.

Belly eyed each of them. He flashed the image of the fall back plan they'd hatched so many days previously, before they crossed over into Washington State.

Harry pulled the van over to the shoulder. The light green Highway Patrol ghost cruiser pulled in behind them. Red and blue emergency lights strobed from behind the grill work.

A stocky Washington State trooper got out. He placed a gray service Stetson on his blond, crew-cut head and with his right hand, reached down to the leather holster at his side and flipped off its safety toggle. Everyone in the vehicle saw the motion.

The group saw an image of the wood grained handle and the silver sheen of the gun turning red as flames jumped from it. It was a communication from Belly telling them that the contingency plan was in motion.

Looking into the rear view mirror, Harry watched the trooper's cautious approach. The old man's nervous tapping cadence of fingers against the wheel matched exactly the trooper's steps. The sound of the fingers sounded like a death drum to the tired youngsters whose senses were on overload.

The big man strode up to the rear of the van. Reaching Harry's window, he raised a beefy arm and rapped meaty, freckled knuckles on the glass.

The old man slowly lowered the window.

The trooper bent down until the perfectly straight brim of his hat filled the upper portion of the window, effectively obscuring his face from those in the back. He wore big wraparound sunglasses with mirrored lenses. "Good afternoon sir!" The voice was authoritative. "Would you please hand me your driver's license and the registration?"

"Certainly officer," replied Harry as he reached into his back trouser pocket. "May I inquire what the infraction is?"

"Standard check sir."

Harry sorted through the jumble of papers and certificates in the billfold. After some more fumbling, he finally located the license and handed it to the officer. "Brenda, could you get me the registration out of the glove compartment?"

The trooper briefly scanned the driver's license. His voice dropped an octave and he said menacingly, "The registration sir!"

"We're looking, officer! Brenda?"

"It's not here!" she exclaimed, running her hand one more time through the glove box, then across the sun visor. Nothing.

Harry said, "I'm sorry officer, this is a rental and there doesn't seem to be any paperwork that we can find."

"Please step out of the vehicle, sir. The rest of you, too. Exit from this side, please."

Once they were all standing beside the vehicle he commanded, "Everyone face the car, hands on the roof. Do it now!"

"Officer, isn't this a bit much? These are children."

With no warning, the trooper cuffed Harry across the side of the head. The doctor fell heavily against Belly and Dickie, who managed to break his fall.

Belly whirled around to face the trooper. Seeing the man's right hand whipping for his gun, he lunged. They all saw a mental image of the gun and gun hand wreathed in red flames. The trooper screamed in agony and dropped the weapon. He landed on his knees, howling in pain, fully believing his gun hand was in flames.

Harry peered at the fallen weapon and before anyone could react, bent down, grasped for it, straightened and spun. The gun smashed at the back of the blond head and the trooper's body crumpled to the pavement.

They stood motionless until Belly barked, "Beebo and Brenda, get Harry into the car! Princess, go open the door of the cruiser. Tell us when you see cars coming from either direction! Dickie, let's get this guy back to his cruiser before someone drives by. Come on!"

They dragged the heavy, limp form ten meters to the cruiser. Grabbing the big man's arms they heaved and pulled him up, and into the car. Belly pushed the legs in and Dickie sat him upright. Warner placed the Stetson back on his head, over his eyes.

As Princess yelled "Someone's coming!" they closed the door and stood facing the trooper, as if talking to him casually. When the car had passed by, Dickie removed his fist from the man's shirt collar and the big trooper slumped over towards the window. Dickie opened the door and pushed him upright.

Belly reached over the wheel to turn off the switch marked Emergency Lights. Grabbing for the microphone cable, he pulled the whole assembly out of the dashboard.

Harry Warner looked in. "Good, you've got the microphone! Dickie, give me your shirt." When the boy handed it to him he started wiping. "Fingerprints," he panted.

"Another car!" yelled Princess.

Once again they all pretended to talk to the trooper. When the car passed Warner finished wiping and handed Dickie back his shirt. They all headed back toward the van.

They were off in a hail of gravel.

"Holy shit!" shouted Beebo. "Now we've done it! They're going to be on to us for sure!"

"We had no choice," coughed Warner. "He would've shot me.

And then all of you. We must get away and activate a plan. He looked into the rear view mirror at Belly. "Have you made up your mind?"

"Yes," said Belly decisively. "Even before the trooper. We'll go with your plan."

"Excellent," said the old man. He smiled with relief, elation, they couldn't tell which. He chuckled suddenly. "You're a resourceful bunch. How in God's name did you come up with that impromptu cleanup back there? I'm impressed."

"Saw it in a movie," answered Belly.

For some reason this seemed hilarious and they all laughed and headed for their next refuge from the forces that seemed determined to kill them.

TWENTY TWO

"What the hell is that?" exclaimed Dickie. "It's huge!" Long, sooty black contrails streamed from the four widely dispersed engine pods of the large military transport jet that lumbered towards them.

"A Galaxy C5," said Harry Warner.

"How could such a big thing stay in the air?" piped Princess.

"Well my dear, I'm not totally sure myself but I do know that until recently, it was the largest aircraft in the world. The Russians then topped it with one of their own, much to the chagrin of the Americans."

"Where's it coming from?" asked Dickie.

"Likely McChord Air Force Base."

"McChord?" queried Belly. "Why is that name familiar? I've heard it some place before."

A mile further along, they passed signs indicating exits for Fort Lewis, US Army. Dickie was the first to pick up on the immense size of the base with its military residences, marshaling yards and motor pools sprawling on either side of the freeway. "This place is gigantic! Dr. Harry, is this Fort Lewis place pretty important?"

"Dickie, this is one of the largest military bases in all of the United States. I think I read once that there are over twenty five thousand personnel here and there must be thousands more back at McChord."

"Place this big would be sure to attract attention, huh doc?"

"And like you said, they're proud of their military and it would hit them where it hurts the most, right?" Brenda chimed.

"That's what I said," answered the old man. A glimmer of a smile creased his face. "What, are you thinking of doing something already?"

"Just thinking about what you said," replied Dickie. "Strategy and diversions. Shake up the white man by showing that he can't control his machines. What were some of the other things you told us?"

"Concentrate on military, internal security and economic targets."

"That was it. Thanks." The large boy's tone changed "Jeez, what time is it? How about we find a place to get something to eat?"

"Sounds good to me, but let's find a place to stay first."

A low budget Motel 6 served as their base for the night.

Once they had registered Warner announced he was going out for a short walk to loosen up his legs.

The youngsters converged on one of the three rooms, ostensibly to get cleaned up and relax before they went in search of a restaurant. The four eldest ended up talking about what Warner had said, and what their plans should be. They just ended up arguing.

Feeling left out, Princess turned on the TV and sat idly watching the last minutes of the Oprah Show. When the six o'clock news came on she got up to switch to something more to her liking. Flipping through the channels, the sight of a familiar image made her stop. Video footage of the conning tower of a Trident submarine was accompanied by a female announcer's voice.

"Hey look!" she shouted over the din.

The five hundred and sixty foot Trident submarine remained sta-

tionary for well over an hour until a tug arrived from the Bangor base. This amateur footage was taken by a passenger on board the ferry. Information from the Navy has been very sketchy but early reports suggested mechanical failure in the vessel's steering system. As to the extent of the damage, we have no further information at this time. This is Lori Nakagowa reporting from Port Townsend.

The kids stared at the TV screen. "Man, I can't believe what a kick today was!" exclaimed Beebo. "It was so *easy*. And you know, if we'd tried anything near what we did with the sub before today, I'd have been sick for days. But not now. No headaches, no nightmares! I feel great. I bet if we do another one, it'd be just as easy."

Brenda looked at Dickie, who looked at Belly who was already being studied by Princess. Slowly, each one of them turned to look at Beebo, the healthy Beebo who for so long had been absent.

"Maybe exercising our powers is good for all of us," mused Brenda as Belly and the others nodded agreement.

"Let's quit arguing and make some plans," said Dickie.

Dinner was a quiet affair at a nearby Mexican restaurant. As they walked back to the motel the kids were in fine spirits, buoyed by the events of the day, and aching to be alone so they could discuss Dickie's plan. Dickie was proud of his planning ability but it bothered him that the plan didn't seem to have any connection with Beebo's dreams.

"Doc, about Fort Lewis and all the people there?"

"Yes?"

"You think it's a good target?"

"Of course."

"So what do we target? I mean, we mentally break into the place, but to do what? It's not like taking control of a sub or a ferry boat. A military base just sits there. We need information about what's in there and what to do."

"What kind of information do you mean?"

"Doc, you told me you were in World War Two, right? Well, there must be weapons and stuff in there."

"Certainly. But I must know for sure what you're up to."

"Doc, it's going to be a piece of cake. Just think about how you and me stole that car from the GM dealership in Mount Vernon after knocking out that trooper who was going to kill us. We don't know anything about stealing cars but it went off real smooth. It'll be the same with this."

"Whatever you're up to, you must remember that your case will be negatively affected if anyone gets injured. I can't stress the importance of this enough."

"Fair enough," answered Belly. "We target machines, not people."

Back at the motel, Warner had some excellent suggestions, particularly concerning the target and media coverage. "You have to remember," he said, "military bases are secret. There's no point in making a spectacular demonstration of your powers if no one gets to hear about it."

They agreed on a time and went to bed.

****

Five shimmering mental ropes wavered out through the early morning fog. Reaching the central parade grounds, each undulated off on a different course like surrealistic snakes parting company.

One moved north, winding its way past office buildings, residences, a sprawling five story building with a tall, faintly smoking stack. Past parade grounds, grass covered humps in the ground, basketball courts, finely manicured lawns, to a barb wire enclosure around a large sized concrete and brick structure. Two armed soldiers stood out front, two more guarded the rear.

The filmy, sparkling mental rope wove through a steel man-door into a wide foyer. As it moved, it sent back a moving image of office suites on either side of a long central hallway. The floors of the hall glistened under bright fluorescent lights. The perimeter of the foyer leading to the hallway was guarded by a large, curved wooden console occupied by a female corporal. A bank of TV monitors faced her.

The mental rope snaked past the front of the desk and registered the name on the fabric tag on the chest of the soldier's fatigues: D. E. Jackson.

The mental rope moved off down the hall, continuing its search, through a steel door at the end, into a cavernous room.

Inside, an image was transmitted of row upon row of vertical shelving units loaded with steel boxes. In the central area, rows of wooden stands held scores of rifles resting on their butts. In the very center of the room, crates of all sizes bristling with serial numbers and manufacture's designations lay neatly in rows. Everywhere, the color was drab green.

The mental rope found its target.

Within seconds, four more mental presences joined with the first to form a filmy, multicolored filament.

The mental rope withdrew, back to the position of the console where a bank of twelve television screens corresponded to remote cameras placed at various positions around the large room the rope had just explored. Some of the images on the screens were stationery while others showed scans of sections of the room.

One screen, in the top right-hand corner of the display, registered human movement as a soldier with a white hip holster walked across the view of the camera. He was black, handsome and waved at the camera as he passed.

The female soldier sitting at the console saw his attentions and shook her head, welcoming the distraction after a dull shift of watching the screens. The mental rope *saw* her sit up straight as one, two then three screens went dead. Her radio crackled, signifying that someone was trying to contact her but when she answered the transmission faded into static.

Camera 4 showed her partner turn a corner of one of the aisleways in the central area of the facility, only to fall to the floor grasping his temples. She saw him twitch for a few seconds then, go still.

The rope saw her bolt from her chair and a finger on her right hand move to the clasp on her holster, freeing her sidearm. Her other hand keyed the 'send' button on her hand-held radio. Passing the right corner of her console, she slammed the butt of her revolver down on the single red button that commanded that area of the desk. Klaxons blared.

She ran for the steel door at the end of the hallway, cocking her gun and yelling into the face of the radio for her partner as she ran. No response — at least none that she could hear. With her radio under her arm and her free hand reaching to unbolt the steel entry door, her conscious world faded away.

Camera 5 recorded her fall to the floor as Camera 31 in the base Security Center also caught it. The shrill sound of the alarm and the flashing red light up on the wall of the Security Center told of an occurrence that no one ever really expected to come — the maintenance and storage depot of the 80th Ordnance Battalion of I Corps was under attack.

Responding to the alarms, the two MPs covering the front entrance of the depot rushed for the door, only to be pushed back by automatic rifle fire pelting the ground at their feet. A rumbling explosion in the bowels of the building shook the foundations as banks of windows high up on a side wall blew out.

Beebo reached over and tapped the sleeping Harry on the right shoulder. "Get up! We're in!"

The old man came bolt upright, alert. Hair askew and a night's worth of beard smudging a haggard face, he glared at the youngster.

"What do you mean you're in? You've done it without me?"

Belly shrugged. "We didn't know how long it would take us to find the place and spec it out. Besides, it's all under control. *We're* in control. We need you to phone the TV station. If they hear a kid on the line they'll think it's a prank."

Warner nodded. "You had no trouble with the different types of weapons?"

"None. We found most of the stuff you talked about. The rifles and ammo were just like you said. Fact is, that's what we held the outside guards down with."

He caught the look on the old man's face and said, "No one's hurt. And none of the cameras work any more so nobody's going to figure this one out for a while."

"So the facility is secure and you're all safe?"

"Yes."

The plan was for Harry to make the call from a telephone booth down the street, just in case the motel switchboard operator might listen in, or the radio station had a call tracing system.

They all briefed Warner on what had happened back at Fort Lewis so he could provide the kind of inside information about the base and the attack that would prove to whoever was on duty that the call was genuine. On the first call he gave just enough information to the station's night manager to ensure that he had the man's full attention, including juicy snippets concerning the security layout of the fort and the names of the submarine's captain and the executive officer.

Once he had the man's full attention, Warner ordered him to get his on-duty reporter ready to receive another call in exactly five minutes, then hung up and went to a different booth.

When he phoned back he gave her more information, knowing she would already have been briefed by the night manager. He kept all the calls, including the subsequent two, brief and always phoned from a different public booth. On the fourth call he was told that a chopper was fueled and a reporter and camera crew out the door. Warner hurried back to the motel room where the kids were waiting expectantly. He turned on the TV.

It's early in the morning and we're reporting live from the western gates of Fort Lewis Army Base in Tacoma. Earlier today, this reporter received a tip that the base had been attacked by a group calling themselves the Patriots of the Raven.

It's not known exactly who the Patriots of the Raven are, but to attack a US base and escape with no casualties suggests a terrifying degree of skill and preparation. The limited information we have at this time suggests that the group is an ultra secret, radical native American organization claiming strong support and membership within all branches of the Armed Services. They also claim responsibility for yesterday's near disaster on board the Trident submarine USS Georgia.

At this time, the Army has denied that anything out of the ordinary has taken place. Yet here at the western gates, it is clear that there is a great deal of activity going on inside. Troops and machinery have been readied and are on the move towards the center of the base.

More information when it happens. This is Lori Nakagowa for KING News, reporting live from Fort Lewis.

PART 3

TWENTY THREE

Slowly Michael Potter swam from the black depths, upward into consciousness. He could see light through his lids, pink-red from the blood vessels there. His eyes felt like they were glued shut but he finally got them open. There was a brilliant light nearby but he couldn't look at it. He tried instinctively to move his arm to shield himself from the glare.

Nothing happened.

He tried again and a cushiony mass slipped by his face. It was several seconds before he recognized it as his own arm, swathed in white gauze.

Slowly, his focus returned enough for him to distinguish a plastic tube protruded from the bandages. Still squinting painfully, he looked beyond the whiteness of the gauze to see that the light was coming from a window, with a woman in white standing in front of it yanking something. The word 'curtains' drifted slowly into his mind.

"Well, well. Like Lazarus, he is risen from the dead. I've spent days wondering what colour your eyes are." She leaned over. "Bloodshot. And how are we today?"

Weakly he shook his head. The woman's voice reached him once more. "Can you remember what happened?"

He struggled to think about the words and the images that came with them. Faces, places, machines floating past, never staying long enough to see properly. "No." Uttering the word caused an agonizing spasm of coughing.

"It's all right. The more you cough the faster you'll clear those lungs. Human beings weren't meant to lie on their backs for a week without moving."

After the coughing fit subsided, he gasped, "What happened to me?"

She bent over him. "Here, it'll help if we raise the bed a bit." An electric motor whined and his head started to rise.

"What happened to me?" he demanded again.

"Try and relax! You've been in a coma for quite some time now."

At first her words made no sense to him. His brain started to fog over again but he forced himself to understand, to fight the swirling storm of darkness causing her image to waver.

"Stay with me," she whispered urgently. "Fight!" He fought.

The woman moved to the opposite side of the bed, out of the direct light. He tracked her movement and slowly saw her features come into focus. She was just a slip of a woman, with long, straight red hair, ivory white skin and a pretty smile.

"What happened to me?" he asked for the third time

She picked up a green binder. "According to this, they found you half-way down a cliff. You sustained a pretty good smack to the head. And you've been shot."

"What?"

"With a high powered rifle. The bullet hit you in the chest and barely missed your heart. It's sheer luck you're still alive."

He lay there in stunned silence, his mind struggling to process the meaning of what he heard. "Who . . . ?"

"I know very little about the police investigation. They've been wanting to talk to you. I'll see if I can find . . . "

"Police?" A coughing fit seized him and again, the pain overwhelmed him and he passed out.

When he next came to the same nurse was there. She smiled. "We can't have a decent conversation if you keep slipping away like that. You passed out before I could ask your name."

"My name?" He struggled to remember. Nothing there at all. "Isn't it in the chart?"

"When they found you, you were in jogging clothes with no ID at all." She looked at him closely. "You don't know who you are?"

He shook his head as a slow sense of bafflement began to battle an undercurrent of fear in his mind.

"Do you know where you are? The city?"

Again he shook his head.

After a moment she smiled and with the cheeriness of long experience said, "Don't worry about it. It'll come back. With head injuries as mild as yours, it always does. I'm Maureen Clancy, by the way, and don't you dare forget it. People call be Mo."

"Mo, where am I?" His was the voice of a man lost and afraid.

"You're on the surgical floor of the University of British Columbia Health Sciences Centre. You came to this ward last evening from ICU. Let's see if you can manage to eat something."

She returned just minutes later and was almost up to the bed before he noticed the uniformed woman following close behind Mo. She introduced the tall, slim, attractive blond.

"This is Corporal Hillary Brown, RCMP. Corporal Brown, this is the man with no name you've been waiting so long to talk to. Now, if you don't mind, I'm going to finish searching for something for him to eat." As she passed the officer, she touched the other's elbow and he could just hear her say under her breath, "Just a few minutes to start with. He's still in pretty bad shape." She started to walk out of the room but the officer stopped her with a raised hand and a smile.

"Actually nurse, there's something you should hear.

Unbelievable though it may seem, your patient actually has a name. It's Michael." The female officer was watching closely as he struggled with the news, then moved to the bedside, pulled out the chair and sat down. She flipped open a small note pad. "Now, can you remember your last name?"

It was an effort, but finally it came. "Potter. My name is Michael Potter!"

"And you'll never guess, Ms. Clancy. He's a doctor."

"Must be one of the only doctors in the world who won't admit to it, right off the bat."

"Now," said Corporal Brown, "I'm sorry I have to tell you the rest, but it has to be done. Do you think you are strong enough?"

He pondered her words carefully and then nodded.

"From what we've been able to piece together, last Tuesday, July 17th, you were running on the cliff trail here at the university. They found you on a part of the trail close to the cliff edge. From the entry point of the bullet and the angle it took, our forensics people think you would've just turned the corner and started heading back towards the road when the shooter got you. Now doctor, try and remember anything about the day. Things like the trail up ahead, the weather, even."

Slowly, bits and pieces of the day started to come back to him. It had been a gorgeous morning. He could remember going for a run but not much else.

"What did you just remember?"

He told the two of them.

"I know this is hard but I have to get you to keep that picture in your mind. When you ran into the clearing, can you remember anything out of the ordinary, say off to your right, towards the road and the buildings perhaps?"

In his strain to remember, he felt himself floating away from the two women. Finally, it was Maureen's voice that reached him.

"Michael! Can you hear me?"

"I'm afraid there isn't much else in here."

"Were there any vehicles?"

"I don't know," he muttered. "If there was, I'd tell you."

Corporal Brown was still watching him very carefully and it suddenly dawned on him that it was an appraising and not terribly sympathetic look. "Okay, let's leave the shooting for now. Is there anything else?"

"I keep having this dream with faces in it."

"Okay, lets start there. Try and remember it. Can you tell me about, size, hair color, any distinguishing features of the faces?"

He gripped her words and tried to bring the images out of the haze. He closed his eyes and tried to remember the water, the pebbles, the faces . . .

Small rolling wavelets slurped around pebbles on a beach. In shining water, fragments of things living, like pieces of human faces, bobbed near the shore.

A hand reached out from the mist to touch a number of the pieces, catching two of them, placing them on a spot just out of the waves. Two more pieces were caught, then two more, until a complete face rested on the stones.

Soon, the waves begin to act unassisted, floating pieces together, molding and forming another complete face. Then, another and then another wash in until five complete faces, their features clear, lay harvested on the shore, drying in the bright sunlight. And, there beside them, yet another face, but strangely incomplete.

He had it! "I remember five kids and another person, an older man. The kids looked like they're Indian or something." He described them all.

Corporal Brown took copious notes as he spoke, interjecting short questions on features or other distinguishing items. "What was your relationship with these children? What's so special about them that they would stick out in your mind?"

He was about answer her but before he could get the words out, a dense black fog closed over his thoughts and in a flash, the five faces were gone. The intensity of the blackness was like nothing he had ever felt, and before he lost consciousness it was as if some unseen hand had snuffed out his memory.

The warm, musical tones of Maureen's voice brought him out of the mist. "You're doing just fine. You passed out ten minutes ago. Just relax."

He closed his eyes tightly in an effort to sift out thoughts that swirled and bobbed in a sticky mental ooze.

"Okay Michael," said the insistent voice of Corporal Brown, "what about the sixth face, the one of the older man you mentioned?"

He didn't answer her question but asked one of his own. "Who did this to me? And why?"

"We don't know yet. The details are very sketchy. Look, it appears you've had enough for now. If there's anything else you do remember, anything at all, please have the medical staff contact me."

As she opened the door to leave, he saw another officer. A thought struck him. "Just a minute!" he coughed. "Mo said that you were right here waiting for me to wake up. And there's another officer outside. Why am I being guarded?"

After a slight hesitation she said, "For your own protection. The whole thing looks like a professional job and whoever screwed it up might come back to finish you off."

As he stared at her in disbelief a male uniformed officer entered the room with a tray and set it on the table before leaving. The aroma of the food made Potter recognize that his stomach was churning violently. He attempted to reach for the plastic mug on the tray but his hand would only move part of the way across the distance before it collapsed on the bed. His reprieve from starvation and a crushing sense of inadequacy and bafflement — came in the form of Maureen Clancy. She pulled up a chair and set to work feeding him the liquid meal.

When he was finished she left him to his thoughts for a few minutes before speaking. Even then, he found it difficult to follow what she said. Much as he tried to hold on, he slipped further away from her words, drawn instead by the recognition of a scent, a scent that didn't belong to the food. A perfume? He reached for the scent with his mind. A face came into view, a female, Indian face.

"By the look on your handsome mug, I'd say you just remembered something. What is it?" Maureen asked.

"A woman I must know. A perfume."

"You get a whiff of my perfume and you start thinking about other women?" As she continued to joke his mind clouded over and soon he was asleep.

He slept fitfully for the rest of the day, spending periods of wakefulness trying to exercise various limbs. His left side seemed to be operating well enough but it was the right side and especially the shoulder and arm which gave him the most problems. Through the pain he kept at it until he regained reasonable mobility in the lower arm and hand. It was exhausting work but as the day progressed he detected minute signs that his physical strength might eventually return.

It was late in the afternoon and he was in yet another of the semi-sleep episodes when a stream of clear thought came to him. He called out to Maureen. When she came he said, "Get Brown. I just remembered something!"

Moments later she returned with the officer. Before she could say anything, he demanded, "What floor are we on?"

"Two. Why?"

"What ward? The ward number?"

"2 A. Why?"

"He's here! Here in this hospital, on this floor! For neurological tests." He paused, the pain in his head building terribly.

"Michael, I don't know what you're talking about! Now slowly, what's the matter?"

"A boy. One of the ones in my dream. He's here!"

"Which one?" queried Brown anxiously.

"The small teen, the well muscled one with the broad features and the blue eyes and bronze hair."

"What about a name?"

"I don't know, but he's the reason I'm here. I mean, why I was near the hospital. He came with me. The others too."

"Does the name Samuel Johnson ring a bell?" A slight glimmer of recognition showed on his face. She stole a quick glance at her notes. "How about a nickname, like Deedo or Reebo—"

"Beebo," he cried out excitedly.

"Bingo," said Brown as she turned to Maureen Clancy. In a low voice, to which she attempted to add a touch of warmth, she asked, "Could you leave the room now, please? Things might get a bit touchy from here on in." Silently and begrudgingly the nurse left.

Brown waited a few moments until she was sure the redhead was out of earshot before continuing. "Besides Johnson, there's William and Molly Lucas, Dickie Cook and Brenda Johnson."

The sound of the names sent his mind spinning. Soon, the names began to link up with the faces on the beach. Their true names came to him, Belly, Dickie, Brenda, Princess!

Brown continued with, "Do you know why they were here, Michael?"

The question made the blackness billow behind his eyes. "Tests. "

"Beebo was here for tests, requested by you! The other four

came to visit him. Seems they were all from up island, Alert Bay."

"Alert Bay. That sounds right."

"Good. It would help if you could remember any details about the boy, his parents' names, addresses, other family members, that sort of thing."

As soggy as his brain was, something she said just didn't sit well. Then it came to him. "You're talking like he isn't here any more!"

"The boy hasn't been in the hospital for over a week. He was checked out the day you were shot. In fact, they're all missing."

"Michael, what about the sixth face? What does he have to do with all this? You said he was older. How much older?"

"Don't know exactly. Why does it matter?"

He attempted to picture the sixth face. He reached and reached with his mind until a clearing in the haze opened up, for just a second. "He's not Native."

"What's his name? It's very important." Potter shook his head. Seeing that she was not going to make further headway she brought the conversation to an end and left the room.

Later that evening, just as she went off shift, Maureen turned on the TV for him and handed him the remote control. He flipped through the channels but found it hard to follow anything for long.

He awoke with a start. He could have sworn he hadn't dozed but in front of him was the proof, the familiar introduction for the CTV Late News.

It's been a bad couple of days for the US armed forces. The crew of the Trident nuclear submarine USS Georgia lost control of the vessel and a disastrous collision with a freighter was barely avoided. Although official sources blame mechanical failure, unofficial sources indicate the possibility of sabotage.

On the screen appeared the video of the submarine racing

though the waters toward the freighter.

The issue is of deadly concern as Trident subs carry nuclear warheads. Greenpeace demanded today what the US government would do if nuclear weapons were sunk in the vital fishery off the west coast. Pentagon officials will only say that an investigation is underway, and that if necessary every Trident submarine afloat will be checked out.

Something strangely familiar about the image of the submarine nagged at Potter but the announcer started speaking again before he could remember.

And the second disaster is even worse. The huge Fort Lewis military base at Tacoma was suddenly and mysteriously attacked by a radical Native American group calling themselves the Patriots of the Raven. The White House and Pentagon are in an uproar as the public demands to know why security at such a vital installation was so lax. More on the story from Lori Nakagowa.

An excited looking oriental female appeared on the screen.

Just moments ago, army spokesperson Major Trudy MacDonald confirmed that members of the terrorist group know as the Patriots of the Raven attacked this military base. She states the group has so far not issued any demands or explained their actions.

Behind me and to my right you can see a steady stream of army and civilian vehicles moving off the base. We have just learned that all non-essential personnel are being evacuated from the area as the army is setting up a five mile safety perimeter. Residents of local communities are also being evacuated from their homes.

Although the Pentagon will not confirm it, there are rumors that the method of attack used by the terrorists is something completely new. As a result, the military is taking its time evaluating the situation. This may be the reason why the US army has not already stormed and retaken Fort Lewis. This is Lori Nakagowa reporting live from the gates of Fort Lewis, a fortress incredibly under siege right here on American soil.

Again, something about the scene seemed familiar to Michael Potter but he was too tired to even try to remember. He clicked off the TV, laid his head back and was instantly asleep.

He slept. And dreamed.

TWENTY FOUR

Potter awoke early the next morning in time to witness shift change. Maureen came back on duty and dropped in to check on him before seeing to her other change-over duties. She commented that he looked surprisingly well considering what he had been through the previous day. He didn't tell her that since waking, he'd been working his arms, especially the right one and the result was that he had gained back much of his original mobility.

He didn't mention his attempt to raise himself up in the bed and put his legs over the side of the mattress. Half way over he collapsed and spent the next agonizing minutes trapped in an awkward and painful slumped position. Occupied in trying to right himself, without passing out, he failed to notice the approach of the male RCMP guard. A strong arm steadied him and guided him back onto the pillows.

He turned on the TV again and there was another update on the Trident and Fort Lewis crises. He tried to remember what had seemed so familiar the night before. He was still frowning at the screen when Constable Brown entered the room. She followed his gaze to the TV screen and an advertisement for a shampoo.

"Puzzled by shampoo, Dr. Potter? Your recovery can't be coming along as well as I thought."

"Just a news story about Fort Lewis." He could tell she didn't have the slightest interest in the subject. As he was about to continue he was distracted by a man pushing a steel trolley loaded with a TV and a video player into the room. Looking visibly distressed, Brown stood up.

The man was tall and solid. He was in his early forties but his close cropped, graying hair and mustache made him look older and suggested a wide acquaintance with some of the more disagreeable aspects of life. His well tailored sports coat and trousers were immaculately neat and precisely pressed, and his pale eyes were as cold as the surface of the moon.

"Michael, this gentleman is Staff Sergeant Baker. He's an investigator with our Special Operations/anti-terrorism section. He'll be sitting in on our discussion this afternoon if that's all right with you?"

"Sure," shrugged Potter. "What's Special Operations?"

"National security," said Brown, deliberately not looking at him or Baker. What Potter could not know was that Douglas Baker had once been an intelligence officer assigned to a section of RCMP that conducted all of Canada's intelligence work. But after the press had leaked details of some dirty trick squad activities — information likely planted by the Soviets — Canadian politicians disbanded the unit to form a completely new entity, the Canadian Security and Intelligence Service, or CSIS. All intelligence officers were given two options: stay in the RCMP and move to a different division or resign from the force and sign up with CSIS. Bitter that Soviet disinformation had been so ingenuously swallowed by the politicians, but unshaken in his loyalty to the Mounties, Baker had opted to stay with the force. But for some assignments that dated from the old days, his expertise was badly needed by the new organization. He always had to be persuaded to help out, with the exception of one old, unresolved and very special case.

The staff sergeant regarded Potter for several silent moments. He had the intent but distanced professionalism of an executioner contemplating a prisoner on death row and trying to figure out how fast he's likely to die.

Corporal Brown cleared her throat. "We'd like you to look at some footage we borrowed from a local TV station." She powered up machines and the TV screen glowed.

"This is a picture of the front of a local restaurant. You might remember it from your time in Vancouver?" said Baker, his voice deep and toneless.

Potter did remember it, vaguely. "Yes. I think I was going to go there. I don't really remember." But the restaurant wasn't his primary interest at the moment. He was trying to figure out why the big man obviously didn't like him and why he was here at all when he was suddenly distracted by the next image on the screen.

The footage showed a large number of darkly dressed, heavily armed men sweeping in to take up positions around the patio portion of the restaurant. The camera's field of view zoomed in on one particular table of five youngsters and a tall man half-obscured by a planter. As the camera closed in further their faces came into clear view, and they were all familiar to him, very familiar. The sight of them turned his vision into a tunnel as everything else around went black.

Baker paused the tape, freeze framing the action with a remote control. "Know them?" he demanded?"

"Yes. They're the ones I described," Potter said hoarsely.

"Watch what happens next." The figures once again became animated and then all turned toward the camera, fear on their faces. Baker turned up the volume on the tape and a tinny, electronic voice sounded. "This is the Vancouver Police Department Emergency Response Team. The area is totally surrounded!"

Potter watched closely, detecting a unanimous state of panic in the patrons of the cafe. Even though the sounds of revving automobile engines in the background blocked out the beginnings of a second loud hailer address he had a good idea of what was being said — the reaction of the five youths told everything.

They flipped their table over as they jumped up, along with the older man, and began running for the interior of the restaurant. In the dark interior he could dimly see four Emergency Response members being bowled over near what looked like the kitchen. There was a lot of incoherent shouting.

Baker stopped the tape and Potter looked at him. "What the hell is this?" Michael demanded.

"Your young friends and their companion bolted from a major police operation. The Vancouver Police were there to trap a man suspected of being involved in a recent holdup. Now I ask you, doctor. Since those kids don't look like members of the Capone gang to me, why would they run? What did they do to make them think that the police were after them?"

"How should I know? I wasn't there."

Baker's cold eyes suddenly blazed. "No. But the dinner reservation was in your name."

As Potter tried to remember, Baker resumed rolling the tape. "Look what happens next. After being chased through the restaurant, across an alley and then out on to a side street, another camera picks this up."

The screen showed a long shot down a street lined on either side by three story apartment buildings. The youths were running away from the camera. They stopped next to a car where they huddled for a moment. The camera zoomed in to show two of them supporting a tall, older male.

I know that face. It's the sixth face in the water, thought Potter.

The action continued as the car disappeared around a corner, just as the back window was shot out.

Baker stopped the video, rewinding it to the scene of the old man. He stepped over to the side of bed and leaned in close to Potter's face. "You wouldn't by chance know this man, would you?"

Potter peered at the face on the screen. The face was certainly familiar but no name or other information was clearly associated with it. "I may know him . . . "

Baker's shout would have given a Doberman a heart attack. "You *may* know him? He *may* look familiar?" He moved his face within inches of Potter's. "Five Indian kids from the boonies run from the police and then steal a car! And then they disappear."

Potter watched as the big man slowly backed away. "I've had people disappear on me before. And god damn it, I really hate it."

He crossed his arms in front of his chest. "And all this happens on the very day you get shot. I think you know a lot more about it than you're letting on. And you're going to tell me about it."

Potter felt his face getting red and his heart start to pound. "All right," he said evenly. "I personally incited those kids to armed robbery, kidnapping and auto theft. But before I did that I went out on a jogging trail and damn near killed myself with a self-inflicted gunshot wound so I'd have a really good alibi."

A nurse entered the room. "What was that shout? This man is very ill and needs his rest."

Baker pointed his finger at Potter. "I don't take lip from suspects."

"Fuck you."

Baker pounded heavily on the end of the bed with the side of his fist and strode, cursing, out of the room.

Brown looked at him. "If I were you, I wouldn't do that again," she said softly as she rose and followed the big mountie from the room. The nurse, quickly assessing that Potter was not going to blow a gasket, stormed out of the room in search of the offending officer.

Potter lay there dumbfounded. No matter how he fit the words and actions together they kept coming back like some insane joke. His heart still pounded, adrenaline surged and the pain in his head and shoulder tore at him. "What is this, Nazi Germany?" he said aloud.

They left him alone for some twenty minutes before returning. Baker strode up to the bedside and stood there, his expression and body language implying that nothing out of the ordinary had transpired.

Brown returned to her seat and regarded Potter blankly. Both officers remained silent and just stared at him.

"I get it," said Potter. "Good cop, bad cop."

Baker looked down at Potter with a cold and steely gaze. "Doctor, I want some answers. What were those kids doing in Vancouver and what do they have to hide?"

He thought of his promise to them, and the strange blackness pressed again on his brain. "They're just kids."

"Let's try plan B," said the cop. "Who's the old man?"

"I don't know."

Baker closed his eyes and rubbed his temples, as if consumed by a great and angry weariness. "You know exactly who he is. He's your friend, your teacher. Dr. Harry Warner."

It came back to him. Harry in his office. Harry rambling on to students but still, magically, holding our attention. Harry laughing with his wide sly slit of a grin.

And then the blackness came and he passed out.

TWENTY FIVE

Potter awoke to feel warm hands manipulating his skin. Slowly, his vision improved and he recognized Dr. David Singh, the resident in charge of his case, accompanied by one of the regular nurses whose name he couldn't remember. Both of them flashed him nervous smiles and continued on with their work. An untouched lunch tray lay on the side table and from what he could tell it had been there a long time.

"You're definitely going to live, but next time watch out for those gorillas you let in here" said Singh. "The last episode stressed your system way too much. We're only now seeing your blood pressure go down. Luckily, you don't seem to have sprung any leaks anywhere. How's your head?"

"It's still there. Can you do something about keeping that animal Baker out of here? I think he's the one who should be taking my psychiatric consults. The guy's a raving lunatic!"

"Nothing we can do. Orders from the Almighty, if you know what I mean. Hang in there. I'll check on you later."

The nurse finished her preparations on the IV and both she and Singh collected up their equipment and started to move for the door. Singh turned and came back to the side table where the tray rested and picked it up.

"You want this? Its pretty cold now." Potter waved him off. Singh was about to leave when he turned back to Potter, his face etched with concern. "Mike, what did you do to get these guys so worked up?"

"Dave, I wish I knew." Singh wavered for a second as if he were about to comment then thought against it. Shaking his head, confused, he turned and exited the room.

The remainder of the afternoon passed slowly. In a desperate effort to keep the blackness from taking over, Potter tried to direct his thoughts to things unrelated to the kids or Harry.

He thought about the woman with the perfume. He remembered her name — Linda Jarvis — and his feelings for her and felt lost and alone.

He tried to dredge up other memories when a familiar rubbery squeak at the door broke his flimsy concentration.

"Oh great. The Gestapo version of the Bobsey twins."

"Good afternoon," said Corporal Brown in a tone that could easily have been confused for cheery. Even Baker offered a brusque greeting.

"Look, before you start in with the truncheons, am I under arrest or what? If so, what's left of my memory tells me that you have to inform me what the charges are. I also remember something about getting to call a lawyer."

"You are not under arrest. You may call a lawyer. You must answer questions."

"I'll ask them too, if it doesn't result in my being put to the rack. How did that video end up being made? Does the Emergency Response Team make home movies of their operations?"

From the looks on their faces he knew he'd made a hit. "You knew they were going to be there! You've been following them."

"Not exactly," answered Brown. "That footage exists because the media was there. It was some sort of setup — anonymous tip, but there was no bank robber hiding in the restaurant. We basically stumbled on the kids. What we showed you was all over the evening news."

"If you weren't following them, then who were you following?"

"At the time, we weren't following anybody. But it's a small world. In fact, we've had you under surveillance for some time now."

"Why, for Christ's sake?"

Brown looked at him intently. "This is far bigger than you suspect. Maybe bigger than we suspect."

Baker suddenly lost patience. "We know it was Harry Warner who asked you to go up to Alert Bay."

"He didn't ask me, he just mentioned it and said I might be interested."

Baker sneered. "We know you had a very promising offer in Victoria, one that would've set you up very nicely. You turned it down. What's the name of Warner's friend, the old English doctor?"

The sudden question took him by surprise. It took several moments, but Potter finally remembered. "Doctor Elliott?"

Brown asked a few more questions about Elliott and other people on the island and he had the strong impression there was another issue that was looming in the background.

Suddenly Baker interrupted. "Did you find what you were looking for up there?"

"I don't know what you mean."

"You were looking for something. It was your real reason for going."

"I don't understand!"

"Cut the crap!" shouted Baker. "You had a hidden agenda because you aren't what you appear to be. Just like Harry Warner isn't what he appears to be."

Brown whispered something to Baker and continued. "We did a background check on you. There's a period in your life of about three months that can't be accounted for. Where were you?"

"It's my life, my business," said Potter.

Baker's face was getting red. Bad cop. "Sure it's your life. I guess it's also your business to make more kiddy friends than adult ones at Alert Bay. You some sort of pedophile?"

Again Brown spoke, this time urgently. Good cop. "Michael, those five kids have families and everyone up there is very worried. We have to find them before it's too late. Only you can tell us why they might have disappeared or what Harry Warner might have had to do with it."

Despite all his efforts, Potter felt his face getting red, and the start of the tears that come so easily to the sick and mentally confused.

Corporal Brown leaned forward sympathetically. Good cop. "I know this isn't easy for you. Here you are, your body and your memory shot to pieces, and you're being picked on. But believe me we have to do this. We have so little time left . . ."

Baker thrust his face into Michael's. Bad cop. "Blubber all you want, but I want you to understand what's at stake here. It's bigger than you, bigger than me. I've been after someone almost my whole career. He's smart and he has powerful friends and he's on some sort of mission and I need to know what that mission is. I think it involves those kids."

Potter tried to pull himself together but Baker was on him again. "You know anything about Siberian shamanism?"

The sick man felt a sudden jolt of psychic dislocation, as if he were hallucinating. "What?"

"You always wear one shoe when you jog?"

The sense of being on a demented inquisitorial rollercoaster intensified. "What?"

Brown leaned forward. "The kids fled the restaurant about two hours after you were shot. When you were found you were wearing basic jogging gear. The only thing out of the ordinary was that one of your runners was missing and couldn't be found."

"Why shoot somebody and take a shoe?" demanded Baker. "Sure, in hellholes like East Los Angeles they'll kill you for your Air Jordans but at least they have the brains to take both shoes."

Brown continued. "Unless there was something in that shoe. There was nothing else on you, no ID, nothing. Not even a key to a locker so you could change your clothes after showering. Seems pretty strange, doesn't it?"

Baker interrupted. "People do it all the time. Take the key and tie it to your shoe lace. Anybody know what was in that locker besides you?"

Potter shook his head. "I don't remember. Break into the locker for all I care, if you can find out which one it was. I wouldn't mind having my clothes. And I don't want to talk anymore."

Baker's face was again filled with rage. "I don't care what you want. We don't have a lot of time."

"Go away."

Baker reached for Potter as Corporal Brown tried to push him away and couldn't. "Nurse!"

Staff burst into the room and shoved Baker away. He moved away from the bed and headed to the corner by the window. There, he leaned against the wall and crossed his arms in anger. His face was livid.

Potter lay there and stared at the enraged cop. Only the fierce pumping of his heart told him that somehow, miraculously, he was still alive. He closed his eyes to fight off the pain that raged inside him as he fought for breath.

David Singh pushed through the crowd at the door and rushed to the bedside. As he prepared a syringe and swabbed at Potter's arm with alcohol, he turned to Brown and Baker. "Out. And as this man's physician, I insist you never come back."

When he came to again, it was just in time to see a uniformed guard place a supper tray on the table. Before Potter could form a sentence the man turned and walked silently out of the room. The odors coming from the food tray made him feel sick and he called for it to be taken away.

Maureen came in later in the evening to do a quick check, dangling her car keys. She looked exhausted from her twelve hour day but still managed a warm smile.

Potter noticed the keys. "Ready to go home?"

"Yes. The only thing I like about leaving at night is that I get to drive home in my new Accord. It's a good thing I'm in the lot right down the street. I don't think I could walk any further than that."

Despite this they talked for over an hour. It was not until she reached across to check a drain tube from his lung did he notice her watch and the time, nearly an hour and a half past the time she should have left.

"I thought you weren't working overtime tonight, Mo."

"Being with you doesn't qualify as overtime. You looked like you could do with some company. Especially since they treat you like you're practically in jail."

Potter swallowed a sudden lump in his throat. "That's a very nice thing to say. And, of course, I'm totally at a loss for a charming comeback."

"That's okay. I can wait."

Gently, he said, "Go home and get some rest. Doctor's orders."

"I'll stay. After what they put you through today, it's the least I can do."

"I'll be fine."

She rose from her chair, squeezed his good hand and walked through the door. She had gone before he realized how much he wanted her to stay, and how much she had wanted to stay.

He was soon asleep.

TWENTY SIX

Potter was awake before first light. He hadn't slept at all well as a flood of memories, thoughts and half dreams poured out. As a means to escape the mental torment he spent the time doing sit ups and knee bends which took him to the edge of the bed. There was no question he felt stronger.

Later he received a visitor — the silent RCMP officer who brought him his breakfast.

And a bag containing his belongings, retrieved from the gym locker.

The lack of visits by regular hospital personnel was beginning to get him down so he was pleased to see Dave Singh and the nurse from the previous evening, although he missed Maureen.

They had just turned to leave the room when Potter called out, "Hey, where's Maureen today? I missed her this morning."

"Haven't seen her today," Singh called over his shoulder. "I can never figure out their schedules anyway."

Bored out of his skull, Potter turned on the TV. Sometime during the late afternoon sleep overtook him, a combination of bad entertainment and fatigue from the morning's unaccustomed exercise. His last conscious thoughts before dozing off were of standing with the children on a windy bluff, viewing first a black submarine and then streams of army vehicles moving past.

Supper came and for the first time he was really hungry. Half an hour later, the empty plates were still cluttering the side tray when a familiar and welcome face peeked around the corner.

"Mo!"

"Hungry boy, I see."

"I'm not sure if I should admit this, but I did miss your particular kind of care and attention."

"I'm on nights for the next forty-eight hours." She frowned. "Speaking of care and attention, you haven't had any more loving ministrations from Tweedledum and Tweedledumber, have you?"

"No. But they followed my suggestion about breaking into the locker, and even had the decency to send my clothes over. Can you give the bag to me? I haven't even looked at it."

Sorting through the contents it suddenly all came back to him. His clothes were all there, so at least he had something to wear when he left the hospital. He frowned. Something was missing.

It hit him like a punch in the face. "Oh no!"

"Michael! What is it?"

"A book. My journal. It contains everything I knew about the kids, the experiments, everything. Six months of evidence and observations, all the people I met. No wonder my shoe was missing!"

"It's important?"

"Very."

As they looked at each other, Potter said, "You know, I'm feeling much stronger. It'd be awfully nice to take a piss on my own."

Maureen smiled. "Well, you have to do it sooner or later. Here, I'll help."

For the first time in over a week, his feet touched the floor. It was a thrill beyond belief. Then came his first steps and while they were less than athletic, they got him where he needed to go. Once she had him back to his bed, she left to attend to her other patients.

That night the dreams came again and one led into another.

White clouds slipped past, obliterated by powerful wings.
Fly closer.

Objects came into clear view by simply looking at them and concentrating. Nothing escaped those eyes. Just the thought of power made muscles quiver.

Gliding down further through the clouds, craggy, tree covered mountains came into view and nestled among them, a glistening, silver blue lake. Swooping down further to land at the lake's edge, stately wings flap over the satin calm water, forming wavelets.

The reflection in the gently undulating water was of fine, ebony colored plumage, a chest proudly puffed and that regal scarlet-purple mantle. As the water calmed, the full magnificence of the reflected form came into view, easily multiplying the pleasure of self admiration.

The image the reflection provided was so magnificent it deserved a mighty cry for all the world to hear. "I am Raven, master."

Many minutes passed spent waiting for subjects to respond to the cry but none came. Then in anger, "Raven, mighty one, push yourself off the ground, into the afternoon sky. Go and find subjects to scold for not bidding this mighty call."

Suddenly the land below was no longer familiar. Gone were the trees and the mountains. Now there were groupings of gray and brown beads had been sewn onto a magnificent woven blanket and then joined by threads of black yarn.

Descending farther, the beads transformed into mighty nests and the threads into trails. The nests were bigger than anything imagined, housing more humans than could be possible.

Swooping further down, one of the nests, pure white and surrounded by green grass and trees, came into view. "Surely, it must be the lodge of some very powerful chief. Nearby is a tall totem that guards it."

In front of the great lodge and all over the wide trails were humans, more than it was possible to count. They stood and waited for someone, or something. Faces looked up. They were afraid.

"Yes, you should fear me! See my power.

"What is this?" The piercing eyes saw a physique, once covered in fabulous feathers and that red mantle, turned to lifeless, dull metal. Above, huge, dark shadows revolved. Gone were the familiar, graceful sweeping wings.

The shadows above became awkward, moving in sickening patterns. Below, the green grass and the beautiful white nest lurched violently.

Somehow, strangely, the view of the dream changes as if time had moved backwards. On either side of the street, crowds cheered.

The crowd's full attention was directed to a slow moving, black procession, like a funeral, a procession of hearses. The cars slowed, then stopped. From out of the third car, a stocky, bare headed man emerged. He mounted the curb. His exit was followed immediately by four men who rushed to surround him, before the crush of the crowd could engulf him.

He waved enthusiastically, moving out to the edge of his protective circle, shaking the hands of any bystander that could get near him. Loud, enthusiastic cheers rang out from the crowd for this special man, this man with the distinctive purple-red blotch burnt onto his lower jaw, stretching down his neck, past his collar.

Rumbling and throbbing, a shimmering wedged shape emerged out of the brilliant afternoon sun. Few eyes in the crowd saw the object, intent on the procession.

It was a helicopter. It thundered nearer and began a long, graceful, gliding downwards swoop. Suddenly, a violent shudder disturbed the smooth descent. The nose pitched skyward and the tail came around with a sickening wrenching motion. The machine continued to pivot wildly, then flipped in the opposite direction, toward the green expanse of a park. The big machine's engines uttered an eerie, strangled, wobbling howl.

One by one faces in the crowd turned skyward, toward the machine's awful gyrations. Screams rang out. Within seconds, panic spread.

The machine screamed as it dropped and tumbled.

One last valiant effort by the doomed pilot brought the craft onto level keel, only to have the flying green demon flip sideways once more, and its whirling blades slice menacingly toward the grass . . .

Michael Potter awoke with a start, soaked with sweat, his mind as dark as the raven dream that had filled it.

Never before had he dreamed like that. His head and heart pounded. It was so vivid, so real.

He thought of his other dreams, of black submarines and troops. He'd never dreamed like that before either.

Suddenly he realized. They weren't his dreams. He was a conduit, a mirror, a TV that could once receive only static, but now somehow could receive vivid bursts of transmission from a source sufficiently powerful.

He thought back to the TV images he'd seen, of the submarine and the sailors on deck. He saw fierce warriors standing in a dugout canoe, then green clad soldiers and a seemingly endless stream of trucks.

Suddenly, the seemingly unrelated events of the past few days, the submarine, Fort Lewis, the dreams, all merged together.

It was them. They've been at each incident, perhaps even caused them, he thought. His five young friends were the Patriots of the Raven, they had to be. But where did Harry Warner fit in?

He frowned. The white nest in the dream of the raven had looked as if he should know it. Think in terms of allegory, he thought. The first half of this dream is some sort of fable, before it turns into a nightmare of thundering modern machines. What powerful creature lives in a white nest?

The fog around his brain thickened then ebbed — and there it was. The answer.

He realized he had to get out.

And find the children before it was too late.

****

At 5:30 a.m. the hospital corridor outside Potter's room was quiet. The night officer shuffled in his chair, long tired of the paperback he was reading.

The silence was interrupted by the faint sounds of a shower, coming from Potter's room. The guard listened and shrugged. So he was finally up and around. Maureen Clancy had told him as much. He settled back in his chair.

There was a shrill scream from the room. In an instant he was at the door and inside. The room was dark and only a slit of light from under the bathroom door showed him the way. He lunged inside as a cloud of hot steam billowed out.

The interior of the small bathroom was engulfed in swirling mist. He moved rapidly over to the curtain and ripped it back. He could just make out a slumped form in the corner of the shower. Reaching in, he desperately tried to turn off the boiling water to save Potter from further burns.

He saw the body slowly move, extending over the floor with the relaxation of death.

Too late, he realized the victim was two drenched pillows hinged with a hanger and disguised by a pale blanket.

He spun around and sprang for the door, just as it clicked shut in front of him. He wrenched at the handle but it was wedged shut from the outside.

****

The night security team was assembled soon after the alarm was sounded. Reinforcements from the university RCMP detachment answered the radio call to block all exits.

Within five minutes there was a tight cordon around the whole building. A check of the prisoner's room showed his clothing and other possessions to be missing.

All pedestrian traffic in and out of the hospital was restricted to the front entrance along side the Emergency Ward. Each staff member leaving the facility, male or female, was questioned thoroughly.

It did no good. Michael Potter was gone.

At 8:00 a.m. a petite redhead stood on the curb, taking a breath of outside morning air before crossing the lane to the parking complex. Having already cleared the single check point as she exited the building, she now passed an RCMP officer guarding the entrance to the multi-level parking structure. He checked her ID and then opened the door for her. Inside, she headed to her Honda.

As she opened the car door a man in the back seat lifted his head.

She stared momentarily, then looked around. Seeing no one, she got in.

"You've got half the damn RCMP looking for you."

"Don't care. It's not like I'm a criminal. I don't know what's going on and I have to find out. Mo, I need help."

"Oh mother of Mary. What the hell am I doing? Damn you Michael! Just stay down." She turned the ignition and drove from the parking lot onto the street.

TWENTY SEVEN

"He what?" shouted Bob Corbett. Behind his desk at CIA headquarters in Langley, Virginia, the boyish, six foot tall agent looked like he was about to burst out of his immaculate charcoal gray suit, and his eyes blazed behind Italian wire rim glasses.

"You told me his memory was so bad he was practically a zombie and that he couldn't even get out of bed to go to the can by himself. And he *escaped?*"

"Early this morning. Fooled one of the guards by luring him into the bathroom, then slipped out and jammed the door behind him. Pretty clever, actually. I suspected all along there was more to this guy than met the eye."

Corbett looked like he wanted to reach into the telephone line and drag Staff Sergeant Douglas Baker through the receiver and strangle him. He had put his ass on the line with his boss to let the Canadians handle this thing, and now they'd blown it. Already he sensed some large boots headed for his posterior.

"So why didn't you guard him better? Jesus Christ, Baker! He was practically dead from a gunshot wound. The only person easier to guard would've been a corpse."

"Trust me, Bob, things are under control."

"Under control? First Reggie disappears and now this. At least Reggie was a pro. I doubt if you guys are in control of your goddamn bladders."

There was an ominous silence at the other end of the line.

Instantly Corbett regretted what he'd said. He and the big Mountie went back a number of years, to when the Canadians first shared with the CIA their find of the Soviet mole named Reggie. As a rookie agent, Corbett had been assigned to work with Baker. He had quickly learned that Baker was a superb operative and a fundamentally honest man in a very slippery profession. Even after Baker's unit had been disbanded they had kept in touch over the Reggie case, because the big Canadian knew the wily mole's psychology inside out. Corbett knew Baker was obsessed with capturing Reggie before he had to retire, and was getting sensitive about his age.

"I didn't mean that and you know it."

"Ya, right Bobby boy. I'll call you back later when I know more details. He can't get far in his condition. And watch your mouth, young pup, or I'll have to come down there and teach you some manners." The line went dead.

Bob Corbett looked at the phone. There was something wrong about the whole thing. It occurred to him that ordinarily Baker would have been furious at the loss of Michael Potter, and wouldn't just have threatened to teach him some manners, but caught the next plane to Langley to do it in person.

Douglas Baker was holding something back.

Corbett replaced the receiver. Deep in thought, he rose from his desk and wandered to the window to gaze at the Virginia forest.

Maybe I'm too young for this game of cross and double-cross, he thought. Damn it, Baker, what are you up to?

TWENTY EIGHT

The novelty of power was starting to feel as stale as the hot-dog buns sold by the city's street vendors.

The late afternoon heat was oppressive, so when Harry Warner said he had to meet an old medical crony, Belly, Beebo, Dickie, Brenda and Princess were delighted to be rid of the old man's now oppressive presence and opted for a bit of freedom.

Harry left them at the Smithsonian Institute, with instructions to find their way back to the hotel. He had developed an obsession with taking them to museums and art galleries, bringing them back late to their hotel and then saying they needed their rest and couldn't watch television. As soon as he left, they agreed to make a beeline back to their rooms at the Capital Hilton. The thought of air conditioned rooms and endless television without supervision was infinitely more attractive than three hours in a museum.

They arrived back at the hotel just after 3:30 p.m. and all but Beebo charged up to the rooms. He said he wanted to look around the lobby for a while, and the others all understood. Beebo's debilitating dreams had returned with vengeance. While the others glowed in the praise and gifts Harry showered on them, Beebo slipped back into his quiet ways, preoccupied with the strange twists his new dreams were taking.

The boy lingered in the opulence of the hotel's lobby. He had never seen anything like it. The light green carpets were luxurious and the rich rosewood wall paneling and thick, ornate columns all whispered quietly of money and class. While none of the splendor he saw around him held any particular fascination, he did wonder about people who lived like this all the time. And like his friends, he'd spent considerable time thinking about their dramatic change of fortune over the past week, from stealing a car and staying in places like the Motel 6, to traveling in private jets and staying at the Hilton.

At first they had wondered where Harry was getting the money from, but his explanations were so convincing that they quickly accepted whatever came their way. It was as if the more jobs they completed, the more Harry wanted to reward them. For five poor Indian kids from Alert Bay, that was just fine with them.

Beebo bought a Wrestlemania magazine and went upstairs. The others were watching TV in one of the other rooms and he turned on the set in another room just in time to catch the news.

The nation continues to be terrorized by the mysterious group known as the Patriots of the Raven. Just an hour ago, they claimed responsibility for kidnapping Blake Roberts, the senior Republican senator from Utah. In a call to the media, the terrorists claimed the abduction was a protest against treatment of Indians on Utah reservations and the presence of military bases and nuclear dumps on sacred ground. Eyewitnesses report the senator was snatched from his limousine by a group of heavily armed men dressed in black robes. And, for the first time, someone was injured by the Patriots. In the resulting gun battle, Secret Service agent Thomas Reardon was severely wounded and remains in critical condition at Walter Reid Army Hospital. The fate of the senator is unknown and no ransom demands have yet been made. As in the six other incidents, from Washington, LA and now right here in the Capitol involving this terrorist organization, they suggest that such actions will continue until Native land claims throughout North America are addressed. The nation is in an uproar over the inability of security services to find and punish the culprits. In a statement to the media, President Clinton expressed outrage at . . .

Beebo watched in stunned disbelief. He called the others into the room so they could watch the synopsis at the end of the newscast.

"We didn't kidnap nobody," protested Dickie. "What the hell is this?"

"We've only done a couple of things," said Brenda. "The submarine, Fort Lewis and that research place outside of Los Angeles. What do they mean, seven?"

When Harry Warner entered the room an hour and a half later he was met with hostile stares.

"Seen the news lately, doc?" asked Belly. "Seems there's two sets of Patriots ... and one of them likes to kidnap senators and shoot people."

Warner looked both apologetic and wily as he spread his hands. "The whole affair was unfortunate."

"Unfortunate?" stormed Dickie. "A guy gets shot and nearly dies and it's unfortunate?"

"We didn't do it," said Brenda, "but now everyone thinks we did. Who did the others?"

Princess's voice chimed in. "You lied to us. We trusted you. I want to go home." She started to sob.

"Now try to calm down, all of you calm down," said Harry soothingly. "It's all part of the plan."

"No it ain't," said Belly, his voice shaking with rage. "We make the plans, we do the deed. All you do is handle the media stuff."

The old man waited before answering, looking slowly at each of them in turn. "I admit I've made a grave error in not mentioning the changes to you. But you must understand that there was so little time, and so much at stake."

"Why don't you tell us about it then," said Beebo through clenched teeth.

"Look, the work we came here to do is so very important I just couldn't let anything go wrong. I believed you had to make a much stronger statement than originally planned. People might care about machines and military facilities, but not as much as they care about other people. It was important to emphasize that you can strike anywhere, at anytime."

He turned and paced the room. "But I didn't want to run the risk of endangering you. That would ruin everything. So I was forced to utilize the services of others. Unfortunately, what you can do mentally they can only do physically, which means there's the risk of people being hurt. It's a terrible tragedy, and I assure you I feel it even more strongly than you do. But it has set the scene for the next job, and because some of the other incidents mentioned in the newspaper happened at the same time as the three you did, it makes it look as if the Patriots can strike in two places at once."

With the slowly growing wisdom of adolescence, Belly and Brenda had been increasingly unwilling to take Warner's explanations and advice at face value. Now, faced with undeniable evidence of duplicity, they got straight to the point.

"How come you know so much about us. And tell us again why you want to help us," asked Brenda.

"And," added Belly, "why didn't you mention this kind of thing to us in the first place?"

"What I told you was and is absolutely true," protested Warner, taken aback by this sudden unchildlike interrogation. "The western world of industrial capitalism is hopelessly corrupt and must be destroyed, along with its lethal machines. I've worked my whole life to help bring it down but could never find the proper tool."

He spread his hands beseechingly. "One that wouldn't hurt

others. Not like the nuclear bombs and biochemical weapons in the arsenals of the West. You five are the answer to my prayers."

He walked to the window. "For many years now I've been searching for people with powers such as yours. Others have been searching too. All over the world."

He turned to gaze at them with an intensity they found frightening. "The first evidence came from the aboriginal populations of Siberia, the homeland of your ancestors, who migrated across the Bering Strait many thousands of years ago. Evidence of strange neural activity in the brain, accompanied by dreams, nightmares, even seizures. And always in those who had traditionally served their people as shamans, magic men with strange powers. And strange appearance."

He could tell from their expressions that the five children were enraptured by this tale. Suddenly relaxing, he threw his lanky frame on the sofa. "My wife Alice became convinced that such powers were hereditary, that they would be carried down through the generations. That they would have found their way to North America with the first emigrants from Siberia. Which, incidentally, is not a particularly pleasant place in which to do research."

Warner made a temple of his fingers. "I emigrated to Canada myself, shortly after the Second World War, after I graduated from Cambridge. Alice was convinced the answer might lie in West coast Native history, so I concentrated my efforts in that area. I studied people up and down the West coast and finally found you. Or should I say, before I found you I found someone like you?"

The five children were staring at him with wide eyes and he continued confidently, his rich English baritone like that of a Shakespearean actor reciting one of the more famous soliloquies.

"It was not until just over a year ago that I found what I was seeking. I was called into the hospital to observe a young man. He'd been severely injured in a bar room beating and subsequent car accident. I had told the hospital staff that I was doing research on aboriginal shamanism and to call me at any time if anything unusual seemed to be happening."

He gazed at them deliberately, his eyes sweeping over every intent countenance. "Especially if the Native person involved had unusual colouring, such as blue eyes and bronze hair."

Four children turned to look at Beebo, who never took his eyes off of Warner.

"Unfortunately, the young man died that very evening. But when he did, the strangest thing happened. I actually saw his soul, his spirit, leave his body, like bronze smoke that spiraled in the air, and as he turned . . ."

"He wore a fabulous cape and hat made of cedar," whispered Brenda. Her face was pasty and drawn. The others looked at her compassionately, knowing each of them could have finished Warner's sentence as well.

"And I knew, as the result of a life long search, that *we* were destined to meet some day."

There was a great silence. Harry Warner shrugged. "As for the rest of it, where you as individuals are concerned, I've already explained. Michael told me about your powers. Again, it was I who suggested he go to Alert Bay in the first place. I knew it would be dangerous if I went myself, because the enemies who are after you have been after me too, for a long time, and they might begin to suspect. I also knew that if there were seers and visionaries such as you in the community, he was smart enough to recognize you."

"So he was cheating us all along?" said Brenda.

"In a good cause," said Harry Warner. "My cause. Our cause. The cause we are fighting now. But he betrayed me as he betrayed you. I thought he was willing to fight the good fight, on the side of light. But instead he wanted money. And other things. He is working for the forces of evil. You remember what happened at the restaurant. Michael Potter's betrayal."

The children were silent.

"Now, the question of why I suggested all of this to you in the first place. As I said at the time, various organizations are after you and it is impossible for you to go home. But as the Patriots of the Raven, there is one final act that you must perform. It will make history. You will have accomplished the biggest possible service for your people, And the rest of the world. After that, you will be able to go home safely, because no one will dare go against you, ever again."

"What is it?" asked Belly.

"I can't tell you at the moment. But it will be soon. You must continue to trust me. And haven't I treated you well, and protected you? Without my help, you might very well be dead."

Despite their growing mistrust, it was impossible for them to counter this compelling stream of information. And they were intrigued at the thought of others like themselves, in far-off lands.

Each wrapped in their own thoughts, they did not resist as Warner shooed them off to bed.

TWENTY NINE

Michael Potter awoke with a start, to see white fabric in front of his eyes. For a moment he thought he was still in the hospital, his bandaged arm in front of his face. Then he realized it was a flight attendant placing stiff, white linen napkins on the tray in front of him.

He turned his head to relieve the kink in his neck, only to have the whole right side of his back convulse in pain. He moaned involuntarily. Four passengers looked at him, alarmed by both the noise and his pallid, sweaty, and thoroughly beat up appearance.

Potter was beyond embarrassment. He continued to straighten himself, attempting to get control of the pain. Twisting his head in the other direction he saw a female form curled there, a mass of red hair cascading over her face and shoulders, fast asleep.

Maureen Clancy.

He twisted his head slowly from side to side as it all came back to him. She had taken him to her apartment and sneaked him in so other tenants didn't see. He'd explained how he had taken the fire exit out of the hospital and walked to the parking lot — hers had been the only new Honda Accord there. She tended to his wounds and put him to bed in the spare room. Then she went out and bought him some personal effects, including new clothes at Eaton's, the shirts one size larger than the ones he usually wore to hide the thick bandages. At 3:30 p.m. she prepared a meal and woke him when it was ready. She changed his dressings again and they ate and he painfully did some stretching exercises. She had tried to convince him to go to another hospital but he was adamant that he would not and insisted he had to go to Seattle.

To avoid suspicion, Maureen had gone back to the hospital to complete her last graveyard shift before taking several days off. In her absence Potter worked out a plan to get out of Vancouver and puzzled over the dream he had had. He knew Baker and the others would be looking for him and he had to find the Patriots of the Raven. And they had last been reported in the Seattle area.

When Maureen Clancy returned home, he told her of his plan. It took a lot of persuading, but she finally relented. She agreed to drive him across the border to Seattle so he could make a passportless entry into the United States.

They left the next morning and made it safely across the border to Seattle. Maureen rented a room at the downtown Mayflower Park hotel and Potter had slept, exhausted from his exertions. That evening, he had turned on the television to see if there were any further reports on the Patriots of the Raven and discovered they were in Washington, DC, where they had kidnapped a senator. Potter's puzzlement over the media's description of armed men in black robes made him more determined than ever to find the kids. He had asked Maureen to call United Airlines and book him a ticket from Seattle to Washington using her own credit card. Not until she was off the phone did she tell him that she had booked two first class tickets — the only seats available at such short notice — because she was coming with him. Over his protests, she informed him that he was not fit to travel by himself.

After finally realizing that she was right, and grateful for the offer of assistance, Michael Potter had called the one person in Washington who he knew could help him find the five children.

The flight had left the terminal at Sea-Tac airport at 7:30 a.m. And now, several hours later, Potter was frowning sightlessly at the gourmet meal of filet mignon on his tray, trying yet again to figure out what the children were up to and how Harry Warner fit into the picture. He was also fretting over how it was possible for him to somehow intercept the kids' dreams.

From the time back in the hospital when he first started to gain control over the blackness, a number of the dreams Beebo had described to him over the months in Alert Bay started to come back. The problem was that they were filled with symbolism he couldn't understand. Not for the first time he wished he had taken a couple of courses on Indian mythology at university.

He started when Maureen touched his arm and pointed at the tiny TV screen. A news program was starting and there might be something on the children or the Patriots of the Raven. Potter put on his earphones and adjusted the volume.

There was nothing new. The first major story concerned the President's cancellation of a planned meeting in London with the British Prime Minister as a result of his concern over the Patriots' terrorist attacks. The second was about preparations in the nation's capital for the long-awaited first visit to the US of the new president of the Russian Federation, a tough former military man named Feodor Vasikov. Potter watched until the end of the newscast, took off his headphones and dozed.

They landed at Washington's National Airport at 6:25 that evening. The night air was humid and stifling and it took all of Potter's energy to put one foot in front of the other. It was only with Maureen's help that he was able to trudge down the jet-way into the dull, flat decor of the old section of the terminal. For some unaccountable reason he felt a sense of doom, as if death was thundering toward him like an express train.

Outside on the concourse Maureen stopped at a store next to a bank of telephones. "I have to pick up some personal things I forgot when we left in such a hurry. Wait for me outside — the night air will do you good."

Potter leaned against a light standard near the curb and looked at the ranks of taxis and passengers with their luggage and trolleys. He always thought of Washington as an exciting place because this was Patti Donovan's territory. It had been his third year at medical school and he'd still had wild oats to sow. And for three glorious months he had sown them with Patti. It had been those three months that Staff Sergeant Douglas Baker has referred to as missing, and Potter still thought of them as something very special and very private. She was the most exciting woman he'd ever met, and now he was about to get dangerously close to his hot old flame.

His eyes searched the crowds and then suddenly he saw her. She walked with grace and elegance and just a hint of a swagger. Although she was ten years his senior, her hair was still genuine chestnut brown and her eyes were still gray and she was still as beautiful as ever.

"Hi, sailor. New in town?" she smiled as she approached. The smile vanished as she got closer and by the time she was standing in front of him it had been replaced by a look of concern. "Mikey, you look like shit. What on earth happened?"

"I got into an argument with a bullet."

Before he could explain, Patti's eyes were suddenly watchful as her gaze slid sideways and Michael realized Maureen Clancy was standing next to him. The women looked at each other like two female leopards about to battle over a kill.

Hastily Potter said, "Patti Donovan, Maureen Clancy. Maureen's the reason I'm alive and free. And Maureen, Patti is the unofficial queen of Washington."

The two women shook hands in a manner that was anything like amiable when Patti said, "Mike has a weakness for Irish women, don't you darlin'? He likes his blood hot."

She turned to Potter. "I'd better bring the car before you fall over." As she strode athletically away Maureen folded her arms across her chest. "I didn't realize the Donovan we were going to meet was a woman. Care to tell me about her?"

"Sure. I first met her at an art show when I was in my third year of medical school. She came through Vancouver because she was running away from her guy at the time. Fellow nicknamed Big Frank, a wise guy type from Washington who was tied up pretty heavy in some shady night club deals, gambling, that sort of thing. She couldn't decide if she wanted to save his sorry ass or hang him out to dry. So she skipped town as he went to trial."

"And?" added Maureen, enjoying his discomfort.

"And we fell for each other instantly. Hell, she was the gorgeous, exotic older woman, led a wild life. It was a thrill. She stayed around for a couple of months. Then Big Frank was sentenced to prison and begged her to come back and look after his business, so she went home."

"There has to be more than that."

"Well, she knew I had my third year practicum coming up and that was why I couldn't go back to Washington with her for the summer. That was when I discovered how well connected she is. Somehow she got me a prestige posting at Bethesda, papers, assessments and a profile from some chief resident. She even got me free airline tickets. So, that's how I spent my summer. Enough said?"

"No," said Maureen. "You didn't keep in touch afterwards?"

Potter shrugged. "You know how it is. I was determined to finish med school and I could only do that in Vancouver. She and Frank had kissed and made up, even though he was in jail for a while. I was on the wards twenty hours a day and we were a continent apart. All I know is that it's great to see her again."

"I'm pleased that you're pleased. But why contact her concerning a crisis like this?"

"As I just explained, she's incredibly well connected. She's got friends in high places because her father used to be head of US Air Force Intelligence and she went to Vassar. And she's got friends in low places thanks to Big Frank."

He nodded at the rapidly approaching BMW convertible. "If there's anything or anyone to be found in Washington DC, Patti Donovan is the person who can."

The silver 325 purred up to the curb and they got in. Patti screamed away onto the street and they spent the next ten minutes on a seemingly aimless, high speed dash up and down small streets and alleys.

"What are you doing?" shouted Potter.

Patti Donovan tossed him a reckless smile. "You spend a lot of time with a guy like Big Frank, you learn to take precautions. To stay on my tail you'd have to be bolted to my bumper."

Finally she pulled up beside Samantha's, a bar and restaurant near the corner of 18th and 'L.'

"You remember this place don't you, darlin'? Name's changed but it's still the safest and most discreet hotel in town. The only people who find it are the ones who already know about it." Looking in the direction of her outstretched hand he saw the small red awning and the even smaller neon sign above it discreetly announcing the Anthony House Hotel. Patti was out of the car and heading towards the door.

Maureen followed and Potter gasped involuntarily as he heaved his still aching body out of the car. At the hotel's dark, rich reception desk Patti smiled at a squat, hairless night clerk the shape of a fire hydrant. "Hey Charlie. You got that room for me?"

"Of course. But I was expecting one person. The room has a king size bed."

Patti looked sardonically at a suddenly uncomfortable Maureen Clancy. Potter cleared his throat. "You read this situation right, Charlie," she said. "They're a couple, and yet they're not. Got anything else? Two beds, north side, seventh or eighth floor?"

"Nothing at the moment." Charlie gazed at her warily as she leaned forward, looked him right in the eye and whispered, "Really?"

The fire hydrant twitched in what might have been a shrug. "Then again, I heard a rumor that the Swedish diplomat in 808 killed himself, oh, five, six seconds ago. I'm sure we could arrange to move his body to another room without too much trouble."

Patti flashed a dazzling smile. "Thanks. I take it he's out?"

Charlie handed her the key. "I'll send someone up right away to move his stuff to another room."

"Give the stiff a bottle of champagne, with my compliments, to soothe any ruffled feelings. Put it on my tab."

She turned and gestured for them to follow her down a richly paneled hallway with tapestries and discreetly expensive antique furniture. The carpet was Persian and looked expensive enough to have belonged to a Shah. As they approached the single elevator an enormous white man in a tent-like dark suit sidled up and whispered in her ear. He had over-dyed, close cropped blond hair and looked like a retired linebacker who could still run through a brick wall if he took a mind to.

"Thanks, Thunder Thighs. I can't believe we haven't found them already." Patti was frowning. The big man nodded and with one massive, gold bedecked hand waved a small 'it's nothing' gesture. He looked at Michael and Maureen as unemotionally as if they were bugs and he was the exterminator.

As they rode up the elevator, Potter said, "Thunder Thighs?"

"All tough guys have a nickname. If you don't have a nickname, you're not a tough guy. Al Capone was Scarface, Salvatore Accardo was Big Tuna, Franco Spinati is Big Frank. Etcetera."

On the eighth floor they followed her along a tastefully decorated corridor covered in plush carpeting. A hotel staff member was just leaving with the Swedish diplomat's belongings. The interior of the room was ivory and gray with the occasional hint of burgundy details. Potter remembered how the hotel was the best kept secret in Washington. It was designed to be discreet and, thanks to Big Frank, had seen more than its share of big time card games and beautiful women you vaguely remembered from third rate movies entertaining men you vaguely remembered from the cover of *Time*. It was also designed to be safe and escapable, if necessary. He smiled as he remembered the maze of passages and interconnecting tunnels in the basement.

"Enjoy the peace and quiet. If you need anything to eat, there's a fully stocked kitchen right around here." She walked across the room and pressed a spot on the wall next to the first bed. With a soft hiss the wall folded back to display a bright, shiny kitchen.

"If you need anything else, call the desk and ask. Don't answer the door unless they say something with my name in it."

She turned and faced Maureen Clancy, hands on her slim hips. "Have you had sex with him?"

Maureen flushed. "No."

"Your loss. Sex with Mike will blow your head off. But I'll be very unhappy if I sense any hanky-panky going on. I'm territorial. And whatever is on my territory is mine. Got it?"

Clancy was speechless. Patti pointed at Potter. "Get some rest. But I still need more information on these kids than you gave me over the phone. A picture would be nice."

Reaching behind him with his good hand, he swung the day pack off his back. He pulled out a wad of papers and retrieved a couple of colour photos. He handed Patti one of the five young figures, all dressed in rain gear. "This is the only one I have and it's not that good." Attempting to put the other one away, she was too quick for him, plucking it from his fingers.

"And who is this dark beauty?"

"A nurse on the island. Linda Jarvis."

"I see," said Patti coolly. "Even for a doctor, you seem to have something of a nurse fetish. Is it those cute little caps or the rustlely polyester uniforms?"

She turned on her heel and sauntered out.

Avoiding Maureen's icy gaze, Potter said, "I think first thing in the morning we should ask Patti to get you a ticket back home."

Clancy snorted. "Forget it! With her around, you need protection more than ever."

THIRTY

The bedside phone chirped insistently. Potter fumbled for it and finally placed the receiver against his ear. "Yes?"

"Mike, we got trouble."

"Patti?"

"Get dressed now and be out of your room in two minutes. Smilin' Irish eyes too. The whole building is surrounded by guys who look like Efrem Zimbalist Jr. Move!"

"Mo, wake up!" called Potter.

A mass of red hair swirled under the pillow.

"Maureen, get up! Someone's found us!"

She threw off the covers and sat up. "Who?"

"Don't know. Let's get out of here." He reached for his clothes.

They darted around the room, gathering everything haphazardly. With a final hasty look around Potter threw open the door and headed down the hallway. At the end Patti beckoned impatiently.

"The stairs," she ordered. She opened the steel door and let them through. "Up. Faster!"

"One more to the roof. Get the lead out!"

They burst onto the roof, to find themselves under a protective canopy. Potter was gasping with the effort and fear also constricted his heart. Patti tugged at an aluminum extension ladder leaning against a concrete dividing wall forming a partition between the stairwell and the hotel's air conditioning unit.

"We have to cross over to the next building and then down to the underground parking lot on 19th Street," she explained. "We'll have to assume that these government types don't know about this old gambler's escape route."

Potter was doubled over, gasping, a thin sheen of sweat forming on his pale brow. Patti motioned to someone at the top of the ladder. As Thunder Thighs descended three rungs at a time, it shook under his weight like a tree in a storm. His enormous legs were obviously strong as well as big. He came to a jiggling halt as his huge body landed on the roof and there was a brief tremor.

"Time to do a little weight lifting," said Patti. "Thighs, if you don't mind."

Effortlessly the huge blond leaned down on Potter's good side and swept his shoulder under the uninjured arm, lifting the smaller man effortlessly into a fireman's carry. Paying no attention to Potter's protests, he stepped on to the first rung of the ladder and started up. At the top he stepped off and carried Potter across the twenty foot long crest to the wall of the adjoining building. The two women followed.

Thighs put Potter down, then with both hands pressed at the base of the aluminum window sill, felt for the hidden catches. He hooked his fingers and heaved upwards. The window popped open and in an instant Potter was stuffed through like a bag of laundry. Moments later they were all in the long hallway of an office complex, moving toward a bank of elevators.

When they were all inside an elevator, Patti reached into her bag and took out a key on a long dangling brass holder. She inserted the key into an aperture in the wall panel and gave it a quick turn. They began a rapid descent to the basement garage. "Big Frank always had a good grasp of logistics," she smiled.

Five minutes later, they were safely inside the smoked glass security of a slate gray Cadillac Seville. Thighs drove the big car cautiously out into an alley at the back of the building, left onto 19th and then a quick left onto 'L'.

They turned on to the street where the hotel was located. For a normally quiet side road, it was crammed with unmarked cars, official looking sedans parked every which way, and clean cut men and women looking up at Anthony House. The big limo slid silently past them.

Maureen sat in the back between Potter and Patti. She hadn't said a word since they left the roof. Now she turned to Patti. "What on earth was that?"

"Big Frank's version of Houdini. He had a thing about being trapped. When he went down, we arranged that I'd take care of business while he was in the Big House. That means using the perks of office." She swept her arm at the interior of the limousine.

Her reference to a Big House reminded Michael Potter of Alert Bay and why he'd come to Washington in the first place. He turned to look out the back window for any signs of being followed. "We can't concentrate on finding the kids and Warner when we're always on the run."

"I agree," said Patti. "Thighs, evasive maneuvers. Let's head for the next safe house."

They drove for a full hour, bobbing in and out of traffic. Thunder Thighs spoke constantly into a radio mouthpiece and it seemed apparent they had a friendly tail who was keeping an eye out.

Eventually Patti leaned forward and tapped on the divider window. Thighs lowered it and she talked to him in a low voice. Minutes later the limo swerved into a back ally and came to a stop alongside a roughly planked fence with two large, old fashioned garage doors cut into it. Thighs punched a button on a remote control and the doors swung back to reveal a darkened garage.

Once the car was parked they entered a brightly lit foyer, leading to a spacious and luxuriously appointed living room. Walking though the room to the front window, they could see that all the surrounding buildings on a quiet street were four story brownstones.

"You can rest here for a bit and get cleaned up. There are bathrooms on each floor. Thighs is going to buy you both some new clothes. And I'm going to try to find those kids. And figure out what the hell is going on."

The soaker tub that Potter filled with bubble bath and gingerly settled into was exactly what the doctor ordered. The water jets massaged the worst of his aches away.

He closed his eyes, counted to ten, and yanked off the dressing that should have been cleaned first thing that morning. He hissed with pain and his eyes teared, but when he looked it seemed to be mending well enough.

The soothing warmth of the tub helped clear his mind of the turmoil of the morning and the past few days. He had almost dozed off when there was a knock on the door. "Patti? Maureen?"

"No, sir," came a deep Southern drawl. "Miss Donovan asked me to bring your new clothes. May I come in?"

"Sure."

He was black, very slim and handsome, and beautifully dressed. As he crossed the room to the chair by the tub, his walk was as casually precise as a fashion model's. He placed a bundle of folded new clothes on the chair and as he did so his camel hair jacket opened to reveal a black shoulder holster and the squat menace of a gun butt.

The newcomer reached over and held out his hand. Taken aback, Potter reached for it without thinking and was surprised at the ease with which he was drawn out of the water. The black man handed Potter a thick, blue towel as he studied the wound. "Looks sore."

"It is."

"You'll have a scar. Too bad. Nice pecs."

Before Potter could respond to this odd remark the man was gone. He dressed clumsily, skirting the pain and had just put on a pair of obviously expensive summer weight beige linen slacks when the black man returned. Now he carried a new bundle of crepe bandages, cling gauze, swabs, antiseptic and sterile saline.

Potter was impressed with the supplies and was even more impressed when moments later, without a word being said, the man began expertly dressing the wound.

"I understand you are a physician, sir. How does this look?"

"A very nice job. Where'd you learn?"

"Rangers. Medic for five years. Finish dressing and we'll get you something to eat."

A few minutes later they were downstairs in the kitchen. Patti and Maureen were sitting at a counter, sipping coffee and eating freshly cut fruit and cheese. "Oh look," smiled Patti. "It's Paul Newman." She walked over and gave him a peck on the cheek. Michael sat down to eat.

"Thank you, Andrew," she said, turning to the black man. "Can you help Thighs out front?"

Andrew smiled and nodded before leaving the room.

"What, no nickname?" asked Potter, eating a croissant, a fig, a wedge of asiago and coffee all at the same time. "Dandy Andy would certainly fit. What's his story?"

"No nickname," said Patti. "Not a professional tough guy, although he is extremely efficient and can take care of himself. The army let him go because they found out he's gay."

The remark about his pecs suddenly made sense. "Gee, thanks for telling me before I was standing in front of the guy stark naked. Any news on the kids?"

"Nothing yet. I'm frankly surprised it's taking this long. And I'm still trying to figure out how they found us at Anthony House.

Thank God Charlie spotted them early when they were just starting to surround the place."

"Who?" asked Maureen.

"FBI, CIA, or any number of alphabet soup organizations you care to name. You can always spot them because they all look like they were produced using a cookie cutter and then dressed in suits from 1962."

There was a stunned silence. "But there's no reason on earth they'd be interested in me," protested Potter. "Even the RCMP in Vancouver couldn't charge me with anything. I haven't *done* anything."

"Maybe it's not you at all," mused Patti. "Maybe they figure you'll lead them to somebody else.

She turned to face Michael. "When you called me you didn't tell me much. I didn't ask because we're friends. I think you know more than you've told me. And it's time for me to hear it. I don't have a criminal record, I keep Big Frank's business nice and quiet, and the last thing on earth I need is to attract the attention of these guys."

"Okay." Potter turned to Maureen. "You know that journal I was looking for? Well, it had a lot of information about these kids. They have unusual abilities. Whoever shot me stole the journal from my locker and now they know almost as much about these kids as I do. Their aspirations, fears, personal psychology, weaknesses. And abilities."

"What sort of abilities would they have that could possibly interest the FBI and the CIA?" asked Patti.

"They have visions in which they can see the future. They can move objects at a distance, with their minds. Big objects. *Really* big. And they can attack people with their minds."

"Honestly, Michael," protested Maureen. "You've had a long time to think up a story and this is the best you can do?"

Patti Donovan's shapely eyebrows were reaching for the sky and her face was a mask of polite skepticism. *"The X-Files?* Is this an original episode written by Chris Carter?"

"I know it sounds ridiculous, but it's true. I've seen it." He struggled for a moment, wondering whether to tell all. He couldn't bear the slowly growing look of mistrust on his former lover's face and suddenly decided.

"You know those attacks on Fort Lewis, the near catastrophe with the Trident submarine, and all those others?"

"Yes."

"I think it was my kids. I think they are the Patriots of the Raven who have been terrorizing this country."

"Five little kids from the wilds of the west coast have the White House, the Pentagon and every intelligence officer in the country with their drawers in a knot? Oh, come on. That head injury has made you delusional."

"I'm not!" insisted Potter. "And they'd never do something like this on their own. I think unscrupulous forces have kidnapped them, and Dr. Harry Warner too, when he tried to help them after I disappeared. Whoever has my journal, if they are clever enough, could psychologically exploit these kids. I think they're being held prisoner."

Patti was frowning and started to pace. "If it's Fu Manchu or whoever is doing this, they must have a strategy, a plan. Some end result that all of this is supposed to accomplish. What could it be?"

"I don't know," said Potter helplessly. "All I know is that suddenly they're here in Washington. And I think the kids are broadcasting to me."

"The evening news, brought to you by the Patriots of the Raven?" sneered Maureen.

"Of course not. But I've been able somehow to share their visions, their dreams of the future. The problem is I'm not Indian or a scholar specializing in aboriginal myth. The visions are mysterious and I don't know what they mean."

At that moment Andrew entered the room and whispered in Patti's ear. Her face blanched. "What, again? That's impossible!"

Andrew made small apologetic gestures with his hands.

Now Patti's face was grim and her gray eyes suddenly glowed with the embers of anger. "Get everything together. We're out of here."

THIRTY ONE

Four hours after leaving the brownstone, another safe house and a dizzying five changes of vehicles, the final one a taxi, Potter finally recognized the Duke Ellington Bridge and the National Zoological Park in the northwest section of the city. When they entered Columbia Road he knew exactly where he was. Old and pleasant memories flooded in.

The taxi stopped on the quiet section of the street monopolized by restaurants in single and double story buildings. They got out and Patti attempted to pay the fifty buck fare, only to have the driver push the money away. "On the house. Maybe you'll do me a favour some day." Before she could protest he gunned the engine and had the vehicle back into the traffic.

They crossed Columbia Road and headed toward a three story brick building at the end of the block. It's sole decoration was a purple fabric awning that said *Perry's*. After passing through alcoves and narrow hallways they suddenly turned into a cavernous restaurant.

Most of the room's light came from banks of TV screens positioned behind a low slung, sit down bar that took up the entire front of the room. The bar was packed with trendy patrons, all eating sushi and watching sumo wrestling on the screens. The remainder of the large room was near deserted, spotted with tables occupied by same sex couples. Patti got familiar waves from the bartenders and sushi chefs.

Past the bar, there was another hallway and another staircase. When Potter and Clancy finally caught up with her, they discovered the whole roof was an open bar. Potter moved painfully to the nearest chair and collapsed into it, chest heaving. After a few moments he'd recovered enough to start taking in his surroundings. It had the feel of a real party spot.

Over on the far side of the roof, beside raised planters that served as railings, Potter saw Patti beckoning to them from a table. He attempted to stand up and found himself being steadied by Maureen. After sitting down next to Patti he noticed Andrew with another black male. Both wore colorful, baggy silk shirts that Potter was pretty sure concealed sidearms. Farther over, directly in front of a fire escape, Potter located Thighs at a table with five others. Even the big man seemed to be having a good time, oblivious to Patti and the people at her table.

A waitress brought three Corona beers. Potter took a long pull on his and continued to scan the panoramic view that the roof top afforded. He peered over the wall to look down at the yellow and black neon sign — the *El Caribe Restaurant*. It caused a warm feeling to rush through him and he recognized he was in the center of Queen Patti's domain.

Patti was grinning at him, and he raised his bottle in salute, savoring the flood of glowing memories evoked by the sight of the little restaurant.

He leaned over. "Think we were followed again?"

Patti shrugged. "I have no idea. But if they get thirsty and want to come up for a drink, we can't stop them, can we? But it's interesting you bring the subject up."

Patti ordered more beer and started telling stories. The one about Big Frank, the alligator and the crate of Georgia peaches had them in tears of hilarity. After her second beer, Maureen asked where the ladies' room was and headed off.

As soon as she left Patti gestured to Andrew and rose to meet him in the middle of the floor. "No rest for the wicked," she smiled at Michael as she left. She was back almost immediately and said she had to go the washroom as well.

Potter sat and watched the people, ordinarily one of his favorite activities. But soon he was frowning, lost in a reverie and half-expecting Patti or Andrew or Thighs to return and say they had to flee once more.

He was roused by a bustle of activity by the stairs. He jerked his head up and saw Maureen storm onto the roof. She looked furious. Patti followed. "Mo, what happened? asked Potter.

"Her purse got ripped off in the washroom," said Patti.

"Bloody hell!" seethed Maureen. "Somebody's arm just reached over the top of the cubicle and it was gone. I didn't even see it, it was so fast. That was my favorite bag, too! Everything I brought with me was in it."

"You can always buy another one," said Patti soothingly. "Let me get you another drink."

A few moments later Potter spotted Andrew coming up the stairs. He walked toward their table, leaned over and placed Maureen's handbag in front of her. Maureen's green eyes widened with relief. "Oh my God. Thank you!" Andrew smiled distantly. He moved around to Patti, whispered in her ear and slipped something into her hand as Thunder Thighs ambled toward their table. Potter frowned. What was going on?

Maureen pulled the bag to her and rifled through it. After a few seconds she looked up, her face drawn.

"Something missing?" asked Patti.

"My car keys."

On the table Patti laid a set of keys with a Honda Accord key fob. "These keys?"

Maureen looked at Patti Donovan and did not appear relieved.

"Yes."

Patti leaned forward and purred like a jungle cat contemplating its next meal. "The ones with the personal locator beacon built into them?"

Maureen suddenly tried to get up and found herself held completely immobile by Andrew and Thighs. Potter stared in disbelief. The two men were so good an onlooker would have simply assumed they had placed friendly hands on an old acquaintance.

Patti dangled the keys in front of Maureen. "Tell Mike about these. It's not exactly off-the-shelf technology."

Maureen Clancy stared defiantly at Patti, trying not to look at Potter. When she finally did, she flinched at the look of betrayal in his eyes. "How could you?" he asked.

"Look, you're a very nice guy, but I had my orders."

Potter turned to Patti. "Can I talk to you for a minute? Alone?" She nodded. Painfully, he reached down for his day pack as Patti leaned over to Maureen. "Big Frank owns this place. I run it. Make a sound and you're dead." They walked over to a corner of the rooftop terrace and sat down at a table. Potter said, "Maybe I'm too trusting a soul to figure this out. Explain."

"We're very good at what we do. If people like the FBI and the CIA find us once, it could be luck, it could be coincidence. If they find us twice in less than a day, it's a god damned setup. I know you. I don't know her. It had to be her."

Patti took a pull on her beer. "Andrew's good at this kind of thing. That's why we bought you both new clothes, in case it was sewn into a garment. It wasn't. The only place she had left to hide it was in her old handbag."

"So Andrew snatched the bag and found the bug."

Patti nodded.

A sudden thought occurred to Potter. "What about my day bag? I never checked it for bugs when I fled the hospital."

"Andrew checked it. You left it on the bed when you took your bath. There was nothing in it. We got suspicious with her because she never let that bag get more than six inches away from her."

"So we're safe now?"

"No. We should get out of here soon. As long as that thing is active they can find us."

"But why?"

"You were in the hospital, confused and wounded. They probably thought they could break you easily, get you to talk. But if they couldn't, they needed a backup plan. Maureen Clancy was the backup plan. Pretty slick."

"They expected me to run from that hospital, didn't they?"

"If you didn't tell them what they wanted to know, sure. If she was convincing enough you'd trust her, and as long as the two of you were together your trail would be lit up like a neon sign."

"But I couldn't tell them what they wanted to know, because I don't know anything."

Patti poured the rest of her drink down her long tanned throat. "I think you do. You just don't know that you know it. We have to have a little talk with Clancy. Privately. And we have to do it fast. There may be more backup plans."

They walked back to the table, where Maureen, looking hunted, was still restrained by Thighs and Andrew. Patti took Maureen's handbag and keys and strode purposefully towards the bar. She threw back the stainless steel lid of the ice tray and threw them in, then slammed the lid down and loped back to the table.

"It's a shame what water will do to expensive electronics." Patti gestured and they followed, the two men holding Maureen Clancy upright. They walked down a flight of stairs to an office. Patti unlocked it and walked in. She took a chair from behind a desk and set it in the middle of the floor. Andrew and Thighs bound the captive's hands behind her back and taped her legs to the chair with duct tape as Potter found a seat and Patti perched on the edge of the desk. She leaned over and opened a drawer, taking out something small and black.

Donovan contemplated the bound Maureen. "Pretend it's spring, and you're a songbird. So sing."

"No."

Patti walked toward Maureen with a casual gait, then when she was in striking distance lashed out suddenly with an overhand right that sounded like the crack of a whip. Maureen's head snapped back and Patti walked away with the same casual stride.

Potter tried to rise from his chair and found that Thighs's hands were holding him down as if he had a couple of anvils on his shoulders. He realized Patti was wearing skin tight black leather gloves. "Wait a minute. This isn't what I had in mind. You can't hit a woman."

"You've got it wrong, sweetheart," said Patti Donovan. "You're such a romantic. It's socially unacceptable for a man to hit a woman. But for a woman to hit a woman, well . . ."

The next punch was a left hook so hard Potter could feel Thighs flinch. "Stop it!" he yelled. No one paid him the slightest attention.

Tears of pain streamed down Maureen's puffy cheeks and her lip was split.

Patti leaned over and stared at her. "I can keep this up all night."

Clancy was still defiant. "Tough talk for a gangster's moll."

Donovan threw her head back and laughed out loud. "You hear that, guys? I'm a gangster's moll."

"Hubba hubba," said Thighs.

"Twenty-three skidoo," drawled Andrew.

"Gangster's moll or not, I assure you my fist will last a lot longer than your face. By morning your own mother will look at you and not be able to stop screaming."

Maureen Clancy's head bowed as Patti once again perched on the desk. "Let's start with the personal locator beacon. Never seen one like that before. You, Andrew?"

The slim black man slowly shook his head. "State of the art."

"Tell me about it while you still have teeth," said Patti. "I hate it when people lisp."

Maureen gave up. "It's a locator transmitter, good for a three mile radius, accurate to within six feet."

"And how do you do the long distance stuff?"

"I use the phone, call an embassy, whatever the contact is."

"Good," said Patti decisively. "Isn't this much more civilized? I don't enjoy this kind of thing at all, but as they say, time is of the essence."

Looking directly into Maureen's glistening brown eyes she said, "Now for the important part. Who do you work for?"

Maureen Clancy looked over at a still horrified Michael Potter. "I don't care what the rest of them think. As I've gotten to know you, I don't believe you're involved in planning this at all. No one is that good an actor."

"Answer the question."

"Canadian Security and Intelligence Service. CSIS."

"More alphabet soup. Never heard of it," said Patti. "Guys?"

"Bunch of Canadian spooks," replied Andrew. "She's a spy. Like a CIA agent."

Patti contemplated her black gloves. "In Big Frank's business we call them snitches, stool pigeons. I hate spies almost as much as I hate damaging good leather. But it wasn't a bunch of Canucks outside of Anthony House this morning, or at the brownstone."

She pointed a black-clad finger at Potter. "What's the connection between him, this CSIS and the CIA, FBI, or whatever? I mean, we're talking international here. What's the connection between your outfit and American intelligence services?"

"It's very big," said Maureen Clancy. "It involves questions of national security at the highest levels for both countries. And possibly others as well. But I can't explain it to gangsters." She closed her eyes and leaned back like a sacrificial lamb expecting the knife.

"Patti, I swear to God, if you hit her once more I'll never talk to you again," said Potter.

His old flame looked at him sadly. "She betrayed you. And depending on how big this really is, how gentle do you think the CIA is going to be with you?"

They looked at each other, trying to read each other's souls the way they'd been able to read them only a couple of years before. They both read, and saw.

Patti Donovan tore her gaze away from Potter's. She sighed and started to strip off the leather gloves. "Okay. How's your history?"

Maureen opened her eyes. "What do you mean?"

"I heard this from my father when I was a girl. World War II. The invasion of Sicily. Before it took place, naval intelligence went to Lucky Luciano, where he was languishing in jail. They said, Mr. Luciano, you are the *capo di tutti capi,* the boss of all the bosses, of the American Mafia. Our maps of Sicily are poor and we have few informants there. You know the country and the people intimately. Will you help us? And Luciano instantly replied, 'Yes. I'm an American, after all'."

Patti threw the gloves on the desk. "So am I. So are these guys. If there's a threat to national security, maybe we can help."

Maureen Clancy searched Patti Donovan's face, then turned to Potter. He nodded.

The spy sighed. "It's Dr. Harry Warner they want."

Potter couldn't believe his ears. "He's famous. He's been in Canada since the fifties. He's been a friend and advisor to four Canadian prime ministers, plus God knows how many Royal

Commissions."

"All of that is true," agreed Maureen. "It's also true he's a long time Soviet mole, recruited by the GRU."

"More alphabet soup," said Patti. "What is GRU?"

"The old Soviet Military Intelligence. Recruited during the Stalin era when he was at Cambridge. One of the ones they plant and leave for decades, ticking like a time bomb until they tell him to go off. One of the important ones, that they don't use for trivial missions. One of the ones, like Philby, Burgess and Maclean, who change everything."

She thrashed in her bonds. "Take these off."

They were all looking at her in disbelief. "He only made a mistake once, and that's how we've know about him for years. He never made another error. And because of his powerful connections we couldn't touch him. So on a casual basis we monitored his friends instead, just in case."

She looked at Potter. "People like you."

"I don't believe any of this," said Michael flatly.

Maureen insisted. "He's the one who had you shot. Damn it, he has those kids!"

The office intercom buzzed quietly. Patti picked it up. "Yeah?" She sighed. "Big surprise."

She put down the receiver. "On the road again. Her with us. Now." As Thighs tore apart Maureen's bonds with his bare hands, Andrew drew his 9mm Beretta and sprinted down the stairs.

Patti faced Maureen. "VCRs I like. Locator beacons, I don't like. You have more songs to sing, so you're coming with us."

As Maureen thrashed, Thighs pressed her carotid arteries and she blacked out. He threw her over his shoulder as if she were a bean bag chair and walked out of the room.

"This cat has a lot of lives, but I never thought I'd use up three of them in forty-eight hours," said Patti. She opened another desk drawer and withdrew a black automatic, then grabbed Potter's hand and pulled him toward the stairs.

When they had finally descended to the second floor, Potter heard loud, angry commands coming from the direction of the restaurant. There was the sound of furniture being thrown around. Patti ran on, pulling him with her.

At the bottom they saw Thighs ramming his body against a locked fire door with the heavy inevitability of an elephant determined to knock down a house. Andrew was behind him. Gun in one hand, the elegant black was looking disapprovingly at the shoulder of his expensive jacket as his other hand flicked at a speck of dust.

The instant they burst through, Potter could hear the throaty rumblings of a truck's engine being revved.

Dashing through the door, Potter could see that they were in a fenced-off area behind the restaurant. The gate was open. There was a Ford Escort inside the enclosure and a huge truck at the far end of the alley. The truck rocked as its driver pumped the accelerator, the engine roar deafening. Thighs had the back door of the Escort open and was stuffing Maureen into the seat as Andrew sat behind the wheel, whistling tunelessly as he tapped time with his pistol.

Piling into the vehicle, Andrew signaled to the truck driver. The engine altered pitch as the driver engaged the gears and the big machine moved past the fence.

The instant the truck's box was clear of the fence, Andrew floored the accelerator and followed the lumbering machine. Up ahead, a wrenching crash of metal and glass sounded as the truck driver wove his big vehicle back and forth to clear a path. Suddenly, the gaping mouth of the alley came into view.

The truck plowed out into the street and crossed two lanes of traffic as tires squealed. Andrew jerked the steering wheel to the left and they careened away from the wildly skidding truck.

Turning around, Potter could see the flashing blue and red lights of police cruisers and unmarked vehicles trying vainly to edge around the truck that was blocking the road. Shots rang out, and there was a thud as a slug hit the Escort.

"Damn," said Andrew. "There's nothing prettier than a clean getaway, where not even the car gets hurt."

They roared off.

THIRTY TWO

Just a few minutes later they pulled up in front of an attractive, two story, federal style home and entered the garage.

As Thighs struggled to extract the still unconscious Maureen from the car, Patti muttered, "This can't go on much longer. I'm running out of safe houses."

She leaned over to Potter. "I know you think I was brutal with her. What else was I supposed to do? Field operatives are trained to resist interrogation. Even now she might be lying. We have to find out what she knows as fast as we can."

Through a hallway they entered a comfortable living room, then walked to the kitchen. All of the curtains were drawn. A long oak table covered in a dull black cloth took up the center of the room. At the far end, two comfortable upholstered arm chairs rested. When Potter came back from the bathroom a handcuffed Maureen Clancy was sitting on a bar stool.

"Okay," said Patti. "Let's pick up where we left off. You say everyone is after this Dr. Warner. You say he's working for the Russians. How do you know?"

"Almost twenty years ago now a large group of Polish sailors defected. The RCMP got a tip that one of them, a guy named Pavel, was a spy so they started following him." She looked at Michael. "The officer on the case was Douglas Baker. One evening the sailor made a passoff in a restaurant to another man, and then they both just disappeared. Weeks later, by total fluke, Baker happened to see Warner's picture in the paper when he won some award and realized it was the same guy who'd done the switch with the sailor. Through the Brits and the Americans we investigated Warner's background. Turns out he came from the same nest of Cambridge spies as Kim Philby. His wife Alice was a traitor too. They gave him the code name Reggie."

Potter's mind was reeling as Patti asked another question. "Obviously your organization knows he has the kids Michael is looking for. Does CSIS know that the children are the Patriots of the Raven?"

Maureen shook her head. "It's news to me."

Potter interrupted. "Tell me again why I came to your attention, if it was Harry you were after all along?"

"We suspected Warner knew he was being watched, so he was very careful. If he needed something done, he always used other people. Like you."

Patti shrugged. "Of course. Standard ploy."

Maureen continued. "We knew you were his student, but so were a lot of other people. It wasn't until you went to Alert Bay that we got suspicious. We knew that Warner had been in touch with a Dr. Elliott on the island, and having you suddenly decide to go there too looked strange. We got really interested when Warner actually went and visited you there. That's when we did a background check and found a three month period in your life that couldn't be accounted for. Just like with Lee Harvey Oswald, we figured maybe you'd been out of the country, secretly in contact with the Russians. And then we found out that someone with a lot of power had pulled some very important strings to get you that summer posting in Bethesda. It looked like a classic Russian setup."

"When in fact it was Patti who got me the posting."

Clancy shrugged. "We didn't know that. All the available evidence suggested that Warner had recruited you as a spy and the two of you were working together."

Potter shook his head ruefully.

"Then you brought the five children to Warner, which really puzzled us. What the hell was going on? And then we found out that Warner had always been interested in Siberian shamanism. Occult powers, that kind of thing."

Patti interrupted. "I remember reading something about that. For decades the Soviets have been researching psychic phenomena."

"And then there was the fact that you made the reservation at the restaurant for yourself and the five kids. All at once, you get shot, the Vancouver police department gets a bogus phone call and surrounds the place, Harry Warner is there, and him and the kids run like they've just committed the crime of the century."

Potter nodded slowly. "When you explain it like that, I can see how from your perspective it must've looked strange as hell."

Maureen continued. "When we looked at the tape of the restaurant incident, there was a fellow in the background who looked a lot like you, only in a cap and shades. Nobody on the force had ever seen him before, so for some reason Warner must have planted him there. And when we analyzed the voice tapes of the bogus call, our experts were finally able to figure out that the caller had a British accent, even though he disguised it extremely well."

Patti jumped in. "But none of this has anything to do with the FBI or the CIA."

Maureen shook her head. "We have a standing agreement with US intelligence services where suspected Russian moles are concerned. We share information and pool our resources. These guys worry us because we don't know what they might be instructed to do. We handled the whole thing because it was happening on Canadian soil. Once Michael arrived here in Washington, the FBI and CIA took over."

The redhead sighed suddenly. "That's pretty much it. We don't know why Warner is here or why he has those children. If what Michael says is true, what's the point of all this terrorist Patriots of the Raven activity? After planting him and protecting him for decades, I can't believe the Kremlin would activate someone as vital as Warner just to play pranks with a bunch of kids."

She looked directly at Potter. "You *must* know something. Warner was doing tests on those children."

Potter shook his head. "Just on one. Beebo."

"Did he find out anything? Anything that would explain what's going on?"

Potter thought hard. "Just that Beebo has unusual bursts of brain activity when he dreams. And I told him some of what I'd witnessed of the kids' powers."

"Did you tell him about your journal?"

"No, no way!" Slowly it was coming back. "Oh man, maybe, indirectly. He would have known I was keeping notes on my findings."

Potter's puzzlement was rapidly overwhelming his embarrassment. "If in fact it's Warner who had me shot and stole my journal, then he would know how to manipulate them. But once again, to what end? What the hell is going on?"

THIRTY THREE

The sight of the beautiful salmon swimming closer and closer brought on a peaceful feeling, one strong enough to make the horrors disappear. The sun's rays reflected off the fish's back to form a beautiful iridescence that alternated from silver hues, to vibrant greens and pinks. The fish called out in a sweet voice, one irresistible to the human heart. "Come here. Touch me."

There was another voice, one that came from inside. It seemed to say, "No, this is a bad thing!"

Suddenly, the fish transformed into a most terrible two headed snake thing with two faces staring out from the woods, burning eyes glaring. The long, wavering necks moved ever closer and as if by some terrible mistake of nature, the two necks appeared as the arms of a man. At the point where the necks came together, a headless human form crouched in the mist. From where the heart should be, a fiendish human face smiled . . .

Even though he'd had this dream before, it was the first time he could clearly see the face. The shock of recognition make him fight to throw off the dream. But some tremendous, unseen power forbade escape. It came from the same place as the voice — the one that warned against the fish creature and the deceitful face where its heart should have been.

Another dream washed in. A sad little girl in Arctic snows, named Nakita, held prisoner but never told why.

And another. A soaring raven, and a powerful creature that

lived in a white nest.

And then the machine, its precision gone dreadfully wrong, dropped and tumbled sickeningly. Rotor blades snapped as they sliced into the lawn and deadly shining fragments flew into panicked crowd of thousands.

And one very familiar face, grinning, insanely.

The dreamer thrashed convulsively. For the first time in this dream, he could see the person, could see what was going to happen. A hoarse scream burned in his throat as he saw . . .

"Beebo! Come on man, wake up! It's us."

He opened his eyes and saw that Dickie Cook and Belly were holding him down with all their might.

A knock sounded on the door. As they turned they saw a blue and silver aura radiating from the door jam. The door opened automatically. With increasing confidence, they had all been using their powers on a regular basis, even for trivial things, sometimes alarming Dr. Harry Warner and on a few occasions almost getting caught when a passersby witnessed doors and windows opening. Despite Warner's admonitions, their relationship with him had never been the same since they discovered he had been lying to them.

Princess and Brenda entered the room and wordlessly stood at Beebo's side, Princess tugging sleepily at her pajamas.

Beebo saw that Brenda had tears in her eyes. It was another few moments before he regained composure enough to speak and when he did he knew instantly that they had shared the same dream, that she had seen what he had seen. "You saw?"

She nodded. "Two snake heads. Sisiutl, Man Eater's helper."

"And its heart?"

"What are you talking about?" demanded Dickie.

"No heart at all. A face. We've made a terrible mistake."

"What!" shouted Belly.

Beebo took a deep breath. "The face in the center of the Sisiutl was Dr. Harry. I've never been able to see it clearly before. He's lied to us and made us do terrible things."

"He won't hurt us anymore" blurted Princess. "We'll stop him. Did the dream tell you how? What else did you see?"

Beebo swallowed hard and looked at Brenda. She bent over the little girl and spoke hesitantly at first. "he saw the little girl again, the one behind the barbed wire fence, the one the soldiers watch. He saw that she's still sad because she can't leave that cold place. She must be one of the ones Dr. Harry told us about, in that place, Siberia maybe."

"C'mon, Beebo," cut in Dickie. "It can't be that bad. We've already talked about it. We can handle that old man easily. He couldn't be crazy enough to cross us."

Beebo rose painfully from his bed and padded to the window. A hot smoky dawn was just breaking over the city. "With residue of the dream still burning behind his eyes and the knowledge that someone would die," he muttered, "I don't know. I just don't know."

****

At 8:30 the five of them joined Harry for breakfast in the hotel restaurant. He gave them his usual cheery greeting, which over the past several days had become rather forced, but stopped when he saw the looks on their faces. He looked at them warily.

"Something wrong? Today's the big day, you know."

"That's what we want to talk to you about," said Belly quietly. "I know it's just fooling around with machines, like we've done before. But we're worried."

The gangly teen held Dr. Harry Warner's eye. When Warner realized he wasn't going to look away, the old physician's lips suddenly tightened as he seemed to come to some sort of decision.

"I was expecting this sooner or later. I was just hoping it

wouldn't be today." He finished his coffee. "You all have to eat something. Order what you like. I have to make a phone call. When I come back, we'll go to the park at the end of street and have a nice chat in the sunshine." He stood abruptly and left.

When he returned more than half an hour later the five children were picking listlessly at the remains of their meals. Warner picked up the check, tossed some bills on the table and gestured impatiently. "Let's go. We don't have all day."

They exited the hotel and walked to the small, flower filled park. Harry threw himself on a bench that faced an ornate chalice-shaped granite fountain with cascading water. "So. What's the problem?"

The change in his manner from friendly, joking avuncularity to unsmiling, cold-eyed professional was unsettling. Belly looked at him warily. "Why are we meeting here?"

"It's a public place. Makes me feel safe."

Belly could no longer contain himself. "You lied to us. You made us think that it was all about Native rights and capitalism and the white man's machines and we believed you. But it's not about that at all."

"Yes it is," said Warner. He frowned. "I explained all of this yesterday and every word of it is true. What brings this on?"

Beebo broke in. "I had a dream. You were in it. You were Sisiutl, Man Eater's helper. And you didn't have a heart."

Warner smiled as if listening to some childish fantasy. "And what else did you see?"

"Helicopters falling. Gunfire. Explosions." Beebo looked at Princess. "And other stuff."

Warner gave a deep sigh of satisfaction. "Helicopters falling. And explosions. Good, good. Everything's all right then."

With the air of an actor who's had to do something else in the middle of a performance, Warner attempted to return to his previous avuncular persona. False warmth emanated from him, but by now the children could tell the difference between this and real warmth the way they could distinguish between the sun and a heat lamp.

"I haven't lied to you. It is still about capitalism and Native rights and the white man's machines. If anything, I've more than lived up to my bargain. And there's only one more thing to do. What we've talked about. And then you can go home."

"No."

"What?"

"We've agreed. We won't do it. This is the end."

The pupils of Harry Warner's cold blue eyes were turning into pinpoints of rage. "My young friend, there are forces of history at work here. Interfere with them and you will be destroyed."

Dickie Cook grabbed Warner's collar and pulled the old man from the bench as if he were an empty suit of clothes. "Never threaten my friends. *Never.*"

Involuntarily Belly's mind was probing Warner's body the way a boxer's jab tries to spot weakness in an opponent's defense. The old physician gasped in fear as he felt it, as Dickie shoved him away. "Are you going to kill me, Belly? The way you almost killed Jimmy Albert?"

The remark stopped Belly cold. "I'm not a killer."

"Are you sure?" hissed Warner. "Absolutely sure?"

"Belly isn't, you old creep. But I wouldn't be too certain about me," said Dickie as he reached again for Warner's neck.

Warner's eyes flickered and he suddenly reached into his jacket pocket and pressed something. Several people in the vicinity immediately turned and converged on the park. Instinctively the youngsters moved closer together at this completely unexpected development. It all happened so fast that they didn't have time to even think about reacting. A burly blond man handed Warner a large unsealed brown envelope.

Without taking his eyes from the children, Warner started to open it. "Thank you, Pavel. Nice hand-off. Just like the old days, eh?"

Beebo stared in disbelief at the big blond named Pavel. "You were the state trooper who stopped our car."

Belly pointed. "And these guys were the sailors at the restaurant in Port Townsend."

Brenda stared at Pavel too. "You saved me. Those Yugoslav fishermen."

The big blond gazed impassively, then touched a scar on his forehead. "The same."

Warner took some photos out of the envelope and shuffled through them. "A certain degree of stage management is sometimes necessary to induce the requisite amount of paranoia to make people pliable. Standard brainwashing technique. But now we must use something a little cruder."

He handed one of the photos to Princess.

"Daddy," she whispered.

"What?" Belly snatched the picture.

"He's such a nice man," said Harry Warner. "My people tell me he put up quite a fight, which is why he looks a little bruised."

Belly stared in horror. "Who's the other guy? My God, his face."

"Blake Roberts, the senior Republican senator from Utah. Some of my people really hate American politicians."

Warner was talking fast, trying to make sure the children didn't have time to think, to act. "They have nothing against Indians, but . . ."

Dickie Cook was breathing heavily and Warner looked at him quickly as he held up a small black box with an antenna and a tiny glowing red light.

Without taking his eyes from the enraged Dickie, he said,

"Belly, notice the rather interesting belt your father is wearing. It contains a kilo of the best Czech plastique. If you do not do as you are told, I simply activate my little black box here and all that will be left of Dan Lucas is a mist of bloody vapor. And although I know you can manipulate electronics, this device is connected with twelve others, and you don't know where they are or how they're linked. Interfere with this box, even for an instant, and your father is dead."

At that moment almost nothing on earth could have restrained Dickie Cook, and had he acted on his immediate impulses even Pavel would have been surprised at this power. But a quick mental flash from Brenda stopped him.

"First Potter, and now you," he said in a voice thick with rage.

Warner's eyes narrowed as if he were evaluating this statement or making a decision. "Yes. And now why don't we go somewhere private and have a little chat about what's going to happen later on today?"

THIRTY FOUR

"I can't believe I'm so fucking stupid!" stormed Patti Donovan as she burst through the door like a brunette hurricane.

Michael Potter awoke with a start. He stared blearily at the alarm clock by his bed and groggily tried to sit up. It was just after ten in the morning.

"What are you talking about?" he croaked.

"I can't believe it!" She was dressed in a sleeveless black tank top and black slacks.

Potter was now fully awake. "Talk to me!"

"When you told me about the five kids, I assumed they were being held prisoner somewhere in a tenement and if anybody saw them they'd assume they were refugee Indians from El Salvador or something. So that's where I've had my people looking. I couldn't figure out why those kids were so hard to find."

She swore like a trooper. "Instead, they were hidden in plain sight. Oldest trick in the book and I fell for it. Naked is the best disguise. My people have been tearing apart every seedy corner of this seedy town, and the whole time they were in four hundred dollar a night suites at the fucking Hilton!"

She threw herself on the bed as Potter swung his legs over, instantly alert.

"The Hilton? Let's go!"

Her beautiful face once again clouded with anger. "For some reason they were in a park down the street from the hotel. My people would've picked them up on the spot but this Warner guy was there too with about ten thugs with bulges under their jackets. They didn't want to get into a gunfight in the middle of the street. And then several cars pulled up and the kids were separated and the cars went different ways and they chose to tail the wrong ones and they vanished."

Potter was baffled. "You lost them again?"

"Only temporarily, I assure you," she said grimly.

"But who are these other people, these thugs you mentioned?"

"Don't know. Apparently they all looked hard as hell. Obviously they work for Warner. My people got pictures of all of them, with hidden cameras, so at least we know what the bastards look like."

Donovan noticed he was thinking hard and frowning. "What?"

"I had that dream again. With the raven and the white nest. It's more vivid all the time. And I recognized a couple of landmarks, even though I can't remember them now. All I know is that whatever the dream means, it's going to happen here in Washington. Soon. Maybe that's why Warner has people with him."

"Describe this damned dream!"

When he had finished she looked puzzled. "Ravens, white nests, then helicopters and explosions. I hate riddles, and this one doesn't mean a thing to me."

After a few moments she said, "My people are looking for the kids. We're going to take a little tour of the city and see if we can spot these landmarks. If we can find them, there might be a clue. Maybe the whole thing will come clear to you."

A sudden thought occurred to Potter. "What about Maureen?"

"I think she's told us everything she knows. And I think she's right. You do know something, you just don't know that you know it. We'll dump her someplace."

Potter looked at her in horror. "You're going to kill her?"

"Have to. It's the only way. If we don't, she'll spill the beans and every alphabet soup intelligence agency is going to be all over us like a cheap suit."

"You can't!"

Patti was appraising him sadly. "Mike, she's a professional spy. They told her the risks when she joined."

"But they already know about us and that we're holding her. How many places are there left to run to in this city? You told me before you don't have a criminal record. Do you want to start with murder?"

"I know," said Patti Donovan. "Already I feel like I'm running toward the old Berlin Wall and someone's just turned a spotlight on me and the guns are being aimed. And Big Frank is going to be thrilled too."

She turned suddenly and took his face in her hands. "All right. We let her go. But at the moment the only thing we have to go on is your dream. You told me these kids can see the future. Do they always see it accurately? Is it fixed? Or can it be altered?"

"I don't know. As far as I know, they've never tried to alter it. Maybe it can be changed."

Patti kissed him, hard. "Harry Warner is a Russian spy, recruited during the days of the old Soviet Union, during the worst of the Cold. He's a traitor. If some sort of disaster is going to happen, and he's behind it, maybe, just maybe, we can prevent it. And then to the FBI and the CIA we'll be heroes instead of victims."

THIRTY FIVE

Thunder Thighs tipped a protesting and well trussed up Maureen Clancy in to the trunk of a Lincoln Continental Town Car.

Twenty minutes later Andrew and the big man deposited the bound, thrashing redhead next to some garbage cans in a deserted back alley. Potter phoned Canada House giving instructions where to find her, wasting valuable time trying to persuade the duty officer that the call wasn't a prank.

Potter climbed painfully back into the vehicle as Patti leaned forward to give instructions to Thighs and Andrew.

"Now what?" he asked.

"We're going to the Hilton, even though they've checked out. But first you get a tour of the monuments. It'll take them some time to debrief Maureen but we still have to be quick. When you see a landmark from your dream yell bingo or something."

They drove around in ever-widening circles in what remained of morning rush hour. It took about thirty minutes for Potter to decide that the view he'd seen in the latter part of the dream was not from a car but a sidewalk, as a pedestrian would see things. The first half, from the air, he simply didn't understand.

"Let me get this straight," frowned Patti. "Whatever's going to happen occurs in broad daylight, on a street. There's lots of people standing on the sidewalk facing the street, but it's not like a rally or a demonstration. Everybody's friendly."

"Yes," said Potter.

"There's lots of traffic, black limos and security. None of that means anything, especially not the black limos. In this town they're a dime a dozen. But the traffic could be significant. It gets that heavy three times a day, morning, noon and afternoon rush hour. And you think it's going to happen soon?"

"Yes."

"I wish your brain was a television. If the two of us could see your dream together it might help a lot."

Potter shrugged helplessly.

Patti leaned forward and spoke to Thighs. As he pulled the big car to the curb, she said to Potter, "We're in the historic centre of the capital and it's lousy with monuments. In your dream you see things from the sidewalk. So let's walk."

Thighs drove off to park the car and Andrew ambled behind them as they strolled hand in hand like lovers without a care in the world. "By the way," said Patti. "Since he's right behind us I don't want to make you self-conscious, but Andrew thinks you have a cute ass."

"Funny, I thought he liked my pecs. And he just sort of volunteered his opinion on my glutes to my former lover and his current employer?"

Patti grinned. "Not quite. He said you had a cute ass after I said to him, 'Andrew, doesn't Mike have a cute ass?'"

It didn't take long for the heat and humidity to make Potter very tired. Donovan looked at him appraisingly and he could tell she was impatient, although she was doing her best to hide it.

"Sorry, Patti. Zilch."

"Nothing to apologize for. Let's get a cool drink and something to eat. It might be the last opportunity we have if Maureen's already told them what she knows." She sighed. "My whole damn life trying to keep out of the limelight, and now this. I keep expecting the screech of cars, the gleam of handcuffs, and film at eleven."

Suddenly Michael Potter saw it. "There!"

She looked where his finger was pointing. "The Washington Monument. Are you sure?"

"Positive."

"In the dream you keep having, can you always see the Washington Monument? I mean, is it in plain view all the time?"

He thought hard. "No. Only at the end."

They had reached their destination, an elegant restaurant called Nolte Lune. They took a sidewalk table and ordered drinks and coffee as Patti rummaged in her purse. She pulled out a city map, spreading it on the circular table. Her finger searched eagerly, then started moving aimlessly.

"Damn. You can see it from just about anywhere in this area. Do you remember the point of view?"

He shook his head.

One of the things Potter loved about Patti Donovan was that she was a positive thinker. "Never mind," she said. "It's a start. Monument number one is pinned down. I bet the rest fall into place like dominos."

She studied the map again. "Here's where we are, 'I' Street and 15th. And the Hilton is very close, on 16th Street. Her finger searched urgently, then suddenly stopped.

"What?" asked Potter.

"The Russian Embassy. One block from the Hilton."

"And Warner is a Russian spy."

Patti's gray eyes darted furiously. "I know. But there's something wrong here."

"Like what?" asked Potter anxiously.

"I'm not sure. But it's something big. It'll come to me."

Potter gazed across the street. Thighs and Andrew blended in perfectly with the crowds. Patti pulled a Motorola phone from her pocket and dialed. Across the street, Andrew responded on his own phone.

"Andrew? Female intuition again. No jokes, I don't have time. Something big is happening. I think very, very big. I don't know what it is yet but we have to be ready. Tell Thighs too and get the others around. I hate to break it to you, but this might be bad."

"What are you talking about?" asked Potter incredulously, as she rang off.

"Female stuff. A sense of things converging. Most men never understand. Big Frank understood. Why do you think he begged me to come back? I got good instincts."

In spite of his worries and fatigue Potter had to smile. "Of course you do. You chose me, didn't you?"

Her smile was as bright as the sun, and as reckless.

Suddenly a squad of four motorcycle police sped past, followed by two police cruisers. Potter watched, transfixed.

"What is it?" she asked.

"Dream," he said as he stood like a robot and walked away. Donovan threw some bills on the table and followed.

A terrible pressure crushed at Potter's temples. He forced himself to keep walking as Patti stayed close behind, not daring to distract him.

They passed the Russian Embassy and Potter speeded up as he saw its stately facade and copper plated arbor roof. So familiar. Behind him Patti looked at her watch. 12:05, and the noon hour pedestrian traffic was reaching a peak.

Potter's heart pounded and he could feel the sutures in his chest. He felt the blood drain from his face. Must go on.

Suddenly he was standing at the intersection of Rhode Island Avenue where it crossed 'M' and Connecticut. Potter stopped and stared at the crowds on Connecticut.

He looked from side to side, trying to remember, trying to think, trying to duplicate the dream.

Suddenly he stared at the news kiosk on the corner. He took a step closer and held his hands to his sweaty face.

"Oh no. No."

Patti was at his side in an instant. "What?"

Potter pointed a trembling finger at the hard face that glowered from the newspaper cover. It was a man in his late forties, with the slightly oriental looking eyes and broad features of a Mongol or Uzbek. He was mostly bald, and the right side of his face and neck were disfigured by a giant purple scar.

In the shape of a raven.

"Oh no."

"Michael!" Patti Donovan shook him roughly by the shoulders. "For God's sake, what is it?"

"The mark of the raven," he whispered. "Feodor Vasikov, the new leader of the Russian Federation. He's here in Washington for the first time, to meet with Clinton." Desperately he tried to remember what he had read about the man. Heavily decorated veteran of the Afghanistan war. Colonel, tanks. Horribly burned in a rebel ambush. A hero for trying to get his men out. Refuses to get the scar fixed with plastic surgery because he sees it as a badge of honor. Hard as nails. Becomes disgusted with corruption in post-Soviet Russia and the connivance of former hardline Communist Party members with the Mafia. Elected president of the Russian Federation on a platform of law and order coupled with liberal economic reform. Had already ordered the arrest and trial of thousands of former Party members.

He put his hands to his eyes. There was something else. It came to him. Vasikov was from Siberia, near Lake Baikal, born of mixed Mongol and Kirghiz stock. He shook his head, trying to clear it. Warner's interest in Siberian shamanism. Staff Sergeant Baker asking him about the same thing. Suddenly the dream he had been having was terribly clear. He looked at Patti Donovan. "He'll meet with the president today, at the White House."

He looked at Patti Donovan. "What sort of powerful creature lives in a white nest?"

"Mike, I'm not a mind reader!"

"The President of the United States. In the White House."

He held out his arms beseechingly. "Patti, he's going to kill Vasikov. Oh Christ, maybe them both."

Patti saw the awful certainty on his face and screamed, "Andrew!" as she snatched the paper out of Potter's hand. "Vasikov's general itinerary. From the Russian Embassy toward the White House from the north. He'll probably go down 16th Street."

Andrew was at their side in an instant. He gazed impassively at Michael. "Figured it out, huh?"

"Yeah," breathed Patti.

"How bad can it be?" asked the black man.

She told him. For the first time Michael Potter saw Andrew lose his cool. "Oh, *man!*"

"Andrew, Thighs, stay with him for a minute. I have an idea, maybe the only one that will work." She dashed off turning down 'M', disappearing around the corner.

Potter leaned back against the wall of an office building and tried to control his trembling body. His two protectors held him up as he rested.

A spike of clarity entered his head. Like an automaton he began a blind, headlong rush along the street.

Three blocks down, along Connecticut he stopped and gazed into the crowd. And then he saw.

It was Belly.

The sight of the boy sent a new charge of energy through Potter, enough for him to throw off his mindless acceptance of the commands of the black doom. He pushed his way through the oncoming stream of humanity. "Belly!" The boy's head flicked like a hawk spying prey and when he saw Potter his lips drew back from his teeth in a feral snarl. The look of hatred on his face made Potter stop in his tracks. Even the resolute Andrew took a step back.

"Belly. What is it? Where are the others?"

"Prisoners. We all are. As if you didn't know."

The weight of disillusioned adolescence was behind the teen's contemptuous words. "Get away from me you lying piece of shit!"

"Belly, I'm here to help! C'mon man, I'm your friend!"

"Like hell! A friend wouldn't have turned us in, sold us out like you did! Get the hell away from me before—"

"Belly, what're you talking about? I didn't turn you in! How could I—"

"You lied to us too many times and now it's your turn to hurt!"

Andrew and Thighs moved in close to Potter, their expressions intense, their hands poised to protect their employer's ward.

"Belly—" The intense pain of some unseen jet of fire blossomed around him, throwing him back forcibly against the wall. The impact was so severe that he felt his knees buckle. Excruciating barbs of mental flame burned into him. Right there, on the corner of that crowded intersection, Potter knew he was going to die, and that there was nothing he could do to stop it.

Then, through the human wall that had formed to gawk at the spectacle, a large, dark figure surged, pushing bystanders away as if they were twigs!

Dickie jumped into the clear area in front of Potter, glaring at him even more menacingly than Belly. The anger behind the eyes burned into Potter. The big lad plowed straight in towards him, a single intent on his mind, to tear the battered form of his ex-friend in two.

Thighs jumped out in front of Potter in an attempt to protect him but Dickie was too fast for even the big man. With a meaty hand, he easily flung Thighs out of the way, continuing his headlong charge towards Potter. Both Andrew and Thighs reached for their guns but were rendered incapable of withdrawing them as an invisible, vice-like pressure closed around their hands. Both winced in pain, while still attempting to move forward to reach Potter's side. One more step each and they were immobilized. Dickie charged on unhindered.

He flung Potter's head back to the wall with one hand as the other was thrust at his neck, pinning the limp form to the wall. "You!"

"Stop it!" Andrew commanded, words that fell on deaf ears. What really caught Potter's attackers attention was what the black man blurted next. "Oh Jesus Dr. Potter, you're bleeding!" He stared at the wound then imploring, back at the two boys. Soon, all eyes were directed at Potter's upper chest and the crimson blot spreading down the fabric of his shirt.

Weakly straining against the hand at his throat, Potter reached up and ripped the shirt back exposing the blood soaked bandages. He pushed his fingers up further, into the layers of bandage and yanking them back, exposed the horrible, open wound. The sight of it caught attentions. No longer held up to the wall by meaty hands he pitched forward toward the concrete. Five sets of hands reached out to support him.

"What happened to you?" demanded Belly.

"He was shot in the chest damn it," seethed Andrew. "Over a damn journal, a journal that Warner probably now has. My god, he was shot trying to protect you! The whole thing at the restaurant in Vancouver was Warner setting you up." Somehow, at that instant, the two boys knew that they were hearing the truth.

Belly turned to Andrew. "Man, I don't know who you and your friend here is but you have to get Doctor Mike away from here, now! Get as far away as you can!" Then without explanation he turned and looked up Connecticut Avenue.

Silently, Dickie turned and darted back into the crowd.

Through a veil of pain, Potter regarded the boy's expression. The trance. At that instant he knew that the reason for his being in Washington was about to be revealed. "Belly! Don't do this! Andrew, Thighs? It's . . . going to happen, here, now!"

He reached Belly and with his good arm, grasping at the boy's shoulder. "Belly! Listen to me! A group of five black limos are coming this way. You know it, don't you? Belly, you're here to stop a man, a very powerful man. I think you're here to kill him! You have to stop it! Harry can't make you do this!"

With no change of expression, the boy's lips began to move in a slow, labored dance. "Can't stop. Harry will kill my Dad!"

The shock of the new information caused the black doom to flood in. "Belly, you have to stop this! Your Dad and who knows how many others are as good as dead if Harry succeeds! Belly, for God's sake, talk to me!"

The shock treatment had its effect. The glaze over the boy's eyes began to clear as he looked over at Potter. "How do you know about the cars? Why we're here?"

"The dream damn it! The dream about the flying beast and the people dying! Now, I dream it! "Harry? Where's Harry?"

"Right here Michael."

Potter spun around. The tall English physician, wearing a deer-stalker cap and wraparound sunglasses, looked every inch the elderly eccentric tourist. He took off the shades to contemplate Potter, then doffed his hat. He had a delirious smirk on his face. He put his hand on Belly's shoulder and the boy flinched. "The game's afoot, eh, Dr. Watson? Just checking to make sure everyone's in position."

"Harry?" Potter uttered beseechingly. "Why are you doing this?"

"It's my profession. My destiny."

"You five-sided son of a bitch."

"Temper, temper. This is much bigger than either of us. It's as big as history."

Potter looked at Belly, knowing the gangly teen could destroy Warner in an instant. "We trusted each other, remember?" Gazing around, labouring to find some way to reach through to the boy — and the preoccupied citizens of America's capital. He wanted to grab out for them as they walked past and tell them an urgent message: "The Russian president, you know, the one trying to change Russia from history's biggest bad joke into a functional modern society, is about to be assassinated by this crazy looking Englishman in the funny Sherlock Holmes hat. This Indian kid is an unknowing accessory who will assist with his mind, using powers you've only seen on *The X-Files*. And by the way, this guy might even make a try for your own president." And he knew no one would believe him for an instant

Inexplicably the boy's eyes flickered dangerously toward Warner. Potter wondered if somehow Belly had made sense of the dazed mush that Potter called thoughts?

Sensing a strange 'twisting' sensation in his own brain the old man quickly pulled a black box from one jacket pocket, and placed his hand in another. Potter could see there was a gun hidden.

"No Belly. Don't! I press this button and Dan Lucas is sausage. Michael, this's how I control them now. And given how pale you look, I don't even think I'd need this gun to control you. The shooter was supposed to be good. But he missed. My bad luck. But now it just doesn't matter. Not at all."

Warner turned to Belly. "You know the plan. Up the street and across the block. Now. Check the others."

"Belly, don't do this!"

"Have to. My dad. And I don't know this Russian president at all. To me, right now, you white people are all the same."

"Move!" commanded Warner.

"I'm not like him!" shouted Potter as the teen moved reluctantly away. "Look," he beseeched. "We trusted each other, remember?"

"Move!" repeated Warner waving the black box, watching as the boy continued to slink away. "Oh my Michael," he clucked. "You must face facts, I control them now. And I must say its been quite a ride, an intellectual challenge. Could I control them, all five, right to the end, through psychology alone? Alas, it wasn't to be. So I had to fall back on sentiment. The love of children for their parents. As if that kind of thing matters in the overall scheme of history."

"What are you talking about?"

"History, Michael. Just as Karl Marx said. History will end when the classless society comes into being. Just as Joseph Stalin said. The class enemies never kill themselves. They must be exterminated."

Potter struggled to understand. "But you're a Soviet intelligence mole. The leader of the new Russia is Feodor Vasikov. One of yours, a military man, a hero. Why kill him?"

Warner grinned and for the first time Potter noticed the glint of insanity in his eyes. "Michael, you disappoint me. I thought you were intelligent. I joined the struggle under Stalin. I've waited my whole life for the call to action. And the call has come."

Warner's eyes suddenly darted up and down the street. "But not from this stupid soldier with his livid scar, dismantling everything we worked for. Arresting my friends and former comrades, indeed. Personally, I thought we should have killed Mikhail Gorbachev right at the start, instead of waiting so long to take action. *Perestroika* and *glasnost* indeed. Stalin treated Western leaders like the capitalist scum they were. That's how we acquired Eastern Europe. Vasikov is just like Gorbachev, a class enemy. He grovels, as if our historic struggle was something contemptible. He is no hero. He is a traitor."

"So who do you get your orders from?"

Harry Warner smiled. "Believers. In the Kremlin. Not like Vasikov or his lackeys. True believers. Like the ones who recruited me, so long ago."

"I'm a physician and so are you, and in my clinical opinion you are insane," said Potter. "How can you believe this garbage?"

Warner smiled dangerously. "Garbage? Do you know how close Kim Philby came to being appointed head of the British Secret Service? If that had come to pass, none of this would be happening. Because it would be over. We would've won. But we'll win now. Better late than never."

Desperately Potter tried to think. How to diffuse this time bomb that Harry had become? He kept talking, desperately hoping something would happen.

"Philby was a stinking traitor, Harry. He died a miserable lonely death in Moscow, surrounded by tin-plated medals and empty vodka bottles, with a woman the Soviets gave to him as some sort of prize for being a liar and a killer. But even they despised him. Everyone despises a traitor, Harry. What are *you* going to win?"

"Everything, you fool. With Vasikov dead, the few remaining hard-liners in the Kremlin will mount a coup and bring back Stalinism. And with Bill Clinton dead at the same time, we might even be able to stage Armageddon."

Warner waved in the direction of Belly, now half way up the block. "And even if it doesn't happen now, it'll happen later. I have my escape all planned. I've learned a lot from your journal, as well as from the past few days with the children. I made some mistakes in interpreting their psychology, but I've learned from it. And I will share that learning with my superiors."

He threw back his head and laughed aloud. "We'll have a secret weapon that no one ever dreamed possible. There are others like young Belly here and the rest of you. In Siberia. The US Navy has its trained dolphins to plant mines on enemy ships. But compared to the powers these children possess, that's a circus act. We will rule the world. It's history in the making."

"What was the point of all this Patriots of the Raven terrorism?"

Warner shrugged. "I had to test the children to be sure about their powers. I had to get them onside. Once I told my superiors in the Kremlin what they could do, we hatched this plan. The terrorism kept that idiot Clinton in this country, doing his swaggering Yank thing, pretending to be in charge. And once the two of them are dead, if anything should go wrong, I need someone to blame it on. Much better the history books blame the unprecedented, simultaneous assassination of the world's two most powerful men on the Patriots of the Raven, rather than Dr. Harry Warner.

"Fuck you, Harry," said Potter.

Suddenly he saw the escort squads of police cruisers and motorcycle cops. They were doing the classic maneuver, leapfrogging each other's position, intersection by intersection. Once the guarded dignitary moved past a security point at a specific intersection, the squad at the intersection would remount, rushing ahead to their next specified security point.

The man with the mark of the raven was on his way.

The dream was turning into a nightmare.

THIRTY SIX

Potter turned back to Warner only to find the old man was gone. Frantically, he looked around pointing at the flashing lights of the approaching guide squads heading up the long cavalcade of black limousines.

Patti burst through the crowd. Thighs and Andrew moved to provide a protective shield for she and Potter, isolating them from the expectant, jostling crowds that lined the street.

"Michael, I told you to stay put!"

"Patti, I've just seen Warner. I know what's going to happen."

"I've figured it out too," she said. "Warner is going to kill his boss as well as the leader of a rival gang. Classic ploy. It's like the movie *The Godfather*. Take out everybody at once. Big Frank would understand."

Potter pointed at the flashing lights of the approaching guide squads heading up the long cavalcade of black limousines.

"Where are the kids?"

"Belly and Dickie, they're the only ones I saw. Now they're somewhere with the others. They know Warner is a traitor, but the old man has Belly's father as a hostage. I just can't believe the kids would actually kill anyone."

As the four of them headed off the way he had pointed, more police and motorcycles roared past. Potter looked around distractedly. "It still isn't right," he muttered. "In the dream, the *raven* flies — and should be descending from the air." Craning around painfully, he recognized the tip of Washington Monument above the trees of Faragut Park. And just ahead, the green glassed towers of the only modern commercial building in the area. It was all there, just as he had seen it so many times before.

The cavalcade with its flashing lights cavalcade entered the intersection. The sole identifying decoration on each of the long, black volga limos was a foot long brass standard attached to the right front bumper, supporting the red, blue and white tri color of the Russian Federation — just as in the dream.

At the end of the block from Potter, right through the intersection, several limos slid to a disorganized halt. Men who were unmistakably presidential security detail, Russians and American Secret Service agents got out and shouted terse commands at each other, and into mouthpieces. It was obvious this was an unscheduled stop. Suddenly the curb-side door of the third vehicle opened and a man got out. He was in his late forties and had one of those faces you vaguely remember from the cover of *Time*. A practiced politician, he waved to the crowd. There was an ugly scarlet-purple smear bracketing the left ear, itself a scared pulpy mess, and continuing down behind his collar — in the shape of a raven, swooping in for its prey. President Feodor Vasikov. He plunged into the crowd, seizing every hand, as worried looking men wearing sunglasses and micro earsets lunged towards him, aghast at this unrehearsed display of spontaneous enthusiasm.

His eyes searching the crowd, Potter spotted Dickie, Beebo, Brenda and Princess, their faces in a trance. And he knew. It could only be them. They had made the limos stop.

Precisely at this place. Why?

A gangly teen who looked like Belly was running up the block toward them. Desperately Potter thought, can this dream be changed? It has to be from the air.

A burly blond was also moving toward the politician, his face as cold as ice. With a sickening lurch in his stomach Potter realized he must be one of Warner's people. As if in slow motion, as if in the dream, he saw other hard looking men moving up the street. Their role was probably to intimidate the children as much as possible, and perhaps finish the job if the kids didn't. As Potter now knew only too well, Harry Warner never left anything to chance.

It was happening.

But something still wasn't right.

Far off in the distance, but approaching rapidly, Potter heard the heavy *whud-whud* of helicopter blades. He looked around, distracted. In the dream there was a helicopter falling out of the sky.

A huge Sikorski helicopter in the dull olive livery of the US Marine Corps approached. The tips of the machine's five blades spun slowly enough for him to see the track of each one as it moved. With each rotation he felt thudding compressions against his chest.

There was a commotion in the crowd near Vasikov. Desperately Potter swung his head and stood his long body on tiptoe to see above the crowd. Passers-by reached out eagerly to touch the beaming Russian President. Looking very anxious, his security team and American Secret Service agents huddled close to him to keep the pressing crowd at bay. Against their urging, the Russian kept reaching out for any hand that made it through the human barrier. He was intoxicated by the crowd.

Suddenly his reach wavered and his mouth opened. His face became a mask of pain and he clutched his chest. Only the tight squeeze of his guards around him kept him from collapsing to the ground in agony.

Potter could just see the still tranced look on the children's faces as Belly managed to slip through the crowd and grabbed Beebo and Dickie by the shoulders. Just as he shouted wildly at them to stop,

Beebo started to push through the crowd toward the Russian. Hearing Potter's frantic voice, Patti, Andrew and Thighs turned and followed. Thighs surged his way to the front using his body like a battering ram to clear the way. As some agents helped Vasikov to the ground, others formed a defensive circle, heads swung in Potter's direction. Wildly he thought, four very intense looking people barging through a crowd with obvious intent to do something, and panicky agents whose charge was dying of an apparent heart attack. He had a sudden vision of dying himself, in a hail of Secret Service gunfire.

Thighs obviously thought so too and suddenly put on the brakes, breathing heavily. Potter searched frantically for the children. He saw that Belly was still shaking Beebo and pointing. The muscular teen suddenly turned toward Potter.

And for the first time in his life, Potter dreamed while he was awake as Beebo focused those bizarre blue eyes directly at him.

In that dream instant, the purple-red mantle of a flying bird, a raven, transformed itself into a huge pulsating monster approaching a Washington street. The rotating clouds that he had seen before, the ones that had confused him, were the blades of the huge chopper swirling in the shimmery air.

Confusion was written on the boy's expression. He looked from the crowd on the street, up to the approaching helicopter.

And then he knew. Feodor Vasikov wasn't dying of a heart attack on a Washington street. He was in the helicopter.

Potter knew then that the dying man was a decoy. But why? And if that was the case, why were the children trying to take the man's life? Especially if they knew the real Vasikov was going to die in a helicopter crash? And what about Bill Clinton? They were near the White House, Vasikov's destination, but as far as Potter could tell the American President wasn't on this street.

There was too much information to absorb so suddenly, and in such confusion and fear. But to Beebo, everything had become crystal clear.

Beebo's flash of the helicopter reached the others. To Brenda, it came as a huge relief — a miracle. She instantly released her mental grip of the nerve bundles of the Russian President's heart. But then came Beebo's confusing flash of an image of Harry giving his orders that morning, *Kill the man in the car — save Dan.* Somehow in the maelstrom of emotions and thought emissions, the message was overlaid with an even more powerful compulsion driven by silver-blue mental threads from Princess, *Kill the man in the helicopter — save my daddy.*

They were committed.

Silver-blue mental threads intertwined with the copper-green thoughts of Dickie and in an instant they were inside the belly of the helicopter, joined by Belly's golden-blue and Brenda's bronze-green.

****

The real Feodor Vasikov peered intently through a small viewing port at the crowd on the street below. He noticed the crowd swarming around the very vehicle he would have used, before a last minute change of plans at the Embassy. Somehow, at the very last moment, those loyal to him at the embassy had been warned of a plot on his life. All he knew for sure was that the warning came by way of the Canadian embassy and that whomever had made the call had been most convincing.

****

Now that the children were no longer squeezing the impostor's heart, he managed to sit up and the crowd gave a sigh of relief.

Potter's own sense of relief was short-lived as he saw an enraged Harry Warner thrusting his long body through the crowd toward the children. He had the black box in his hand and held it up in front of him like some Satanic talisman.

The helicopter thundered closer. Potter started to move toward Warner, bending slightly as if stalking prey, staying out of the man's line of vision.

As he wove closer and closer, there was sudden change in the pitch of the helicopter's engine. Suddenly, the graceful arc of the chopper was interrupted by a series of sideways jostling wobbles each more violent than the last until a tremendous shudder gripped the machine. The nose pitched skyward as the tail came around in a sickening, wrenching motion, transforming the powerful throbbing of its rotors into an eerie, strangled howl.

The machine was thrown in the opposite direction, flipping on its side as it fell directly toward the trees in Faregut Square. The noise was deafening. All eyes turned sky-ward, toward the deathly aerial dance.

People began to scream and bolt. Within seconds, there was pandemonium.

For an instant, the pilot managed to bring the craft onto a level keel. Then, another jolt, and the howling machine lurched toward the gray granite statue of Faregut standing among four snub-nose mortars, his sword raised in brave but hopeless defiance against this enemy from the sky. It seemed sickeningly inevitable that the whirling blades would smash into the statue.

In the mass confusion induced by the chopper's deathly dance, all eyes in the crowd were trained on it.

Except Potter's. All he could see was the black box, and Harry Warner flinching and looking skyward. To Potter the black box with its shiny red, crystalline light had become the center of his universe. The black doom that engulfed him, compelled him against all reason to possess it! Moving in he suddenly saw the Englishman's eyes bulge incredulously and his mouth open as he caught a good look of the Russian President in the chopper. Breaking free of his pain, he deftly snatched the box from Warner's numb grasp and darted away. The old spy looked around wildly and saw Potter holding up the box. Michael could see in those enraged blue eyes that his teacher, his mentor, realized he had been duped, loosing his chance to revenge himself on the children.

Suddenly the look of rage was replaced by one of indescribable cunning. Warner's head turned toward the machine, hope again dawning in his eyes. But miraculously, at the very last possible instant, the chopper's downward dive was halted and it righted itself. Slowly the chopper settled on the grass, to be instantly surrounded by a shouting, heavily armed melee.

****

Beebo, driven by the powers of the others, concentrating on their deadly task, heard fragments of an old and familiar voice in a remote corner of his brain. Torn by duty to the others, to Dan, the voice cried out to him, pleading for him to remember the other who would die. He had to alter the dream. The man in the raven machine could not be as important as the other, one who was so much a part of them all.

Remembering what had happened when he last ignored the voice, the warrior that he was in his dreams took command.

He flashed the others to cease. To no avail, nothing. Then slowly, colored mind filaments fell away from the machine.

It was over.

****

The failure of his mission unhinged Harry Warner's mind.

He looked around wildly and pointed at Potter as the chopper's thunder died away to a high-pitched whine. "Kill him!"

Sunlight flickered off polished metal as hand guns emerged from the pockets of Harry's men, who as if on cue, broke out of the crowd to move in to protectively surround their leader.

But not before Dickie burst through the crowd near the impostor's location and ran to position himself between Harry and Potter, slashing the old man to the ground with a vicious backhand.

"Michael!" Patti yelled. "Get away from there! Over here!"

Potter looked around. There was fresh swarm of men all converging on the scene, and cars screeching to a halt on the street. Andrew yanked on Potter's good arm to pull him into the panicked crowd on the sidewalk. Dickie, Beebo and Belly turned to face Pavel and others who were coming at them fast. Brenda and Princess came running out of the crowd to join the retreat.

Suddenly their pursuers stopped as if hitting some invisible barrier, as the three boys brought their powers to bear. Writhing in agony, the first few attackers were thrown back bodily and those behind them tumbled to the ground.

Patti kept them all running until they approached the corner where "K" crosses Connecticut, cradling Potter as they went. At the intersection Andrew directed them to cross "K," wanting to put as much distance as possible between them and Harry's now rapidly approaching men.

Half way across the street, two Ford sedans, so nondescript they had to be ghost cars, peeled around the corner into the intersection. One of them skidded to an angular halt to the north while the second swerved over two lanes, thumped up onto the curb and came to a ragged stop on the south side of the street. Simultaneously, the doors of both cars opened and plain clothes agents surged out, with hand guns drawn. They ran for cover behind the vehicles, their weapons directed at Patti's team.

From behind them, Harry's men were rapidly gaining on the group's position. Harry was keeping up the pace admirably. Spotting the parked sedans and their armed occupants, they sought cover.

Across the park, on 17th, two police cruisers came to screeching stops, effectively blocking off the last remaining escape route. The cordon of metal and flesh was drawn shut. They were trapped.

A voice on a loud hailer sounded from behind one of the parked ghost cars. Though the words were unintelligible amongst the traffic noise, Potter detected a hauntingly familiar tone in the voice.

A shot rang out from Harry's position, the bullet shattering the windshield of the cruiser where the bullhorn originated. Return fire rang out.

Belly and Dickie hunched down around Potter, protecting him, while the others dropped down low behind a concrete flower pot. Only Andrew could break the spell of the gun battle. Pointing vigorously at the edge of a concrete and steel lattice wall at the corner of the building he yelled, "down into the subway! There's enough fire power on this street to wipe out an army," he panted. "And we're in no man's land. Let's go!"

The subway entrance was fifteen feet away. As they gained its protection the bullhorn blared, it's message directed at bystanders. "Get down! Get down on the ground!"

THIRTY SEVEN

Held up in the subway entrance, to assess the developing situation on the street — and to give Potter a much needed breather — Andrew grinned as he took a couple of spare clips from the inside of his coat and stuffed them in his pants. "It ain't the cavalry, but it's close."

Potter turned to Patti Donovan. "Who?"

She smiled. "When we figured out Warner's plot was to kill Vasikov and maybe even Clinton, I knew real quick there's no way my people could handle a situation that big. So I called these guys."

Potter was shaking his head in amazement. "I don't get it. What guys?"

"Alphabet soup. CIA and FBI. CSIS too. And for good measure, D.C. Police. Most of them who've been after us wanted Warner. And they still thought you were in on it too. That's when I demanded to speak to one Maureen Clancy at the Canadian embassy. You know, I really think she's still kinda soft on you, even after what she's been through. Anyway, I told her she was the only person who'd seen the two of us together and did she really think that we were in on this kind of thing. She was silent for a while and I knew she was sore so I asked how her face was, that it'd been nothing personal. She said she was fine, and then at the end of the line I could hear her having a screaming fight with some hard case that she kept cursing out, some guy named Baker."

It dawned on Potter. "That's him on the bullhorn."

Patti continued. "They didn't believe me at first, so they checked with the Secret Service. I have clout in this town, you know. They'd just been informed that Vasikov's supporters had discovered a possible plot on his life. It was them who must've made a last minute switch and used the chopper instead of a car to get to the White House. Of course the change came too late for any friends of Warner's at the Russian Embassy to inform him of the switch. That's why he concentrated on the car. He just didn't know."

"But the decoy. He looked so much like Vasikov."

Andrew smiled. "Even in Washington, actors are a dime a dozen. A little makeup, and presto. No one on earth who wasn't in the know would have looked at that scar and thought it *was* anyone but Vasikov."

"But what about Clinton? He was nowhere around."

"That's true," frowned Patti. "But I think I've figured it out."

She turned to Beebo. "You weren't planning to kill the decoy, the real Vasikov or President Clinton, were you?"

The teen shook his head. "Warner's plan was to stop the convoy, force the man out of the car and into the crowd, and then give him a heart attack. We were pretty much desperate so we came up with our own plan. We'd pretend to do what Warner wanted, just enough to make the guy from the car completely unconscious."

Potter grinned in spite of himself. "And it's not like any of the Secret Service guys are going to yell, 'Is there a doctor in the house?' and give Harry a chance to check the decoy' s pulse."

Belly interrupted. "Warner would think we'd actually done it. All we hoped was that it'd buy us a little time so maybe we could come up with another plan and save my dad."

"Jesus," said Potter, remembering. Gingerly he took the black box from inside his shirt."

"Whoa," said Andrew. "Let's have a look." He popped the back off and studied it closely. "Wait here." He charged down the steps three at a time and disappeared. He came back moments later, without the box.

"Don't worry about it," he said to the five sets of terrified children's eyes that stared at him.

He turned to Michael and Patti and grinned. "Toilet. It's amazing what water will do to expensive electronics."

Moments after they all sighed with relief, a heavy burst of gunfire made them all flinch. Potter turned back to Donovan. "How did you figure out how Warner was going to kill Clinton?"

"I don't really know for sure but try this one on for size. You told me Warner is a world-famous shrink, right. Everybody knows Clinton is a ham. So for Warner, reading Bill's psychology should be easy as, 'See Dick, see Jane.'"

It was starting to dawn on Potter. "So Clinton is in the White House, ready and waiting. He receives word Vasikov is dead just blocks away."

"Right. And immediately rushes to the scene to cradle the dead Russian in his arms as the cameras roll. The photo opportunity of a lifetime."

"And then, bingo. Heart attack number two. The guy eats Big Mac's by the dozen and with the excitement no one would be surprised."

Potter was frowning, "But the dreams — your dreams! Well somehow, now, I'm having them too!"

Beebo looked up, astonished, suspicious. "No way! Really? This is way too much." Eyeing Potter warily, he added, you understand them?"

"Hell no. And what about the helicopter back there? I saw people dying, horribly. Yet no one really did die. May be no one will?"

Much as Beebo wanted to believe that to be true, a terrible shadow of death crossed over his thoughts, powerful enough to make him cringe in pain. Brenda saw it and of the group, only she understood. Reaching for him, her eyes wet with tears of under-standing, she held him close as he broke down in helpless anguish.

Patti, her instincts on full power tood his face in her hands. "Beebo, I've asked Michael this before. When you see something in a dream, does it have to happen? Can you really change it?"

The boy's face lit up. "Don't know. Never really tried."

Suddenly there was a deafening series of explosions above their heads and the sound of running feet getting closer.

"Grenades," yelled Andrew. "They're moving up there! Down the stairs."

Reaching the bottom they heard thundering feet far above their heads. Potter turned and saw Harry and his men explode through the entrance. Four large support pillars blocked the attacker's view of the bottom until they were almost around the corner. Warner saw Michael and fired from the hip. The bullet ricocheted inches from Potter's head.

They ran to the left, into the long access tunnel leading to the Orange Line. Half way along the tunnel loud shouts rang out."

"We're too bunched up. Spread out!" shouted Andrew.

More shots. Thighs grunted as Potter was sprayed with blood from a wound to the tough guy's left shoulder. Thighs started to fal-ter as they tumbled over the turnstiles, down the escalators and onto the train platform of the huge Faregut North station, running the length of a full city block.

The platform ended a hundred yards away in the gaping entrances of two train tubes. The only other breaks in the long expanse were seven narrow, regularly spaced advertising pillars. The group separated and ducked behind two of them.

An approaching train whistled as it pressed a gush of hot sum-mer air down the tunnel. The platform was filled with commuters terrified by the sound of the gunfire.

Harry's men flooded onto the platform and immediately

moved up behind the panicked commuters trying to get onto the train.

On the deck above them, Baker and his companions ran toward the bank of ticket machines. Even at a distance the redness of Maureen Clancy's hair was unmistakable.

The train squealed to a stop and its doors swished open.

Within seconds, it disgorged its load of passengers and immediately sucked in a new set of struggling ones, frantic to get away. In the chaos of bodies, it seemed impossible that any of Harry's men weren't making a move to get on the train and get the hell out of what was turning into a very ugly scene. Incredibly to Potter, to a man, they held their ground — and took hostages instead.

Thighs and Andrew both aimed, trying to get clear shots but couldn't. Neither could Baker or the other intelligence people up on deck.

A bullhorn sounded. "Doctor Harry Warner, this is the FBI. You are totally surrounded. Let those people go. Throw down your weapons and surrender."

It took some seconds before Harry's imperial British accent wafted up from the platform. "If I must speak, I wish to speak to someone I know. Staff Sergeant Baker?"

Potter saw Baker behind one of the ticket machines. Without a hint of fear or hesitation the big cop took the bullhorn and spoke. "I'm listening."

"We've never met," said Warner conversationally. "Although you may feel you know some things about me, I probably know as much about you. I'm surprised you had the diligence over all these years. A question, if I may?"

"I'm listening."

"I was always so careful. How did you ever suspect me in the first place?"

"I saw you make a hand-off one night in 1981. Of course I didn't know who you were, but then I saw your picture in the paper."

From Warner there came a sigh of what sounded like satisfaction. "So it was an accident. What a relief. And couldn't you find some sort of code name other than Reggie? It sounds like some lower class footballer."

"If you're going to play field operative, Warner, don't expect the additional excitement of having your picture in the paper. It isn't professional."

Warner's voice hardened and rose. "Don't tell me how to do my business. And you're a bit off your turf, aren't you?"

"I shared you with them. And now it's over and I've got you," boomed Baker's voice. "I wanted to be in on the kill. I've won."

"You haven't won anything. Because I'm going to walk out of here."

Jamming his gun into the mouth of his terrified hostage, the old man carefully pulled something from his pocket and held it aloft. Horrified, Potter could see the journal in which he had written down every aspect of the kids' lives and the experiments they'd done together, along with his conclusions.

"Didn't have time to make a copy," came Warner's voice. "Didn't expect things to turn out quite this way. But I have my escape all planned. This is just a temporary setback. And I'm taking these hostages with me. And the children. They'll come willingly, you know. And so will Dr. Potter. Won't you lad?"

Potter couldn't believe his ears.

Up on the deck, CIA agent Bob Corbett, the liaison officer on the long running Reggie case, moved over to Baker's position, crouched down and turned off the bullhorn. With a look of total confusion on his young looking features he whispered fiercely in Baker's ear. "What the hell's he talking about Baker? What's all this mumbo jumbo about a book?"

"Beats me Bob!" replied the big Mountie.

Turning his head back to the platform, the CIA man missed seeing a sly grin crease Baker's mouth.

THIRTY EIGHT

H arry began to speak again, in the rich baritone he had used to keep the five kids near mesmerized before. "Children, remember what we talked about? You've seen the movies, what the CIA does to people like you. They'll lock you in solitary cells and pump you full of drugs. It's called brainwashing. And believe me, if you wash someone's brain often enough it just falls apart like an old rag."

There was dead silence.

"Physical abuse is a big part of it too. The girls will be raped. They do it all the time."

Bob Corbett was fuming and very worried. "Baker, God damn it! You know this guy's psychology better than anyone else. What the hell is he up to? He's still got the senator and the kids' father. This could be a blood bath. Not to mention a public relations disaster for the agency. I hope to hell you know what you are doing with this maniac."

Baker turned off the bullhorn lowering it as he gazed impassively below, trying not to let his lip curl at Corbett's last two sentences. "Bob, right now I know as little as you do. We need information. I plan to keep him talking."

"Potter. Tell the kids not to listen to this nonsense," boomed Baker. "He's trying to manipulate you all."

"Pavel!" called Harry Warner. The big Pole carefully edged around so no one could get a clear shot.'

"Brenda! Remember him? When those two Yugoslavs tried to

rape you? Pavel and I fight for the victory of Karl Marx's vision of history. We don't hurt little girls. Remember how he saved you, and got badly hurt doing so? And did I ever lay a hand on you?"

"It's true," she whispered.

"Louder, my dear. So they can hear you. Remember, Dan's life depends upon it."

"It's true!" she shouted.

Pavel smiled at Brenda and she gave a faint appreciative nod in return. Then the big Pole looked anxiously at Harry Warner, as he saw his old boss fight for his life and his beliefs with everything he had. Wasnoski sighed. Loyalty was the supreme virtue, he'd always been taught. He looked up at the hostile faces and muzzles that peered down. Too late to change now.

Potter was aghast. He turned urgently to Belly and Beebo. "Do you believe any of this?"

Belly spoke first. "Harry has a way of being very convincing, so right now I don't really know what to think. What I do know is they still have my dad. I think they'll kill him. I can't let that happen."

"Beebo?"

The teen looked lost and haunted at the same time. His eyes flickered. "I have other things on my mind right now."

Potter was about to ask him what he meant when Warner spoke again. "I know true love when I see it. Dr. Potter here is a romantic and an idealist, to the same extent I am, just not for the same cause. He loves these children. Which is why he will come with us."

"Cut the crap Warner,' boomed Baker. "Get to the point! What is it you really want?"

"My my, such manners! What I want is for all of us down here to leave . . . unscathed! It's quite a simple request really!"

"That, Doctor," replied the RCMP officer, "is going to be totally up to how you behave in the next few minutes. These are the terms. Release your hostages and then let them come up the escalator! We can only negotiate if we see a sign of good faith from you! No harm will come to you if you do this peacefully!"

"Good faith is it?" yelled the old man. "No harm will come to us? Are you listening to this Michael? You of all people know better—" His rantings were cut short as Baker's voice echoed again.

"Potter, talk to him before someone gets killed! Your people will be safe! Remember what Maureen told you . . . it's Warner we want!"

A howl of sarcastic, crazed laughter filled the cavern. "Michael my lad, are you listening to this drivel? 'Just me they want,' ha!" He waved the book aloft again. "Michael, because of this, you and I both know that neither of us . . . or our entourages, will be leaving this platform . . . alive." Warner held up the journal again. "And I won't lie to you. There are only two detailed sources of information here in the West about the abilities of these children. One is in Michael's head. The other is in this journal. And I'm sure by now the media is swarming all over this area with cameras, just waiting to see who gets out and who doesn't. There might be a certain amount of explaining you gentlemen must do."

"What's going on?" hissed Corbett. "Baker, you know this guy's psychology better than . . ."

"Bob, shut the fuck up. You say one more word and I'll ram this thing up your ass."

Baker rubbed his eyes and decided something. Two can play at this game.

Warner was still talking. "I treated you well. I bought you clothes and we ate at the best places and stayed at the Hilton. If you come with me you'll live like royalty." He shrugged. "For the time being, of course, it can't be in Russia, but that will change once we finally get rid of Vasikov. Cuba's nice. Why would we treat you any other way from the way we've treated you before?"

Beebo's head slowly rose and his blue eyes blazed. "Nakita," he whispered.

"What," asked Potter. "Is that an Indian word?"

"Warner, you old fraud," boomed Baker's voice. It sounded like he was almost laughing.

"What?" said Warner, startled.

"I said 'you're a fraud.' You talk all that stuff about Karl Marx and the classless society, but you've got that plummy English accent because your family was upper class, loaded, and could afford to send you to Cambridge. Remember the fifteen year old maidservant you screwed in the pantry and got pregnant, and then sent away without a dime? Man, you're a true proletarian. The only reason you joined the Party was to piss off your parents and because you thought it was the cool thing to do in the Forties."

"Shut up!" screamed Warner. The sound reverberated through the cavernous station.

"But what was cool fifty-odd years ago looks pretty pathetic today. Nothing is more laughable than yesterday's hipster. All your life you've drunk the best wines, stayed in the best hotels, gossiped with the rich and famous, betrayed your country and sneered at proletarian footballers . . . with names like Reggie."

"Shut up!" shrieked Warner.

Baker's voice was inexorably calm and full of humor. "You're not a communist, you're a goddamn snob and always have been. We've known all along. That's how we describe you in our files. Everybody laughs about it."

Warner's voice was thick with rage. "I'm the best Soviet spy that ever was," he shouted."

"No you're not. You got caught. You're a dope. Just like your old pal Philby. At the end he was so drunk most of the time he couldn't even stand up and died in his bed soaked in his own piss. You're old, Warner. Because you're old and creaky you can't see how creaky the Soviet system was, and how different the new Russia is going to be.

Gorbachev, Yeltsin and Vasikov are just the beginning."

Warner was shaking with rage as he jammed his pistol into the neck of his hostage. The psychological battle had reached its peak, and the old physician was overwhelmed by anger, fear, fatigue and humiliation.

A train was approaching.

Baker turned to Corbett as he turned off the bullhorn. "The trains are supposed to be stopped. It's the perfect way for him to get out of here. Stop that thing!"

There was a look of slowly dawning respect in Bob Corbett's eyes as he picked up his handset and gave the order.

Baker gazed down, trying not to show emotion. It was now or never.

****

In the short time since she was reunited with Baker, Maureen Clancy noticed that the big Mountie had skirted any mention of the kids' involvement. His discussion with the FBI centered exclusively around Reggie.

At the time, she wondered what the Americans knew about Potter's kids, and what, if anything, Baker had even told them. On the other hand, she knew that whatever Baker knew couldn't have been too much.

First brought into the case immediately after Potter's shooting, Baker had approved her full access to all the video and audio tapes taken from the surveillance on Potter's apartment. One chance call made from Warner's office phone to Michael Potter had started it all.

Once traced, a judge's orders was issued and Baker had Sergeant Jim Glinnen of the Alert Bay RCMP detachment sent to check Potter out. It only took one visit to the apartment before Glinnen discovered that the place was rigged for sound — there were bugs everywhere. Someone other than the RCMP had Potter in a fish bowl.

After some extensive electronic sleuthing — compliments of Baker, who sent a crew in from Vancouver — they finally tracked down the listening post to a fish boat run by three Yugoslavs living in the village. One of them turned out to be Pavel, a direct connection to Reggie.

From that time on, everything that was said in Potter's apartment was heard by Baker's people. Unfortunately, Potter and the kids had started to restrict their discussions and it was that reign of secrecy that set Baker off. He smelled 'cover-up'. It frustrated him that he couldn't get a clear handle on what was going on between the kids, Potter and of course, how Reggie fit into the picture.

The question in Maureen's mind was what Corbett, a self centered ass but no slouch, had figured out.

Within earshot of Baker and the CIA agent, she had heard their whispered exchanges. She had her answer. She knew then that at least some of Reggie's rantings were true. Potter and those kids didn't have much of a future. But she knew Potter and the lengths he had gone to protect their secret. Even if they did make it out of the station, alive, they would be no better than caged laboratory rats if either side got hold of them.

Maureen made her decision.

****

She walked across the deck, automaton-like, her eyes dull, her steps rigid. A Smith and Wesson .38 dangled from her hand. Stepping up to Bob Corbett, she turned and placed the muzzle of her gun in his ear. Holding him around the neck, she rigidly, bent down and mumbled in the CIA agent's other ear, with words that only he could hear. Together, crab-like they scuttled backwards to a ticket machine so no one else on deck could shoot her without killing him too. But she was still in full view of Harry and his people.

Slowly, in agony, Corbett turned toward Baker whose own regulation issue Walther .380 was trained at Maureen's head. The look on the big cop's face was one of total disbelief. "What the hell are you up to? Woman, you're dead meat!" Ignoring him completely, grimacing, as if in great pain herself, she mumbled in Corbett's ear.

Corbett spoke in a strangulated voice. "Give her the bullhorn, for Christ's sake!" Baker passed it to her and, she raised it. She whispered again. He raised his radio receiver. "This is Corbett. Power up the tracks. Let the train through."

Staring straight ahead, not flinching or reacting in any way Maureen spoke into the bullhorn. A voice, normally lilting and pleasant now sounded monotone and coerced blared across the cavern. "The children want to leave . . . with Dr. Warner. They're forcing me to do this. They're making Potter leave with them too."

Potter turned to look at Belly and Beebo for any sign of trance activity, and saw none. He stared at them questioningly mouthing, "you?" Both boys shook their heads, confused.

Then he had it. A diversion! Maureen was giving them a diversion! "Belly!" he whispered, "I don't know how or why but, she's helping us! Get that train moving! Back it up to our position, and," nodding to the knot of Harry's men and their hostages, "hold all those guys off!"

Corbett blurted out to Baker, "W-what the fuck is going on here? Call your bitch off—" The grinding of steel against bone shut him up.

Again, Maureen's voice blared. "Michael! Make . . . them stop! They're making me do this! I-it hurts so bad! They'll make me kill this man if he doesn't allow the train to move! Please Michael! Please make them stop!" Then, in a shrill scream, "noooo please, no more—"

Maureen collapsed in a heap. The bullhorn rolled out of her hand, plummeting to the platform below.

Potter looked up to the white-gray vaulted ceiling of the station. "The concrete, do something with the concrete!" There was no need to say more.

The dull background echoes of the cavern were split by ear wrenching *SNAPS* coming from above. Particles of concrete spiraled down.

The sounds intensified. A ten foot section broke loose from its anchors and began to fall, from directly above Harry's men.

The train hummed and vibrated as current surged through its motors. It started to move back towards the group.

At the first sign of the slab about to give way, Harry's men ran for the escalators. Those with hostages dragged them along.

The huge block broke completely free and began its deadly plummet downward. Many of Warner's men, knowing they were doomed with the hostages slowing them, pushed their prisoners down to the ground, and lay spread-eagled across them, providing what little protection they could. Theirs was a totally irrational display of gallantry, of truly committed professionals.

Harry and Pavel were among the doomed. Too far over from escalators to escape, the burly blond pushed the elderly woman he held ahead of him, towards the escalators. With his other arm, he grabbed Harry and in a last desperate attempt to save the man who's dream he had long believed in so deeply, pulled the old man down and lay over him!

A deafening roar thundered through the station as the huge concrete slab impacted with the platform. Shards of cement rifled off in every direction, demolishing the glass of the near side of the slowly moving train. A plume of dust rose off the crater in the platform.

In the explosion's aftermath, the near side of the platform was left littered with moaning, struggling people. Death and carnage was everywhere.

What remained of Pavel's body lay in a mound of bent iron and cement chunks. Two other motionless bodies lay scattered nearby. Miraculously, the old woman he catapulted over to the escalator was grabbed out of harm's way by one of the men who'd played Navy drunks in Port Townsend.

With the sounds of the collapse still reverberating through the cavern and clouds of dust billowing up to the ceiling, the group used the intense confusion as a shield.

Up on the deck, forms moved around hesitantly, searching the wounded, assessing damage. Those who could, began running for the escalators.

From the far end of the station, squads of uniformed, M16 rifle toting DC Police reached the platform and ran towards the mess.

Under the fleshy rubble that was once Pavel, a bloody hand moved. Then a leg. Someone was still alive there, moving to escape from under the pulpy, dusty mess. Warner.

In jerky fits and starts, the train picked up more momentum.

Warner, dazed and bloodied, staggered to his knees. In his hand, he still clutched the book, now soaked and soggy.

The train was moving faster, its doors remained closed, requiring the attention of a driver, who, due to an unseen force, couldn't move his limbs.

Dickie let out an animal yell. "NOW!" He was in motion, dragging the injured Thighs with him. Before him, the doors of the first car, its windows blown out in the explosion, swished open. Without any further urging, the others swept into action. Two knots of people surged for the open door.

Dickie with Thighs cleared the door post. Depositing the big man's limp form on the train floor, the boy turned to reach for Brenda's hand.

Brenda and Patti, pulling Princess along with them, sprinted the distance from their column. Belly and Beebo propelled Potter through the door.

Through his already blurred vision Potter saw a staggering, weaving, bloody mess he somehow recognized as Warner. The old man's arms were raised, his mouth moving in some desperate plea. In one hand he still clutched the blood soaked book. His approach, strangely rhythmic was suddenly jarred! Shots rang out. He pitched forward and as he fell, the book came loose from his hand, flying free in a graceful arc.

To Princess, with her child's view of the world, the book meant exposure of their secret and therefore, them. Blindly, she lunged out of the door to catch it.

Warner's hand rose up, his gun aimed . . .

In some recess of his mind Potter heard the voices of Beebo, Belly, Brenda and Dickie meld together in a hideous cry, "Princess . . . nooooo—

The little girl's hand grasped the book and at the very instant she made contact, her tiny body twisted in mid air as a rifle's bullet sliced into the base of her neck, exploding out the other side in a pulpy mess, forcing her tiny form backward, into Belly's outstretched hands.

He caught her and dragged her through the door, just as the platform slipped by, and Harry's prone body, framed for that instant in the open door, was assaulted by multiple explosions of flesh.

The bullet that hit Princess was meant for Reggie.

The train screamed out of the station.

THIRTY NINE

In that instant when Potter saw Princess's doll-like form assaulted so grotesquely he witnessed a part of the group die.

Praying for a miracle was useless. Nothing he or what remained of the group could do would save their Princess, the damage was just too severe.

She died in her brother's arms after keeping herself alive long enough to help them escape the station. As her small heart stopped beating she closed her eyes and with no sign of fear, simply slipped away. The sight of a bronze aura, with blue and silver flashes crackling from it, rising out of her small form was her parting gift to them. In a blaze of yellow-bronze brilliance, she was gone.

To the outsiders, the sight was truly a wonderment, powerful enough even to allow the badly injured Potter and Thighs some brief relief from their pain. To the remaining group members, the aura's flare left a huge, black hole that swallowed their emotions. They sat there, unable to react in any way to what was going on around them. It was Patti who acted.

The train was rapidly gaining momentum and she knew that their only chance was to stop it between stations. She directed Andrew to run to the front of the train to take care of the driver, to ensure that whatever the group had done to him, didn't wear off.

Numbed into nothingness it took her slapping Belly across the face to snap him and the others out of their state. He regarded her for a second as anger formed. Then reason took over and he understood.

Patti quickly explained that in order for the plan to work and for them not walk into an ambush at one of the next stations, they had to move quickly! Telling them to get ready to get off the train when she gave the signal, she put Belly in charge, and scrambled off to join Andrew.

The train started to decelerate. Andrew had been successful in his task.

In the control cab Patti scanned the numerous vertical ventilation tunnels in the system. Designated by violet colored electrical indicator lights spaced every five hundred feet along the line she located what she was looking for.

She returned to the car just as Andrew brought the train to a jerking halt, then opened door directly across from ladder rungs that led straight up to the surface.

Patti tested her cell phone to determine if her people topside could receive the signal. They could. She called out terse commands for them to arrange transportation and to be waiting on the street above.

In the very short time that Patti spent in the presence of the group, she had came to understand a great deal about the strange youngsters Potter had been so hesitant to discuss. She knew that the success of her escape plans depended on the mental powers of four very shaken kids. There were no other options.

With Potter's help, she convinced them there was nothing they could do for Princess except to help themselves. Time was of the essence. They had to get out of that car!

When Andrew ran up to them, she called out to the youngsters, "do your stuff with the train!" Still not convinced that they could overcome their mind numbing grief, she added a final curt command, "NOW, damn it!"

The distraction was exactly the verbal slap in the face they needed.

The train started moving. Patti called out to them again. "Take it through the next station and then stop it half way through to the next! We need a decoy!" A decoy for the ambush she knew would be waiting. "Can you do it?"

"Oh yeah," answered Dickie, up to the challenge.

The long black shaft that rose above them appeared as an impassable barrier, everyone knew that the two injured among them had to be assisted.

Patti and Brenda went up ahead as Andrew slung Potter over his shoulder. Dickie took his lead and did the same with Thigh's heavy and now unconscious bulk.

Refusing to leave Princess behind, Belly swept her body up in his arms and ran for the ladder. Beebo took up the rear.

After the first twenty rungs, both Dickie and Andrew could go no further, their limbs taxed beyond belief. The acid stench of fear filled the air. Escape with the injured was going to be impossible. At least by conventional means.

Incapacitated by grief and the weighty guilt of having foreseen Princess's death and then not being able to prevent it, Beebo's mental pattern, up to that point, was only a faint glimmer of his normal self. Then, giving himself over to the old familiar voice again, he marshaled the same strength he used to defeat his dream, demons, and broke free.

The group's survivors saw his new strength stream up around them in the blackness. One by one, they joined his mental rope to form a fabulous rainbow of swirling, dancing color that only they could see.

The weight of the injured and the dead became as insignificant as a feather.

They knew then that they would survive.

At the top of the ladder, Patti pumped at a well maintained

hydraulic lifting system. Two opposing steel mesh grates in the sidewalk expanded open.

Patti got her bearings and coordinated the pickup.

Within minutes, they were all safely inside two taxis.

EPILOGUE
Alert Bay

U nder the watchful eye of the giant painted thunderbird soaring overhead, guests crowded through the front doors of the Big House. They moved slowly, somberly, grieving for the one who could never return.

The celebration was to have been the last major festival of light before the dark season descended upon them. Now, the darkness began far too early. Death, particularly that of one so young, was a reminder to be forever vigilant against the warriors of darkness.

An attendant closed the doors, dashing the large room into inky blackness and total silence.

Match explosively touched gasoline as the pile erupted and sparks flew. Tridents of light bolted to every corner of the room, and soon a citadel of light stood over the raging flames.

In his ceremonial robes, Thomas Albert, Chief Councilor of the Nimpkish Band, rose. He nodded gravely at the grieving family, at Belly and his parents, Dan and Yvonne Lucas. He nodded as well to Dickie and Brenda and Beebo where they sat with their families. And to Dr. Michael Potter who sat next to Linda Jarvis. And to Staff Sergeant Douglas Baker and Maureen Clancy . . .

With the CIA, FBI and CSIS all testifying to her courage and initiative, Patti Donovan now had more clout in Washington than ever. Maureen Clancy had refused to press kidnapping or assault charges and her face was now completely healed, as was Thunder Thighs' shoulder. At Patti's request, a grateful President Clinton was arranging a pardon for Big Frank.

Despite lavish enticements, Michael Potter had taken a vow of silence, never to reveal anything to anyone about the childrens' powers. His journal had been the only documentation, and he had taken it from Princess's shattered body and thrown it down a sewer.

It helped that virtually every law enforcement or intelligence official he encountered didn't seem to believe it could have happened anyway. And people who had actually witnessed the children's powers and talked about them soon learned not to. As Staff Sergeant Baker had advised Bob Corbett and the others who had been on the subway station's upper deck that day, it was like telling your superiors you believed in UFOs, and discretion was the better part of future promotion.

That was before he and Maureen were escorted out of Washington, discreetly asked never to return.

Locating Dan Lucas and senator Blake Roberts had been easy. Upon hearing of the failure of their mission, the four guards watching the two prisoners in a house near the Russian Embassy simply left. The two men were able to free themselves. Lucas had helped the badly beaten senator onto the street and they were soon whisked away to hospital and later debriefed.

The corporate Lear jet and the flight back to Canada was all Patti's doing, the result of a favor owed her that even she was hesitant to discuss.

For Potter, leaving her again was particularly difficult. This time, like never before, they knew they still shared a passion that distance and time would not kill. Yet, sadly, they knew that their particular callings were in worlds so totally different. Her haunts were still the back streets where she was still the queen of Washington. For Potter, his hideout was a small island where sunshine was a rare commodity.

At an upstate Maryland airport they held each other long and hard. As they parted, they knew they shared something that was bigger than the two of them. With Andrew and Thighs, they knew they had all been touched by the group's magic. And they all knew that the fight wasn't over yet.

. . . As Chief Councilor Thomas Albert struggled to describe the indescribable, Potter was roused from his reverie by the warm, tender touch of a hand. He turned to look at Linda Jarvis, whose dark glistening eyes gazed lovingly at him. He squeezed her hand and smiled at her. He didn't know how long he might stay in Alert Bay, he wasn't making any plans. He suspected he might stay as long as she did, even if it was forever.

Suddenly the Chief's voice changed. Many of the elders sitting near Michael and Linda sat up to listen closely to the words. His voice was that of an old woman, scratchy and weathered, speaking in Kwakwala, their mother tongue.

Trance-like, Chief Thomas Albert spoke. The words that at first seemed so foreign somehow made sense to all in the Big House.

"Many dark winters have passed since the first Spirit Talkers stood together as a group to fight the spirits of the season of darkness and its chief, Baxbakualanuxsiwae, the Man Eater. Many have died to protect the secret powers against discovery by those who would destroy the delicate balance between light and dark. Too often, their deaths were fraught with violence."

They all listened intently and somehow, by listening, with minds cleared of all external distractions, so to could they see, her image, speaking from her hospital bed, propped up, looking out with those black, wise eyes, her fingers stroking her long, sparse hair, calming everyone who saw her.

"We are always searching for new Spirit Talkers to take over the fight. If they are not found in this generation, the Guardians of Light will be cast from the earth by the powers of darkness. Now, four are amongst us who have completed the tests. They trod the path between light and darkness and at any time could have taken a wrong step. But they didn't take a wrong step. They fought the warriors of darkness, and triumphed — this time."

Still in a trance, his eyes closed, the Chief with Aunty Mary's voice turned toward Michael Potter. "And they were helped on their journey, which is why they didn't take a wrong step. There will always be guardians, who fight a good fight against the powers of darkness." Potter felt his eyes fill with tears as Linda gripped his hand and kissed his cheek.

The fire suddenly flared and filmy trails of bronze smoke marked the passage of ghostly images through the darkness. They spun and spiraled, then plunged back into the flames. Soon, they took on recognizable shapes, all dressed in rich ceremonial clothes. Those in the audience who recognized the faces, cried out the names of people long dead. Names dusty and half-forgotten lived again as they were named.

Suddenly the audience saw the image of a young man in a splendid, wedge-shaped, woven cedar helmet. His image spun slowly, as if blown by some gentle wind. He smiled as he looked down at his family.

Dorothy Johnson stood, reaching out for the image of her dead husband. The sight of him, so splendid, so happy brought peace to her broken heart. In her hand, bunched next to her heart she clutched the gold amulet given to Constable Reinholt the night her husband was killed, the one with the carver's signature, her husband's signature, B. Johnson, the one carved by his own hand and depicting his family spirit protector, the Raven.

Next to her, Brenda, tears filling her eyes, turned to Potter and mouthed, "That's my dad."

. . . . "But while this battle was won some had to die. One of the chosen left the world of the living, to dwell in sunlight forever."

Up from the fire jumped a smaller image. Swirling joyfully, her head thrown back in silent laughter, she was dressed in a copper necklace and abalone shells that glinted like diamonds. A sweet, smiling little girl dressed in the finest of cedar cloaks. Princess. She was truly their Princess.

Mary's voice rustled through the building again, like a calming summer wind. "Now, that there are others to carry on the battle in the realm of the living I can claim my time of rest . . ."

The image of her in that hospital bed was one of peace and contentment. Those intense black eyes continued to look out at the audience, but soon, the sparkle turned to a dull glaze. Her head dropped forward.

The hovering images over the fire began to disintegrate, bit by bit, until they simply faded away, leaving only the light of the fire to twist and bob in the darkness.

****

In the darkness Brenda and Beebo sat enthralled as the image of an old friend appeared, only to them.

She looked so lost standing there, her face framed between the strands of wire. The cold wind blew at her severely cut bronze colored hair, exposing her dirty face. Behind her, the soldiers stood expressionless in the cold.

She had came to Beebo many times before and to the other, the girl named Brenda, only twice. In each of her comings, she always appeared the same way, until now. A broad smile spread across her pretty face and for the first time ever, Nakita spoke. "You are not alone. There are many others. Soon we will be together, united. So do not be afraid. . ."

Her message complete, she turned away from their view and walked through a hole in the barbed wire out into the expanse of the frozen Siberian night.

The End